A LONG WALK WITH FATE

a novel

Liz Torlée

Library and Archives Canada Cataloguing in Publication
Title: A long walk with fate: a novel / Liz Torlée. Names: Torlée, Liz, 1950- author Description: First edition. Identifiers: Canadiana (print) 20250230917 | Canadiana (ebook) 20250230925 | ISBN 9781998494118 (softcover) | ISBN 9781998494125 (Kindle) | ISBN 9781998494132 (EPUB) | ISBN 9781998494149 (IngramSpark EPUB) Subjects: LCGFT: Novels. Classification: LCC PS8639.O78 L66 2025 | DDC C813/.6—dc23

There are no wrong turnings, only paths we had not
known we were meant to take.

Guy Gavriel Kay

Coincidence is the language of the stars.

Paulo Coelho

Other Books by Liz Torlée

- *The Way Things Fall* (2020)

- *In Love With The Night* (2022)

Dedication

To my brother, Mark, for the love and the laughter

Table of Contents

PROLOGUE...1

PART I — THE PORTRAIT 3

PART II — THE PHOTOGRAPH 73

PART III — THE CHAOS OF ISFET 109

PART IV — THE FEATHER OF MA'AT.............193

EPILOGUE..237

PROLOGUE

Aiden Quinn took out his phone, not at all sure he wanted to make this call. He read the letter a second time.

My dear Aiden,

I found out my sister Dorothy has gone. I know she raised you as her own, and how much you loved her. Years ago, she made me promise I would never bother you, and I've kept my promise. But things are different now. I have been better for many years. I married a good man, and he'd love to meet you.

Please, Aiden … one day soon, please let me see you, so I can tell you face to face how sorry I am.

Maggie

Aiden put the letter aside and stared at the ceiling. He couldn't do it. The pity he had tried to muster was not enough to wipe out twenty-five years of resentment.

He slid the phone back in his pocket.

PART I—THE PORTRAIT

CHAPTER 1

Aiden's mother, Dorothy, had always put him first. She even died considerately—on a Sunday, so he didn't need to take time off work. The nurse called to say his mom was agitated, asking for him, and it probably wouldn't be long now. He leapt out of bed and rushed to Vancouver General. Squeezing onto the elevator and hurrying through corridors, he grew impatient with the trivia of life: comments on the weather, a birthday cake for one of the kitchen staff, the cost of a recent car repair. At the door to his mother's room, he became aware for the first time of the bare patches on her scalp and the deep hollow in her neck. The room smelled of disinfectant and open wounds. He sat on the chair beside the bed, bending close to hear her garbled words.

"Don't be sad, you hear?" She lifted her hand and stroked his face.

The machine at the side of the bed beeped on. He wondered what happened at the end, if it made one long beep, or if that was only in the movies. Through the gap in the drapes, he could see the woman in the other bed, her family gathered around her. They were leaning their heads on each other's shoulders.

***

Dorothy Quinn was not his birth mother. That was her sister, Maggie, who left his life for good sixteen years ago when he was nine. Dorothy told him Maggie went to pieces after his father died, but from what he learned as he grew up, she was in pieces long before that. He was in and out of foster care in Toronto until Dorothy took him home and eventually adopted him.

He had only vague memories of the rare times Maggie cleaned up, and they acted like a normal, happy family. She might let him make cookies with her or take him to the park, and buy him an ice cream.

Mostly, he remembered being alone and scared, hearing her pacing at night, kicking furniture and slamming doors. He always felt he was in the way. "Go find something to do. Watch TV." "Go play with your friend Tommy." He tried, but the TV didn't have the right channels, and Tommy went to his cousin's on weekends. Some nights, Maggie flopped on the couch, pulled him close, and fell asleep watching YouTube, then struggled awake and got mad. "How come you're still up? I told you to go to bed." He'd say he hadn't had any supper, and she'd bring out a bag of Cheezies or stale crackers. It was his school that blew the whistle. They could tell he was always hungry.

Dorothy made excuses for her sister. "Your mom, she was the pretty one, but she had a tough life, a lot of bad luck. Then she met your dad, and he made her well. She was so happy then." Lots of people have bad luck, he thought. Dorothy didn't have it easy, either. She'd never married, had no support from anyone, but she took him in and raised him like he was her own. "No way I could give you back to foster care," she told him. "That cheeky smile, those crayoned pictures you did for me. You were my little angel."

It came to a head the day he fell down the stairs. Maggie was on the landing, getting all tangled up in the blanket she clutched around her, yelling in frustration. He came out of his room to help her, but she couldn't stand straight. She tripped and knocked into him, throwing him off balance. He reached for her hand, but there was only air and emptiness. He tumbled down the whole flight, twisting his ankle and banging his head on the linoleum floor at the bottom. His cries must have brought the neighbours. The doctor said he was made of tough stuff—lots of bad bruises but nothing broken, no concussion. Dorothy took him home.

A couple of nights later, he heard Dorothy on the phone. He climbed out of bed and listened at his door. "Don't keep telling me it was an accident," she was saying. "He could have died. You were drunk or high, or both. I'm having the papers done. That's why those people came to see you. Not my fault you were wasted again. Empty bottles, trash all over the floor. They wanted to see what kind of mother you are. Well, now they know."

Aiden crept into the kitchen. Dorothy took off her glasses and reached for a paper towel to stem the tears. He had never seen her cry; it scared him. He wrapped his arms around her, laying his head on her shoulders as she hunched over the kitchen table. She smelled of flowers and fresh laundry.

"Your mom, Aiden. Things don't look too—"

He tightened his grip. "I want to stay with you. Please. Forever and ever."

She stood and gathered him in. "We're leaving this place. I'm tired of the fighting. We're going to Vancouver. People I know there, they'll help us. The sea and the mountains. You'll love it, you'll make new friends." She seized his shoulders. "D'you think you could be happy there?"

Aiden wanted to sob with relief, but forced himself not to cry. He was going to be alright.

His last memory of Maggie was when they went to see her before leaving Toronto. He remembered her apartment. Maybe it wasn't hers, maybe it was some place where she hung out. There was a pile of dishes in the sink, plastic cutlery, and the smell of beer. She was wearing a white tank top, jeans, and flip-flops. Her hair was tangled, her face sweaty.

"Aiden, my baby, look at you. Give mommy a kiss," she wailed, bursting into tears.

The sisters argued and cried a lot, Dorothy constantly scooping Maggie into a hug, telling her not to fret, everything was going to be fine.

A man yelled from the bedroom. "Shut the fuck up. Can't a guy get some sleep?"

"Watch your mouth. The kid's here," Maggie yelled back.

"Not my fucking kid."

When they were leaving, Maggie put a hand on Aiden's arm. "I'm gonna get better, Aiden. I promise. You'll see." Ash fell from her cigarette. She ground it into the rug with her heel and turned away, coughing.

When he and Dorothy walked across the car park to the bus stop, he looked up at the third-floor window, but there was no one to wave to.

"Your mom was too sad to say a proper goodbye, Aiden," Dorothy said, squeezing him.

"I hate her. She's not my mom."

***

The clatter of a trolley in the corridor made him look up. A nurse came to change the saline drip over Dorothy's bed. "No breakfast eaten?" She eyed the untouched tray of food on the rolling table Aiden had pushed away.

"She's not hungry. Why do they bother?"

The nurse shrugged, wrote a note on the clipboard at the foot of the bed, and left.

"So many hours your mom waited," Dorothy said, her voice more forceful now. "Your poor dad." She clutched his arm with the fierce, unexpected strength of the dying. "He loved you."

Not enough, he wanted to say.

"Code blue, room 503."

Aiden jumped at the loud voice on the P.A., but his mom didn't seem to hear it. He held her hand and felt a stab of guilt at the sight of the cheap watch hanging loose at her wrist. It was the only watch he'd ever seen her wear. He wished he'd noticed before, that he'd saved money and surprised her with a new watch on her birthday. He was angry with himself for the loss of that chance.

Dorothy sank back onto the pillows, her eyes fixed on the corkboard on the wall with its fire alarm instructions, roster of nurses, and various notices. "Aiden, you gotta do something . . . all that talent." She began to gasp, as though in a panic. "Promise me. Don't let it go to waste. You hear?"

He squeezed her fingers. "Promise."

Another nurse came to check her pulse. "Hanging in there," the nurse said. "A real trooper."

He stood for a while at the window, watching the cars crawling in and out of the parking lot. Hanging in, that's all that goes on here, he thought—the rest of us are only biding our time. He looked back at Dorothy. She was still staring at the whiteboard, her fingers clutching and unclutching the sheet.

CHAPTER 2

Aiden had no one to share his feelings with … his anger and resentment. "Sorry, man," his few friends muttered at the sad little funeral. They shuffled, slapped him on the shoulder, and hastened away. Death is embarrassing for them, he thought. When he told his girlfriend his mother had died, she shrugged and said "Shit. Life sucks." Only sex drew them together. After each scurried encounter, she sat on the couch, smoking a joint and tapping at her phone. Two days after the funeral, cleaning out his mother's apartment, he found her going through Dorothy's jewellery box. "There's neat stuff here, kind of vintage," she said. "You might get something for it."

"*What?*" *Jesus.*

She shrank back against the wall. "Hey, cool it. What's the problem?"

"Get the fuck out of her room."

They had a big fight. Afterwards, back at his place, she was all simpering and contrite, but he knew deep down she was ice-cold. He wrenched open his wardrobe, threw the few clothes she kept there onto the bed, then strode to the bathroom and tossed all her lotions and lipsticks to the floor. She screamed and swore, shoving everything into a garbage bag. On her way out, she grabbed boxes of pasta and bags of chips from the kitchen.

"Give me your goddamn key," he yelled as she stomped down the stairwell.

"You think I want to come back? Fuck you. Change the lock."

***

Aiden wept on his way to meet the lawyer, a few days later. It came over him in an unexpected rush, and he couldn't stem the tears. His mother was gone. He had been so consumed with the bureaucracy of death, there had been little time for grief. It began to rain. Despite the new growth of spring, the city had its veil of grey despondency, low clouds blocking all hope of sun. From one of his pockets, he fished out crumpled brown paper napkins from some fast food joint, dabbed at his face, and blew his nose. The rain grew harder. It squelched into his shoes as he strode through black puddles. He didn't care. Nothing mattered.

In the lawyer's corner office, flanked by floor-to-ceiling mahogany bookcases laden with legal tomes, he felt dwarfed and inconsequential. Aware that his wet shoes were soiling the pristine cream carpet, he stared at the framed certificates on the wall and tried to keep his toes raised.

The lawyer, head bent over a file on his desk, barely acknowledged his presence. When he finally pushed the file aside and looked up, Aiden caught the flash of raised eyebrows and realized how dishevelled and unkempt he must appear.

"Have you been through all the paperwork? Letters? Bills?" the lawyer asked. "You don't want to find out later you owe money you didn't know about."

"My mother paid every bill on time."

"There are no other relatives to notify?"

Aiden held his gaze for a heartbeat. "No."

"Your mother's will was simple. Once this paperwork is filed, you will have access to the money." He handed him a form to sign, indicating where. "She was smart enough to make you a joint account holder, so you will have no problems with the bank. It's not a great deal of money, but I'm sure it will help."

How the hell would you know, Aiden thought, sitting behind that enormous desk, with its artfully displayed photos of family, cottage, two friggin dogs. He wondered why Dorothy had bothered with a lawyer, but it was so like her, wanting everything neat. The guy was likely trying to justify the fee, handing over one page at a time. There would be barely enough money to cover the funeral expenses Aiden had put on his credit card.

The lawyer's assistant gave him a set of copies in a manila envelope and said she'd bring him a list of organizations he needed to notify. He should wait in the lobby.

He sat on the low couch in the reception area and took out his phone. The battery was down to seven percent. He slid it back. After five minutes with no sign of anyone, he stood to leave. "I don't need the list," he told the receptionist. "I've called everyone I need to."

"It'll be here any moment. Best to be sure."

He picked up a glossy home décor magazine from the pile on the coffee table. As he flicked through it, an image embedded in an article caught his eye. He thumbed the pages back to find it again and peered closer, his brain scrambling to make sense of what he saw.

"Aiden, sorry for the wait." The assistant came over and gave him the list.

When she was gone and the receptionist distracted, he carefully tore the page from the magazine and stuffed it with the list into his backpack.

The elevator in his building took forever, and the door wouldn't close properly. He forced it shut with both hands. In his apartment, he kicked off his shoes and headed straight for the bedroom.

From the top shelf in the closet, he retrieved a battered cardboard box of childhood memories, and tipped the contents onto the bed. Out spilled crayon drawings, a first report card, boy scout badges, the Game Boy console he couldn't part with, and a bundle of birthday and Christmas cards from Maggie. Dorothy had written dates on each of them. Her neat writing, every letter plump and round, brought back the tender comfort of her presence, the way she would smother him with kisses until he squirmed to break loose. In those early days, Dorothy always knew when he was lying awake at night, scared he might not be allowed to live with her anymore. She would snuggle into bed with him and read a story, or bring him a chocolate brownie and hot cocoa, staying until he fell asleep. Now she was gone. *Gone.* The little word was a gaping hole in front of him. He felt he was teetering on its edge, struggling to keep his balance.

He flicked through the cards from Maggie.

- *When I'm better, we'll go someplace nice. Niagara Falls, maybe. Or Wonderland.*
- *Dorothy's looking after you now, but I'm your mom. I'm trying hard.*
- *I forgot the day, baby. I've got a job now and it's nights, and I get muddled.*
- *All these years gone. Bet you're a handsome boy now, just like your dad.*

Dorothy tried to convince him that his real mother was a good person. He would listen and nod, but he never believed her. Good people don't run away.

The last card was dated 2016, one of those *Greetings of the Season* cards which came with charitable donation requests. On the front was a sleigh piled high with gifts. The holidays had ceased to matter to Aiden. Over the years, he made an effort for Dorothy's sake, but felt dead inside. Christmas, in particular, made him angry: the shopping fever, grinning plastic Santas, and endless loops of *Deck the Halls* and *Joy to the World*. He couldn't believe people followed these phony traditions without question, like it was a duty to be happy. Later, he knew the cynicism was a way to protect himself from disappointment, but it never left him.

He was sure somewhere in this box were the two photos he sought. He found one: his father standing with a group of work colleagues, his hand on Maggie's shoulder. Was that before he told her he was married, Aiden wondered now? Rifling through the mess on the bed, he found the other, a head and shoulders of his father, alone. He studied the features of the man: cheerful, a glint in those blue-grey eyes, laugh lines, messy brown hair. Maggie used to tell him he looked like his dad, especially when he laughed. Problem was, he thought now, there was never anything to laugh about.

From his backpack, he retrieved the crumpled page from the magazine and laid it on the bed. The photograph in the magazine article and this shot of his father were identical. He took big, slow breaths to stifle the jackhammering of his heart.

CHAPTER 3

Gabriella Mazhar needed a husband. More importantly, she needed children. And time was running out. She was already in her thirties and knew it could take a while for her to meet and marry a guy, and get successfully pregnant.

Gabi's parents, her father Egyptian American, her mother Canadian, were born into the horse-breeding and training world. They had met at a horse show in Alberta, where Gabi was born. When her father and his brother inherited the Al Sayed Stud, an equestrian centre south of Cairo, the whole family moved to Egypt and settled there.

Gabi loved the country, both the sparse wildness of the endless desert and the happy chaos of Cairo. She found the people proud and generous, despite the hard lives many of them endured. Over the years, she had learned rudimentary Arabic and assumed the lion's share of responsibility for the family business. Her father and uncle were more or less figureheads. They left staff matters to their wives and the breeding and training to the professionals they'd hired, convinced that flaunting their wealth and entertaining lavishly would sustain them. Her two cousins, both men, married with children of their own, were, in Gabi's view, nothing but freeloaders. They swanned around the property, throwing parties for the rich and famous, getting drunk and high, and contributing sweet fuck all to the organization. The behind-the-scenes work—shows, competitions, auctions, and accompanying temperamental animals to far reaches of the globe—all that, Gabi handled. She could spot both the potential and the weakness of a horse before it had taken two steps forward. And she could ride better than anyone in the family.

"You're good at all that," her father said. "It comes easily to you."

Even when he flattered her, it felt hollow, like something he was obliged to say, possibly at the urging of her mother. She knew he was disappointed he had only one child, a girl, and had to deal with the self-satisfied gloating of his brother, who already had five grandchildren.

Gabi would inherit fifty percent of the business on the death of her parents. Convinced her cousins would drive it into the ground, she fully intended to buy them out or somehow gain control of the other half. But she needed a husband to support this, especially in this part of the world where women entrepreneurs were still viewed with suspicion or amusement. And she needed kids to ensure the business would flourish well into the future, and her role in it would be secure. Her friend, Sally, claimed she had a dynasty complex. "And what if I do?" she had countered. "I've worked hard enough for it."

But she was getting desperate. There were few appealing North American men available in the Middle East, and the wealthy Europeans and Arabs were probably looking for something more exotic and compliant.

So it was with some surprise she discovered Masoud, unattached, on a film set in the Moroccan town of Ouarzazate, a magical oasis of terracotta buildings and palm groves, famous for its Taourirt Kasbah and extensive film studios. She had arranged for the transportation of two horses her family had contracted for use in the film and had flown to the set to take care of them. She was drawn to the quiet man with curly hair and short, trimmed beard, huddling with art directors as they pored over enormous stage plans and drawings. Being Egyptian made him an excellent candidate, someone she could feel self-righteous about. He was dressed European style, in sharply tailored jeans, the collar of his well-pressed shirt turned up against the sun. He had a slight limp that somehow added to his enigmatic appeal. She learned he was an Egyptologist, hired to help with set designs and ensure their authenticity. He barely noticed her, or so she thought, being nothing more than a stable hand in the eyes of the crew. And besides, the "desert bunnies" were making eyes at him—young, film set groupies in khaki shorts, their long hair twisted into colourful Moroccan scarves, nursing the hope of being discovered.

Many of the films shot in the region needed horses, and Gabi had been several times, always at the beck and call of an imperious Executive Assistant. This time, it was a slight, redheaded woman with a big voice, who knew next to nothing about her equine actors. From behind a fake concrete pillar, decorated with hieroglyphics, Gabi observed the art design team, partly because their work was interesting, but mostly because the man from Cairo was usually with them.

One afternoon, so hot even the seasoned crew sought the shade of the canopied tents, she watched the filming of a scene against the backdrop of desert dunes. She had a good Leica camera and took shots for the extensive portfolio the family kept. Take after take, stunt riders urged her two horses from standstill to full gallop, fell sideways in the saddle at the sound of gunshots, and slid to the ground, grappling with the reins. Both horses reared in an attempt to break loose. Gabi watched the riders with disdain. They were good and knew how to fall, but neither was an empathetic horseman.

When the director insisted on yet another take, she couldn't hold back. "These horses need a break."

She caught a few raised eyebrows.

"It's my job to worry about them," she said. "They're highly strung. You can see they're upset. You won't get more from them today."

"She's right," said a voice behind her.

Spinning around, she came face to face with the Egyptian.

"These are purebred Arabians," he said. "They demand respect."

The redhead looked like she'd swallowed a lemon. After a huddled consultation, the director backed off and called a break.

Gabi took the reins from the stunt riders and approached the Egyptian. "You sure know horses, and you obviously have some pull here. Thank you. My name's Gabi."

"Masoud Burhan," he said. "My family has a horse farm not far from Cairo. We raise Arabians. It's more of a hobby now. I'll walk with you to the stables, if I may."

For a moment, she could barely speak. Here was a guy who was not only Egyptian but knew horses … a gift from the gods. "How strange," she managed. "We might be neighbours."

He knew Al Sayed, claiming it was "in a different league," and she thought how much her father would appreciate that opinion. The pandemic was apparently a disaster for Masoud's family, and he wasn't sure how much longer they could hold on to the property.

They talked a little about their work and their love of horses. He told her she was an excellent rider, confessing to having watched her exercising the horses in the paddock. She couldn't see his eyes behind the reflective sunglasses and was unsure how pleased she should be. *Come on,* she thought, *he admires your riding skills, not you.*

"You grew up with horses," she said. "You must ride, too."

He explained he'd had a serious fall some years ago and stopped riding, not wanting to risk another. If the injury flared up, he had to use a cane.

As they reached the stables, unsaddled the horses and hosed them down, he told her about his fascination with Ancient Egypt, the digs he went on in Luxor and Aswan, the papers he'd published on the Dendera zodiac in the Temple of Hathor. A friend had referred him to someone in the film industry. He'd done one project and then more offers came in.

"I enjoy it. And it enables me to help my family. Unfortunately, it's unpredictable."

They chatted for a while about the film being shot and the personalities of the crew. He told her the ones who were easy to work with and those it was wise to stay clear of. She found she liked this man. He was a good listener, gentle, with no obvious ego, happy with his own company, his own life. When she asked if he was married, he shrugged and said the chance had passed him by.

In the coming days, Gabi managed to get her hands on the master production schedule. She knew when the horses, and therefore she herself, would be on call, but she wanted to know the specific times Masoud would be working. With this knowledge, she devised several more apparently casual encounters.

Masoud seemed flattered by her interest in his work and impressed with her knowledge of the Ancient Egyptian paraphernalia relevant to the shoot, little knowing she had googled it all the night before. During these discussions, she learned he was seriously worried about his family and whether they could hang on to their business. So he was poor, she thought. *Perfect.* Her family wealth would be a big draw. She told him he should get in touch with her when the film was done. "We know people who know people," she said, wanting to sound vague at this point and not play all her cards. Although he appeared genuinely interested, she wondered if he was playing a game, acting proud, or not wanting to appear needy. Despite this—or perhaps because of it—she found herself increasingly attracted to him.

The scenes with the horses were finished within a week, and Gabi left the Ouarzazate studios reluctantly.

CHAPTER 4

When Masoud emailed her a few weeks later, Gabi could scarcely believe things might be going her way. Almost as though they were scripted, her father and uncle suggested she invite him to Al Sayed. She had told them about Masoud's family's horse farm and his worries about the future, and swore she could hear the numbers clicking in her father's head.

It went fast: Masoud's visit to Al Sayed, she and her father travelling together to see his property. The horses were healthy and well-cared for, but many of the buildings were in disrepair, and there was defeat in the eyes of the family. Her father told her the parcel of land was too small to be useful, but the horses were world-class, and Masoud's family had contacts, people whose needs they could no longer fill for lack of money.

When the contract was signed, the two families gathered at Al Sayed. To her surprise, Masoud pulled her into a tight hug, lifting her off her feet. For a long time afterwards, she felt the quiver of excitement from the press of his fingers on her back, the soft bristle of his beard against her cheek.

As the horses were shipped and the land and equipment readied for sale, Gabi drew the net tighter. She made Masoud feel part of the family, consulted him about business decisions and the management of the stables. He was courteous to her parents, treating them with diffidence and respect, and let the other men dominate the conversation, never offering contrary opinions, even though Gabi knew he often harboured them. He told her he hated arguments. They were a waste of breath and time. She noticed the look of guarded anticipation in the eyes of her cousins ... here was a man who not only knew the business of horses but could relieve the two of them of the few responsibilities they still grudgingly shouldered. For the first time in her life, Gabi felt worthy and valued.

She and Masoud shared a mutual respect, almost an "understanding"—at least that was the way Gabi explained it to Sally when she told her friend they were getting married. Sally questioned Masoud's motivation. "Are you sure he's not just after your money?" "So what?" Gabi responded. "We like each other. We'll be good for each other. I'll finally get the kid I need to shore everything up for the future. And what the hell, the sex is good. So far."

***

Gabi faced her first challenge when it became clear Masoud did not want to leave Morocco. Because money was no longer an issue, she assumed he would gradually let go of consultancy work and they would live at Al Sayed, where he could establish himself as a key player. By fathering a child, they would secure their future. And she would spend her time doing what she loved best: taking care of horses, riding, teaching her children to ride, and planning how to eventually assume ownership of the entire estate. But when she raised this with Masoud, suggesting that, as an Egyptologist, he would surely prefer to live close to Cairo, and near his own family, he dismissed the prospect out of hand. He loved his work in the film industry, and that would usually be in Ouarzazate. *He* had assumed they would buy a new home there together and would fly to Egypt to help out her parents when he was between projects.

"Gabi, you complain all the time about the workload. If you don't live there, the rest of the family will have to step up and help out more. Those cousins of yours are getting a free ride."

She could not tell him she worried about the cousins being more involved. She wanted to keep them on the fringes where she felt they belonged.

In the end, they compromised. They bought a home on the edge of Ouarzazate. If a consulting project looked to be long and time-consuming, Gabi flew to Egypt and carried on with her work at Al Sayed. She did not like being apart, especially with her pressing need to get pregnant, but it became clear that when Masoud was immersed in his film work, there was little room for her.

Her father resented Masoud's absence, claiming he needed the help at Al Sayed, and he had not given them a huge financial wedding gift to fritter away in "Nowhere town, Morocco."

Gabi felt compelled to defend her husband. "He's an Egyptologist, not a farm hand," she said. "And an expert in his field. It's important to him."

She was embarrassed that her father, who claimed to be proud of his Egyptian heritage, had little interest in its ancient history. Contrary to her earlier hopes, it was clear he felt no particular bond with her husband. "Don't be fooled," Masoud told her. "Your father is American. The Egyptian half is simply good for business."

Getting pregnant was now her sole objective. She thought it would be easy. At first, as each month went by, she shrugged her shoulders and told herself maybe three months, maybe six, maybe it would take a year. But as the twelve-month anniversary passed, and the monthly pain seemed to grow worse, she became anxious, and then obsessed. Masoud told her getting stressed out would only worsen the problem, but she could sense he did not share her yearning for a child. For him, his family being bailed out and the two of them having enough money to live well … that was all he needed. She wanted so much more.

***

Gabi could pinpoint the exact moment she knew something about her husband was wrong. From an upstairs window that overlooked the small courtyard of their home, she saw Masoud leaning against a wall. At first, she thought he was on the phone, but the way he was hunched over was odd. Perhaps he'd had a dizzy spell, she thought— it was hard to stay focussed and hydrated in the unforgiving heat. He had lost weight, but she put this down to his busy schedule and his tendency to skip meals. Now, as he straightened up and moved off, using the cane, she was startled by how gaunt he looked.

She tackled him that night, but he dismissed her concern, claiming it was only an occasional shortness of breath, and his doctor was arranging tests. Knowing he was unlikely to elaborate, she didn't press him for details and, as the days went by, took comfort from the absence of bad news.

But he did not improve. Despite the generous meals she prepared, he didn't gain weight, and began to endure sleepless nights, often struggling for breath. Sex became less frequent and this added more stress to Gabi's frenzied need to get pregnant. He became irritable and increasingly preoccupied with work, spending hours on Zoom calls with art directors in other parts of the world, discussing worlds and languages and customs she knew nothing about. If she protested, or pleaded his health, he claimed she was fussing.

One night, when his restlessness woke her, he admitted he had a heart condition. The doctor had reassured him that it was manageable with medication, and he must cut down on salt and fat, and get plenty of rest. She wanted to ask what kind of heart condition, and what did "manageable" mean, but when he came back to bed, they made love, slowly and tenderly. As he slept, she watched him for a while, struggling with unfamiliar emotions. She had once joked with Sally that they had an arranged marriage, and it suited them both. Now she realized she had grown fond of this quiet man. Perhaps she had never been truly in love, but she felt a guarded tenderness toward him, a desire to make him happy. A child would not only shore up her own future but would surely give her husband something to be excited about.

She thought about their last visit to Al Sayed. A wealthy family came to buy an Arabian hunter jumper for their son, who was competing. They had a seven-year-old daughter who, the mother explained apologetically, suffered from an anxiety disorder and had trouble communicating. With no hesitation, Masoud approached the girl and asked if she'd like to ride. The parents protested, claiming she would not be able to handle the horse. Gabi offered to ride beside her. The elation on the girl's face as she sat astride the gentle mare Masoud selected, the way she listened intently to his instruction, and how she petted the horse afterwards … all these made Gabi feel both happy and desperate. She and Masoud were meant to raise children and teach them to ride, to pass on the passion and skills they shared.

Each month, if her period was late, she went from cautious hope to nervous anxiety and then anger and resentment. Her cycle grew unpredictable, with increasing pain.

Masoud seemed oblivious to all her emotions. She had no idea he was dying.

CHAPTER 5

Steven moved from Toronto to Vancouver a year after Rachel left him. Now, five years since her death, he still felt her presence in his life. Sometimes, a soft footfall on the stairs or a movement in the room would make him pause and glance over his shoulder. Probably only the creaking of the house or the wind in the trees, he thought, chiding himself for his paranoia.

This morning, searching for material for an art course he would be teaching at the local college, he found a box of old photographs and spread them out on his desk. They were taken in Italy when he lived in an old, crumbling house in the hills outside San Gimignano. He'd forgotten he had them. Here was the house itself, a fading creamy yellow, caper flowers growing tenaciously in cracks of stone, frothing mounds of wild lavender in the garden at the side. The pictures showed terraced vineyards and lilac skies, the medieval towers of the walled city in the distance. They were distinguished only by the degrees of intensity of light behind a cloud, or the length of shadow thrown by tall, proud cypress trees marching down the hillside. He used to sit for hours with his camera, enthralled by the subtle changes in the landscape, waiting for the sky to turn a bruised purple, or for the wind to make the olive trees shimmer in the late sun.

At the bottom of the pile were photographs of Rachel. Steven hesitated, telling himself to put them back in the box, but decided there was no harm in a little nostalgia. In one photo, she was pouring coffee for an elderly man in a tiny garden full of fallen yellow leaves. In another, leaning over the terrace wall to gaze at the distant hills. There must have been a strong breeze that day because strands of her hair were lifted into thin spirals. Her long skirt hugged her legs closely on one side, but floated freely on the other.

There had been many women after Rachel, none of them able to fill the void she left, none with her ability to sense his moods and coax him to release the bottled up feelings he wrestled with. Although he'd gained international recognition for his painting since she died, he could never shake the feeling she was still looking over his shoulder. All his brief relationships died on the vine. Until Natalie. Natalie was an investment banker, far removed from the rarefied air of the Canadian art scene. They got married two years ago. Steven found her straightforward manner invigorating, and succumbed willingly, if not always enthusiastically, to her breezy attempts to organize his life.

Trying to shake the flush of sadness, he separated the photos into two piles. The landscapes he threw in the trash; those of Rachel, he put in an envelope which he addressed to Lukas, her son. Lukas, he thought … the son of the man she *really* loved.

He painted all afternoon and would like to have continued through the evening, but he and Natalie were to attend an auction and dinner that night. As one of five guests of honour, there was no way out. He propped his easel and canvas against the wall, regrouped and stashed paint tubes according to colour, and opened his laptop to check emails.

One of them, from his friend Dominic in Morocco, needed a thoughtful response he didn't have the energy for right now. The email gave details of an arts festival to be kicked off in the city of Fez, and included an invitation for Steven to attend. The festival was designed to boost tourism to the country and, no doubt, to improve business at the hotels Dominic and his brother Hadir owned. Like everyone in the tourist business, they had suffered through the pandemic, but this family had money and no shortage of ideas. Betting on a resurgence in recreational travel when the Covid scare abated, they invested in boutique hotels in two other Moroccan cities, and had eyes on more. Morocco needed to get on more bucket lists, Dominic said when they talked on the phone, claiming it was tough competing with Egypt's pyramids, the Valley of the Kings, and Petra in Jordan. "But we have a whole different cachet," he declared. "It's you who gave me the idea. You said it was a painter's country."

Steven had visited the family at their hotel, the Riad Capella, in Fez a few years ago. Everything he saw on his walks through the old, walled medina—spice markets, fruit and vegetable stands, stores spilling their goods into narrow cobbled alleyways—was richly coloured and highly textured. In the early evening, the Atlas Mountains in the distance shone like burnished gold in the lowering sun. The people were dark and sensual, some of the women heavily jewelled. When he returned to Vancouver, he spent months capturing these memories in a series of paintings, all of which sold quickly. He sent photographs to Dominic, and it was these that sparked his friend's idea.

Natalie called up the stairs. "Steven, you need to get ready. We have to be there by six."

"Coming."

The email went on to say the festival planning had begun. The art and photography of tourists would be collected and showcased. All entries would feature elements of Moroccan life, its landscapes, towns, and people. Local artists and photographers would choose pieces to be featured in a website and a huge coffee table book, and help judge competitions in several categories. Tourism organizations and sponsoring hotels, airlines and other parties would feature and exhibit the chosen work across the country in a full range of promotional material. An amazing collaboration, Dominic stressed. The advertising had already begun, mostly through social media, and they were getting strong interest. But there was a lot of work to do. Assuming all went well, the Riad Capella would plan *Artist Retreat* packages in the slower season.

Steven marvelled at the organization and the kind of money it would take to pull all this off. He skipped to the end: the renewed invitation for him to stay with the family and be "an honoured guest" at the gala launch of the festival.

He let out an exaggerated sigh. He disliked travelling. The thought of crossing the Atlantic, pressing on to the Middle East and performing in a star capacity was well beyond his comfort level. He wondered how he could gracefully decline.

Then he noted the PS: *Toronto trip confirmed. Can we meet there?*

Shoot, Steven thought. If his friend was coming to Canada, he'd better do the graceful declining quickly so he wouldn't have to endure face-to-face pressure.

"Steven, what are you doing?" Natalie stood in the doorway, her coat over her shoulders, holding his dry-cleaned jacket.

He closed his laptop, acknowledging to himself he was the quintessential party-pooper, and slid into the jacket, pulling at the neck of his shirt. Natalie complained he smelled of turpentine, but agreed it was too late to fix that. She ushered him down the stairs and into the car.

CHAPTER 6

A gallery on Vancouver's north side was featuring portraits from Steven and four other artists. The faces of people from many walks of life smiled, cried, laughed or grimaced from the walls: a baker kneading dough, a florist finessing an arrangement of tall white gladioli, a truck driver leaning on his wheel and wiping his brow. A fundraising dinner and auction would cap the evening, profits going to the expansion of the arts programmes at the local college. The five artists, all well known, delivered one or two portraits exclusively for auction and a few for display only.

Steven had developed a greater affinity for portrait work in recent years. His new interest began when Dominic asked him to paint his wife, Amina. He doubted he could do justice to that enigmatic face, the mystery behind those dark eyes. There was such innocence in her smile, and yet another quality, hard to define … beguiling, even dangerous. He worked on the portrait for weeks, using photographs for reference. Dominic was thrilled, Amina pleased and flattered, and this gave Steven courage to pursue his portrait style. He discovered a new talent, a way of revealing not only a subject's state of mind, but deeper dimensions of their personalities and emotions.

It was Natalie who persuaded him to exhibit the first portrait he'd ever painted. She found it in a closet and was amazed he'd never displayed it. It was of his half-brother, Colin, ten years his senior. He painted it many years ago in Italy as a form of exorcism, a way to rid himself of the guilt connected to Colin's death. Once it was done, he felt lighter, freer, but he could never extinguish the grief. He'd lost not only an older brother, but a companion, someone who was always on his side. As a child, during Colin's weekend visits, he would sneak into the bathroom, take his aftershave, and spray it on his pillow. He found comfort in the lingering scent after his brother had left.

He became possessive about the portrait; it embodied the soul of a man he'd loved dearly, and he didn't want to share it. It took Natalie's persuasive powers to get him to exhibit it at the exhibition, insisting it would be a way to honour his brother. "You don't have to sell it. Just show it," she said. "Your fans will be astonished you've kept it under wraps."

Eventually, Steven relented.

He glanced at his wife now, chatting to the gallery owner. She wore black leggings and a long black cardigan, claiming she wanted only to blend in. But her openness and readiness to smile made that impossible. He caught one of the other artists, a younger man, making a beeline in her direction, and had to stifle a flutter of jealousy.

Taking two glasses of champagne from a waiter, he went over to break Natalie loose. She linked an arm through his as they made their way around the gallery, admiring the work and greeting friends.

When they paused before the portrait of Colin, Steven questioned whether his brother really would feel honoured to be on display here. The art world was far removed from Colin's life. As a social worker, he dedicated a good deal of his life to helping people down on their luck, the marginalized of society. As a sports nut, his idea of fun was coaching minor league baseball or meeting at the home of another die-hard Maple Leaf hockey fan to watch the game over beer and pizza. He'd be embarrassed to be here, Steven thought now, regretting he'd given in to Natalie.

"It was painted with a lot of love," she said. "That's easy to tell."

As he squeezed her closer, he became aware of someone standing behind him. He turned to see a young man, arms hugged around his chest. He wore jeans and a sweatshirt with the hood well forward over his face, setting him apart from the fastidiously dressed wealthy people attending the function.

"I wanted to see the portrait," the young man said, taking a step back.

"Sorry, do we know each other?"

"My name's Aiden Quinn."

Steven was disconcerted by the hostility in his eyes. *Quinn.* He searched his memory but could bring no one to mind. "Aiden? I don't think we've met. I'm sorry, maybe you didn't know. This is a private functi—" He stopped, realizing how condescending he sounded.

"So, you don't know me?"

"Please forgive me if I've forgotten."

"It's a good likeness," Aiden said, pointing to the portrait.

"You must have mistaken him for someone else. This is my brother. He died years ago."

"I know." Aiden looked back and forth from Steven to Natalie. "Guess I shouldn't be here." He turned away sharply and bullied his way through the crowd.

Steven followed. "Hey, don't run off." The high-pitched chatter in the room fell silent. "Let him be," he yelled at the security guard who was trying to block the exit.

He caught up with Aiden on the street, walking briskly, hunched against the cold. Grabbing his sleeve, he forced him to stop. "Wait. What is all this? Who are you?"

Aiden wrenched away from him. "Did he tell you, and you didn't want to know, is that it? Or maybe he never told you. Maybe he was a fucking coward right to the end."

Steven fought to take a full breath. "What the hell are you talking about?"

Aiden reached inside his jacket. For a moment, Steven thought he was going to pull a gun. It was a photograph. He shoved it in Steven's face, then turned and walked on. "Your brother, Colin," he shouted over his shoulder. "I know all about him."

Steven watched him disappear into the evening crowd, feeling his peaceful life had veered abruptly off course. The sidewalk was surely at an angle. He held on to a storefront window, wondering if he'd already had too much to drink.

Natalie and his agent, Hugo, were standing in the doorway of the gallery, white with concern. It was probably an elaborate scam, he told them, or the guy was delusional. Colin had been dead for over twenty years; there was nothing more to know.

CHAPTER 7

At breakfast, groggy after the sleeping pill he'd taken, Steven sat with his head in his hands, trying to reconstruct the events of the previous evening. He had a dim recollection of enduring another hour of small talk at the gallery, picking at his food during dinner and, with nudges from Natalie, beaming with appreciation at the applause and final auction prices for the work. Hugo ran interference for him, dismissing questions and expressions of concern from gallery patrons, calling the encounter with Aiden a misunderstanding.

"Are you sure you don't know this guy from somewhere?" Hugo asked when he called to follow up.

"I've never seen him before in my life. How could he know Colin? He couldn't be more than twenty-five. How come he has that photograph? It's the same one I used for the portrait. Years ago."

"People can find photographs anywhere these days. But you're right. It's probably some kind of scam. Can't be too many Aiden Quinns in Vancouver. Should I give the name to my IT guy? He can hack into anything. Or d'you want to forget it?"

"Let's forget it." Steven pocketed his phone with a muttered curse.

Natalie poured him another coffee and spooned fruit and yogurt into a bowl. "He didn't say he *knew* Colin. He said he knew all *about* him. Right?"

"Hugo thinks he's up to something." He cupped his hands around the mug.

"So why did he run off? What if he does have a connection to Colin?"

He searched his wife's face for doubt, but her arched brows told him what he feared, breathing life into the gnawing possibility that had taken root as Aiden left him on the sidewalk.

"What are you thinking?" he said. "Spit it out."

"I mean, you have to admit ... didn't you notice? There *is* a resemblance."

"Colin and Amy were married for fifteen, sixteen years. He wasn't the sort of guy who cheats." He rinsed his mug in the sink. "I don't want to think about it. If this guy has anything to say, he knows who I am. He can find me. Meantime, I've got other things to do, like the course I probably shouldn't have agreed to teach."

Despite his determination to forget it, the strange meeting with Aiden Quinn played heavily on Steven's mind. For a week, he looked through old photo albums, reliving memories of his brother, searching for clues. He trawled social media sites but found no one fitting the guy's description. Every time his phone pinged, he thought this Aiden person might have tracked him down. Steven knew he would be easy to find. He was a public figure with information on the internet and at the gallery too. But he heard nothing more. Devoting himself to preparing for the course he was teaching, he blocked the incident from his mind.

***

He was not convinced painting could be taught, believing a person had the gift and the right instincts, or they didn't. But, as he grew more successful and developed new skills and approaches, he felt the time had come to give back. He liked the idea of helping younger, optimistic artists who hoped to make their mark in the art world one day.

As he walked through the college, he wondered if he should warn them about the dark days, those creeping doubts and insecurities, and the desperation that comes when you realize your stifled potential won't pay the bills. But when he entered the classroom and took in the forest of easels and the smell of turpentine and linseed oil, he put aside such thoughts. The chatter stopped, and twenty sets of hopeful eyes turned toward him. He smiled at the happy chaos—piles of sketchpads, random benches with multicoloured tubes of paint, jars and mugs stuffed with brushes. These people loved to paint. Nothing else mattered.

A few had registered as online students, but only one showed her face. The others used avatars and nicknames, like *Van Goff, Dilly Dali, Little Fire*.

After all the introductions, he took a plump yellow vase of cornflowers from a shelf of props, announcing the first exercise was for him to understand his students' *approach* to a painting. He sent a photograph of the vase to those online.

"A golden rule of mine: there is no such thing as still life. I don't care if you paint a pencil. If it looks lifeless, the painting is a failure." He pointed to the cornflowers. "There is nothing 'still' about this. Even the vase is alive. See the handle, the way it curves and clings to the side. Paint what you feel, not what you see. It's only an exercise. Have fun. I'll start the serious stuff next week."

As the students worked, he was struck once again by the fabulous versatility of art, how a simple thing like a vase of flowers could be interpreted in so many different ways.

Two of the online students were particularly talented. One painted exuberantly, overplaying the fullness of the vase and its blue and yellow intensity to dramatic effect. The other, the printed photo taped to his easel, painted as if the flowers were communicating with him, willing themselves to more vital expression. Steven thought of himself as a contemplative painter, seeking harmony with his subject. But, at times, he felt a different kind of energy lying deeper, suppressed, unpredictable, something yearning to be let loose. That's what he sensed with these two students. He clicked their chat buttons: *Can't wait to see more.*

No response.

No question, he thought, turning back to the class. Most artists want to be left alone.

CHAPTER 8

Hugo texted the next day: *Good news, maybe. IT nerd found three Aiden Quinns in Vancouver, one is right age.*

Steven called him. "Hugo? What are you doing? I thought we agreed to forget it."

"Whoa. *Excuse* me. Natalie asked me. Said it couldn't hurt. I thought you both wanted to check further."

"Natalie asked you? That's news to me."

"Oops, sorry. Well, you know women. Pretty tenacious."

Steven took a second to calm himself. "Where did your guy find these Quinns? Facebook? I didn't see anything there."

"Not Facebook, Steven. Get with it. It doesn't matter. But here's the interesting thing: there was a woman in Vancouver General, Dorothy Quinn, who died a few weeks ago. She was sixty-two. Cancer. It's in the obit records. Maybe no connection … or could be the mother. You know, mother dies, kid decides to get to the bottom of a few things. Want me to keep checking?"

"What I want, Hugo, is a peaceful life."

"Hey, he might be a relative. And, not to be crass, but if Ms. Quinn was indeed 'the other woman,' at least she's out of the picture. Puts a different slant on things."

The other woman. Trust Hugo to put it so succinctly, that niggling worry Steven had swept under the carpet. It couldn't be, he thought. Colin never admitted to problems of any kind. Steven sat at his easel, looking into the middle distance and wondered if, deep down, his brother had been unhappy and he, Steven, so self-absorbed that he never knew what was going on behind the scenes.

He tackled Natalie when she came home. She tossed her briefcase on the couch and appraised him, hands on hips. "Steven, you're like a bear in a cave, growling with annoyance if anyone disturbs you. Something is happening outside the cave, you know. It's called life. There are people in it. The guy might be troubled, he might need help. Maybe he's scared to approach you again. If his mother has died, it's even sadder."

The unpleasant implications of this possibility crowded into Steven's head: Catherine, his daughter, her eyes widening over yet more family drama; Lillian, his ex, going into an almighty freak out and talking about rubbing salt into old wounds. Worst of all, having to tell Amy, his brother's widow, "Gee, Amy, so sorry you and Colin never had kids, but guess what, we think Colin had an affair years ago, and he has a son. Isn't that wonderful?"

"I bet Catherine would love to know she may have a cousin," Natalie said, guessing his thoughts.

"There was a lot of heartache in the past. Everyone is over it now. What they don't know—"

"What they don't know won't hurt them. I hate that expression. Truth might hurt, but silence is far more destructive."

Steven ran his teeth across his tongue, a habit he had formed to prevent himself from blurting out words he would later regret. He went to the kitchen for a beer, playing for time. The whole thing could be a scam, he said. They should do nothing, wait and see. But Natalie insisted they make an effort to find the young guy and give him a chance to explain. "He can't show up with such a cryptic statement, then disappear, and expect our lives to go on as normal."

That night, sleep eluded him. At three o'clock, he crept downstairs and poured a stiff Scotch. His finger-wagging doctor had told him alcohol in the small hours was a serious no-no, guaranteed to ruin not only his liver, but any chance of a proper sleep. He resolved to store the bottle out of sight. It had been too frequent a companion in recent days. Slinging a blanket over his shoulders, he stepped onto the deck. The trees were dripping after a heavy rain. A flutter of wings and scurrying in the undergrowth made him feel he was trespassing. One of the neighbours saw a black bear at the edge of these woods a couple of weeks ago. The BC Wildlife people had now posted warning signs. He went back inside. At least let them have the night to themselves, he thought.

Settled into a leather chair, his whisky-fueled thoughts led him once more to the last time he'd seen his brother, at their summer cottage north of Toronto. Colin took a call and announced he had to go back to the city that same evening. He asked Steven to go with him, claiming he'd like the company. Steven could still feel the warmth of that late summer afternoon. He could hear the whirr of a lawn mower farther along the road, and the crunch of his feet on the gravel as he chased Colin's muddy, battered van, yelling "…okay, okay, I'll come." Too late. Old memories churned relentlessly: Amy, his sister-in-law, hysterical with denial; Lillian, his ex, grabbing Amy as she sank to her knees; the cop in the living room … *an accident, so sorry*; his daughter, Catherine, three-years-old, neglected in all the trauma, letting out a full-throated wail.

Decades ago, and still that night came roaring back, poisoning his new life.

***

When Natalie came home from work the following day, she slid into Steven's studio and thumbed a sticky note with a phone number to the side of his easel.

"Aiden's number," she said.

He peeled off the note. "How on earth …..?"

"Dorothy Quinn, the woman who died in Vancouver General … the hospital is a client. Don't ask. And don't *ever* tell. She had a son. Aiden."

Steven wavered between reluctant respect and annoyance. Now he would have to act, take a step along that other road. "Shit. You're amazing."

"Will you call him?"

"I'm in the middle of something. It's not exactly urgent."

But his desire to paint drained away. The painting was a commission he was not fully engaged in. It required planning, strategy, and second-guessing, none of which was conducive to passionate work. He told Hugo he'd take no more commissions, but received a lecture about sitting on his laurels, and the importance of staying in the game.

He cleaned up, went to his study, and attended to emails with slow progress, forgetting to copy the appropriate people and getting confused with attachments. After an hour, finding no further excuse to procrastinate, he called the number, half hoping there would be no response.

"Hello." The voice sounded irritated, as though he, too, would rather not have to deal with this call.

"Aiden? Steven Farrow. We met briefly a couple of weeks ago. At the gallery."

The silence at the other end was disconcerting. Steven fell to apologizing that they didn't start off on the right foot. He tried to explain it was all a bit of a shock for him.

"How did you get my number?"

He fudged an answer, cursing himself for not preparing for this, and stumbled through expressions of regret at the death of the guy's mother.

"You know who I am, then?"

"No, I don't. I want to know why you have a photograph of my brother, what you think you know about him." Steven regretted the challenge in his voice.

"It doesn't matter. I don't give a shit anymore," Aiden said.

"Do you think Colin was your father?"

"I know he was. He died when I was two."

Steven felt a door had slammed behind him, the one which led to his own version of the past. He'd tried so hard to come to terms with that version and wanted only to carry on with his quiet life out here, each day unfolding predictably. Now, an unseen force was pushing him forcefully onto another path, one surely filled with new anxiety and discomfort. He swore the fat moon was glowering at him through the window, waiting impatiently for his next response.

He let out a long whistle. "Okay. I guess we should talk. Can we meet?"

CHAPTER 9

In Aiden's building in the impoverished downtown east side of Vancouver, Steven's determined optimism quickly dissipated. The elevator wasn't working so he had to climb three flights of stairs littered with used tissues and rank with the smell of piss and stale pizza. He worried once again if his nephew—if indeed this guy was his nephew—had sought him out because he needed money.

Aiden's face had scarcely registered in the gallery or on the dark street outside. Now, in the doorway, under the harsh fluorescent light from the hall, his lanky frame, untidy brown hair, and the wary curiosity in those blue-grey eyes were so familiar that Steven took an astonished step backwards. Colin's face. The shock rendered him unable to mutter a greeting.

He looked around the kitchen while Aiden made coffee. It was tired and ill-used: boxes of cereal on top of the fridge, coffee stains on the countertop, an open margarine tub scraped almost empty. The door of one cupboard was missing, revealing a mess of cans of spaghetti sauce and boxes of pasta. His nephew was living like a pauper, though he seemed resigned, even comfortable in these humble surroundings. A flowery apron hanging from a hook was evidence of a mother's influence. It must have been a happy relationship, Steven thought … mom coming round to cook once in a while, concerned her son was not eating properly. A single photograph on the fridge door showed a young woman, her arm around a teenage Aiden, with what was probably a school in the background. The woman had shoulder-length dark hair, big glasses, and an ill-fitting pale blue jacket. Aiden was clutching a rolled-up paper. Graduation day, Steven guessed. They both looked proud, beaming at the camera. Steven wanted to ask about her, but held back, unsure of Aiden's mood, and hoping *he* would start the conversation.

Aiden pushed a big mug of coffee toward him. Pointing to the logo on it, Steven asked if he was a Canucks fan. No. Apparently, the mugs were free with some burger promotion. They sat for a minute in awkward silence, the heavy clouds and a drizzle at the window filling Steven with a growing sense of gloom.

Aiden took the photograph from his shirt pocket and passed it to Steven. "It says Colin on the back. You knew it was him. I could tell."

"Who gave you this?"

"My mom, of course. I've had it since I was a kid."

Years ago, when Steven lived in Italy and was still trying to come to terms with Colin's death, he'd taken a photograph of his brother from his wallet, overcome with the urge to paint him. The portrait spilled from his brush quickly, flawlessly, as though finally given air and light after years of suffocating darkness. Now, here was this young guy in a scruffy apartment in downtown Vancouver with that same photo.

"What made you go to the gallery?"

"I saw an article in a magazine. About the auction. There were photos of the portraits being shown. I recognized him. The article said he was your brother. I knew he had a brother, but I didn't know anything about you."

This is a dream, Steven thought, convinced he would snap awake any moment and it would be a weird memory. "Your mom? Who was she?"

"You really knew nothing? About my mom and me?"

Steven handed the photo back. "I'm sorry. I didn't have a clue. Shit. You're my nephew."

"So, you believe me?"

"It's a real shock, Aiden. I was suspicious of you. I'm sorry. Goddamnit, you look so much like him." Steven concentrated on his coffee, unsure what his next move should be.

Aiden stood abruptly, pushing his chair back. "There's something I guess I should show you."

He led Steven along the hallway into a living room. The room was filled with drawings, paintings and intricate designs, some stuck to the wall with masking tape, others propped against furniture: surreal landscapes, dreams and nightmares coming to life, leading the eye through layer upon layer of colour and texture. Some were large abstract pieces of raw, unbridled energy, paint running or splattering off their edges. Others were small, crammed with detail, ripped pieces of newspaper, paper clips and safety pins glued into their design. He picked up one painting—a red door, a few inches ajar, revealing an intricate labyrinth of pathways across a vast landscape. The door beckoned him, making him want to push it open and step across the threshold into that strange new world.

The clear promise of enormous talent made him gasp. "Oh my God," he kept saying, over and over. He knew these feelings; he knew the way a brush could soar across the canvas with a life of its own; he knew how one thoughtless daub of the wrong colour could spoil an effect and ruin a day.

He pivoted, casting his eyes around the whole room.

And then he saw it. On an easel jammed into a corner: an unfinished painting of a yellow jug, bright cobalt blue cornflowers spilling from it, glowing with new life.

What the fuck? Steven stared, his heart fit to burst through his chest. He collapsed into a lumpy armchair. "Holy shit, Aiden. You're taking my course."

"My mom always wanted me to take a course. She said I had talent."

"Why didn't you come to class? Why didn't you talk to me?"

"Is it any good, the work?"

"Answer my question."

Aiden's face was set once more in the sulk Steven saw on the street outside the gallery.

"When I saw you, I hoped maybe you knew I existed," he said. "But the way you looked … like I was a total loser. I googled you, found the course. I figured it would be a good way to see what you're all about."

"A good way to see what I'm all about—without getting anywhere near me?"

"You didn't want me anywhere near you."

Steven covered his face with his hands. "Jesus Christ. I'm sorry. Okay? I'm sorry."

He wanted to say being ambushed at a function wasn't a good way to start a relationship, but he didn't have the energy to argue. He got up and looked at the painting again. The jug was solid and heavy, handle exaggerated, spout like a tongue, one drop of water, clear, translucent, poised to fall. The thin green stems of the cornflowers competed for space, many squashed or folded over. He moved closer, astonished by the sheer number of shades of green, the vibrancy of the star-shaped blue petals, and their black, fuzzy stamens.

"I guess you're *Little Fire*, right? Your avatar?"

"It's what my name means. Aiden. From Gaelic."

"Your mom was right. You've got talent. Are you going to tell me about her?"

"She and my dad worked together at the community centre. When they knew she was pregnant, he said he was going to leave his wife. So much for that."

"I'm sorry, Aiden. And I'm sorry for your loss." Steven berated himself again for having missed such a huge chapter in his brother's life. "What do you want to do with it, this talent?"

"Do with it? I can't make any money from it, so I do it to feel good. What did you do with your talent before you were 'discovered,' before you went to Italy to find yourself?"

"Guess you did your research."

"It's not hard. You're everywhere on the net."

"Where d'you work now?"

Aiden began to tidy the canvases, stacking them on the coffee table or against the walls. It was clear he didn't want to discuss this. An IT company, he said, eventually. He could get electronic equipment at a good discount and could sometimes work from home.

"So I have more time for this." He gestured to his work.

Steven scanned the room for clues to help him understand his nephew. Jars of brushes and tubes of paint, most rolled tight to extract their last few drops, sat along the windowsill. Stacks of sketchbooks and drawing pads lay on a sagging set of shelves. The furniture was dated and mismatched, out of place for someone of Aiden's age. It must have belonged to the mother, he thought. A bewildering confusion of AV devices and cables was pushed against a far wall. Two laptops stood side by side on a makeshift desk, the screen of one of them cracked.

"Didn't you know *anything*?" Aiden said, sitting again and picking at the threadbare arm of his chair. "I mean, about your brother's marriage, like what was going on?"

Steven felt strangely robbed, as though he was always meant to be part of the life inside this cluttered room, and had been thrown off course. He could have played an integral role in this young man's life, but was never given that chance. Either that, or some greater power had deemed him unworthy of it.

"I knew nothing about another woman," he said, "let alone a child. He gave me no clues. Maybe he did, and I never picked up on them. There was an accident. I guess you know that."

"I know what my mom told me. You were all up at a cottage."

Steven crossed his arms over his chest, feeling a need to protect himself from this strange young man who was making him relive a past he had long tried to forget.

"My brother got a call," he said. "He had to go back to the city to help find a kid who'd skipped probation. I watched him drive off up the hill." He hesitated, reluctant to replay every detail of that night. "A deer jumped onto the road. I saw Colin swerve to avoid it and carry on around the bend, so I thought everything was fine. But he must have lost control. His car crashed into a ravine."

"When he left, did he say he'd be back that night?"

Steven was startled by the challenging look in Aiden's eyes. "That's a strange question. I don't think he actually *said* so. It wasn't a long drive. We all expected him back. Why?"

"He never meant to go back. He called my mom from that cottage, told her he was going crazy, couldn't stand his life anymore. He was going to ask you to go with him, so he could tell you everything, so you could meet us. Guess he wanted you onside."

Steven felt drunk, as though the room had tipped upside down. "No, Aiden. There was a kid who didn't show."

"That was a lie. They cooked it up. My mom and him. So he could get away."

Steven tried again to hold on to his own version of the past, but it fell away in fragments like a dream he was desperate to remember.

"Who told you this?"

"My mom, of course. When I grew up. She waited all night. She was excited about meeting you, couldn't believe it was happening, that we'd be a family. When she heard about the crash, she thought you'd died too. But there was only one body. She figured either he didn't tell you, or he did, and you refused to go with him. That's what she had to live with."

"Fuck." Steven wanted so badly to unlearn what he'd heard, wipe the slate clean again. Now here was yet another reason to feel guilty about that night, a reason so cruel, so twisted, he doubted he'd ever feel normal again. He got up and started to pace, then he stopped and supported himself with both hands on the back of an armchair.

"Aiden … your dad *did* ask me to go with him. But he didn't say why. We never had much time together. I was pissed he was leaving. We argued. If I'd gone with him, we'd have left sooner. Minutes. It wouldn't have happened, the accident." He thumped the chair with his fists. "And now this. I'm not saying I don't believe you. I'm saying it's a punch in the gut. There's a lot more about that night—" He started pacing again. "It doesn't matter, unbelievable stupid stuff, a whole bunch of lives truly messed up. And now yours too. You'd have had a father. You would have grown up with us. Jesus."

They looked at each other in silence, Steven recognizing the features of his dead brother in the face of this young man who seemed to have fallen from the sky. He wanted to scream with frustration, rail against the unfairness of it all, the horrible twist of fate that turned one night into a never-ending nightmare.

"Could he paint, my father?" Aiden said, his voice a hoarse whisper now.

My father. Colin's boy. For the first time since arriving, Steven felt a shiver of joy.

"Your dad was into sports. He used to tease me about painting when we were young, but he'd show me off to his friends, kind of proud. It was our grandmother who painted—your great-grandmother. She was very talented." He gestured to the artwork around the room. "That's where we got it, you and me." His voice broke. "Guess it runs in the family."

He took a step towards Aiden. "I need to know something. You're my nephew, goddamnit it. Can we make this work?"

On an impulse, he seized Aiden by the shoulder and drew him into a clumsy hug. He could smell lemon shampoo in his hair and feel the coarseness of his denim shirt. This guy was his flesh and blood, his nephew. He felt, as though his brother were up there laughing, wondering why it had taken so long, slapping him on the back and saying, "Yep, that's my kid. Look after him, bro, okay?"

CHAPTER 10

Aiden shielded his eyes from the lowering sun and gazed over Bowen Island to the long, forested ridge of Vancouver Island on the horizon. Even after several visits, he had trouble believing he was here, and welcome, in West Van, at the home of his uncle, one of Canada's best-known painters. In the past, all West Van had ever meant to him was golf, tennis, wealth, and privilege.

On his first visit, he'd nearly missed the house: an elaborate log cabin looking like it had grown organically from the woods. Trees huddled protectively around it and plants strayed over the front steps. It had giant wooden beams and tall, wide windows, peaked gables on the second floor, and a massive grey stone chimney. Aiden's battered Honda Civic looked pitiful on the driveway next to the shiny BMW. He felt awkward, sitting in the cavernous living room on the plump leather couches around the fireplace. It smelled of cedar and pine, salt from the sea... and money. Steven had brought out a couple of photo albums and shown him pictures of his father when they were younger, and some of a young woman, a year older than Aiden ... Steven's daughter, Catherine. Steven said she was artistic too, but with no appetite to follow her father. She taught art history and loved it. So he had a *cousin*. The word had sat in Aiden's head with nothing to anchor it. He felt no family connection, rather a sense of detachment, as though he were a voyeur, sneaking a look at a past life he could never lay a serious claim to.

The last couple of weeks had gone by in a blur: various meals with Steven and Natalie, visits to art galleries, introductions to Steven's agent and a few dealers and gallerists. He felt completely out of his league, but everyone had been so kind, so encouraging. He wouldn't be surprised if Steven had put them all up to this, and couldn't shake the feeling he was being patronized. His uncle insisted he show up at the art course in person, although they did not reveal their relationship. He had hung out with a couple of the other students, and felt, for the first time in his life, as though he were, indeed, an artist.

Now, here he was sitting on his uncle's deck, his feet on the big, square coffee table on the deck, feeling *almost* at home.

He had been invited tonight because Steven had something important he wanted to discuss. His wife was out of town, this would be a good night to get together. Aiden assumed the discussion would be about his job and how he should start thinking about another field. His pay at the IT company was not great, but it covered his expenses. The thought of taking a chance on something else did not sit well. Steven told him he mustn't worry about money, but that was a thorny subject; he was not prepared for the role of grateful poor relation.

They'd had a difficult conversation over lunch one day, Steven telling him he'd done freelance advertising when he was about Aiden's age. It was well paid, and he'd learned a lot, he said. But Aiden imagined the humiliation of walking into some hotshot ad agency, sitting in the glass office of a creative director who wore a tight black T-shirt and had yellow spikes in his hair. Maybe the guy would have his feet on the desk while he flicked through Aiden's work, not changing his expression. A colleague would come by and say he had a meeting. He'd apologize and tell Aiden he had to go now, they'd keep him in mind, and good luck and all that.

"You're so creative," Steven persisted. "One day, you could make good money from this talent. You're got a gift for design, too. You work with different media, you know how to blend technology and art."

"I do it for fun. I can't imagine making a living at it."

"What about architecture? Interior design? Website design?"

What kind of world did his uncle live in, Aiden thought, offering careers like fortune cookies? All you had to do was pick one. *You will be a successful architectural designer.* He wondered if a father figure in his life, someone giving him advice through his teens, would have made a difference to his pessimistic outlook. Even if he'd dismissed the advice at the time, it could have been life-changing.

The sky was darkening now and a light rain blew through the trees. Aiden picked up the beer glasses and bowls of chips and handed them to his uncle through the window.

"We'll eat in the kitchen," Steven said.

Dorothy would have loved this blue and white kitchen, Aiden thought, the reality of her absence hitting him again. He'd never be able to tell her about his new relationship and what Steven said about his work. He'd never again endure one of her embarrassing squeezy hugs, and hear her shout, "What did I tell you?" How much did she know, he asked himself for the thousandth time? She knew nothing of his father's brother, had no idea what he had become. *Or did she?*

"So," Steven said, settling himself on a swivel chair opposite Aiden at the kitchen island, and pushing a big slice of pizza toward him. "How would you like to go to Morocco?"

It took a while to sink in. Aiden assumed he was being asked to join his uncle on a visit to his friends in Fez. While cautiously pleased with the idea, he protested about money and taking time off. But then came all the details of an arts festival, how these friends wanted Steven to get involved, or at least to show up at the end as a guest of honour. But they had a more immediate and pressing need, which was where Aiden would come in: the development of websites and promotional literature for the different events and for their own hotels. The objective, his uncle explained, was to promote Morocco as an artist's country, a country which stimulated and rewarded creative exploration. Aiden would stay at the hotel in Fez, the Riad Capella, his meals would be covered, and he'd be given an expense allowance. Because he had both artistic *and* technological skills, he'd be a great asset for this project. It would be a good experience and a resume builder for him, and he could paint in his spare time.

"But they don't even know me. Why would they be interested in me?" Aiden said, struggling to work out whether to be thrilled or terrified.

Steven claimed he'd be doing him a favour, a peace offering to make up for his own lack of participation.

"Look," he added, "it's not settled. Obviously, you need to hear a lot more about the expectations, and they need to get a sense of what you're all about. Dominic's coming to Toronto. They have a hotel there, the Darija. It's a fabulous place. We'll go see him, stay there a couple of days. You guys can talk. You're under no obligation. See how you feel. Besides, you'll get to meet your cousin, Catherine, and my artsy friends in the city. What the hell. It can't hurt."

When he drove home, Aiden couldn't focus on the traffic. He pulled into a side road leading to Point Atkinson lighthouse, and walked to the headland facing south over Burrard Inlet. As the beacon flashed through the darkness, the city skyline in the distance came in and out of view.

He stood for a few minutes and let the wind and fine rain blow his hair back. Morocco. Holy shit. He thought about how his life had changed in a few short weeks, how he'd been catapulted into a privileged world where people had talent and money and influence. He did not believe he could belong in this world. Something would surely go wrong, one little part of it would be unstable, and the whole lot would come tumbling down.

He had driven to his uncle's, resolved to tell him the truth about his birth mother and his childhood, admit the woman who had died at Vancouver General was one of the most wonderful people in the world, but not his mother. Now, he was glad he hadn't. He was going to Toronto to meet his cousin. He may be going to Morocco to work on a dream project. If all these people knew his mother was once a drug addict and was still alive, they might have a different opinion of him.

But his reluctance to tell the full story ran deeper than that. Maggie had written again, almost begging to see him, as though with the death of her sister, she had the right to reassume her role. Through all his formative years, he'd been at the very bottom of Maggie's priorities, and yet here she was, thinking a couple of pleading letters could undo her devastating neglect.

He turned from the sea and walked back to the car. Well, now *she's* the one who doesn't matter, he said to himself, and I'm the one who doesn't give a shit.

Sometimes, he thought, as he drove back to the main highway, the truth is not the most important thing.

CHAPTER 11

As the plane cut a wide arc over Lake Ontario, Aiden wrestled with both optimism for the future and unpleasant memories of the past. He could recall little of his years in Toronto, only the loneliness and constant disruption of his childhood, his envy of kids who had two real parents and regular meals. Dorothy told him Toronto was no match for the natural splendour of Vancouver, boasting a mountain at the end of its main street, but as Aiden grew up and started work, Toronto took shape in his mind as a city of consequence. He had to stifle a yearning for the action and stature it represented.

Steven closed his laptop. "Shit. Guess we're here."

He knew his uncle wasn't keen on the city, claiming to be a country boy at heart. In his view, Toronto was judgmental like New York— shape up or ship out. He used to have a condo here but swore it felt like a Venus flytrap; he could feel the hinged lobes snapping shut when he stepped inside. But he insisted Aiden should take no notice of him … it was a whole different ball game when you're young.

Through the window of the limo, Aiden gazed at the turmoil of construction. At every corner were enormous cranes teetering on the edge of craters, palettes of steel beams swinging on cables, guys waving their arms to guide the loads. He marvelled at how everyone knew who did what, and what went where. Somehow, another tower would emerge, proud and defiant, from all this chaos. If only building your own life could be as methodical and predictable, he thought.

When they pulled into the Darija Hotel carport, Aiden was confused. This was not like any hotel entrance he'd ever seen. The Moorish archway, tiled in more colours than he could name, was a singular attraction. A doorman was taking a photo of a couple posing in the centre.

The bellboy who ran out to take their luggage stopped in his tracks. "Mr. Farrow. So good to have you back."

Aiden was introduced and ushered into the lobby. *Holy shit* was all he could think, pivoting on his heel, widening his eyes in amazement at elaborate lanterns, Moroccan wall hangings, chairs and sofas in turquoise, red, yellow, purple.

"Wait until you see the one in Fez," Steven said. "Sorry, shouldn't get ahead of myself."

Aiden was embarrassed by the check-in process. His uncle had assured him the trip was paid for, and to put money out of his mind, but he felt like a freeloader. He'd never stayed in a nice hotel before and wondered what a night in a place like this would cost—likely close to a month's rent back home.

Steven was in conversation with the receptionist and a man who looked like he could be the manager. One of the bellmen offered Aiden a glass of mint tea and suggested he sit and wait in the arched corridor at the edge of the courtyard. He leafed through a coffee table book with photos of Morocco. What struck him most were the colours: no boring greys and whites, no steel and glass. It was indeed a painter's country, he thought, landscapes of rich gold, cadmium red and cobalt blue already playing in his mind.

"So, you approve?" Steven said, handing him the key card for his room.

"Blown away, man," was all he could say.

In his room, Aiden lay on the couch and took stock of his life, wondering if he might actually have a *future*. He used to think a future was only for people who went to college, people whose parents invested in education savings plans, whose grandparents would ask, "What do you want to be when you grow up?" No one had ever asked him that. He grew up knowing that if you wanted to eat, you got a job and, if you had a job, you were lucky and shouldn't waste time thinking about getting a different one. Now, he had a family. And he was an "honoured guest" at an expensive hotel. He forced himself to keep a mental distance from it all. Too many times in his childhood, he'd been promised something exciting—a visit to the zoo, a meal at McDonald's with a classmate—and it never happened. Only when Dorothy adopted him, did promises come true, but she rarely had enough money for anything special. He learned to live with low expectations.

From the pocket of his jacket, he withdrew the latest letter from Maggie. He had plucked it from the mailbox in Vancouver as the taxi came to take him to the airport. The letters had been coming more frequently in recent weeks.

Aiden … I keep writing because I keep hoping.

I got a call from Amy, your dad's wife. We used to be friends before their marriage went sour, and everything went wrong between us. But that's all water under the bridge, and I think she feels bad for me now. She told me what's happened, that you met your uncle and you're both on a visit to Toronto. I'm so happy for you, Aiden. I only ever wanted the best for you. I know it sounds trite, but I mean it.

It would be so easy to get together here in the city. Even for just a minute or two.

"Why would my father's widow give a shit about you?" he said out loud.

He did not like the thought of these women talking about him and, worse, knowing his whereabouts. Steven told him he'd spoken to Amy about Aiden coming on the scene, and she was cool, almost as though she'd known of his existence for a long time, and it was of little relevance to her now. She had remarried and moved out east some years ago, apparently. But the fact that she and Maggie used to be friends and still had some kind of relationship was weird and troubling to Aiden. He wondered how either of them knew he was in Toronto. He hoped Amy didn't blab about Maggie to anyone in the family or he'd have some explaining to do; he didn't want to be put on the defensive.

Of course, he reasoned, if he confessed now, maybe it wouldn't be such a big deal. But he couldn't face it. He tossed the latest letter aside, unwilling to let it spoil the pleasure of this visit. Steven had lined up several people for him to meet. Nigel and Philippe, two very good friends for years, were apparently beside themselves with the news about Aiden, and were putting on a gourmet feast for him later in the week. They owned an antiques store in town and were thinking of selling it because Philippe's health wasn't good. So a visit to their store was also on the agenda.

Today, Steven was going to introduce him to his cousin, Catherine. Tomorrow, the three of them would visit a pilot project gallery of Penelope Pagonis, a well-known art dealer friend of Steven, with homes in both Vancouver and Toronto. He had met Penelope briefly three weeks ago. Steven encouraged him to show her photos of his work. Knowing most artists would willingly grovel for five minutes of her time, he expected her to make a few encouraging remarks, then wish him well for the future. Penelope was a flamboyant, colourful creature, sporting jet black hair, big jewelry and long purple fingernails. He was suspicious of her intense focus, the way she zoomed in on certain pieces, asking him about the materials he used, what inspired him, and he wondered if Steven put her up to this, wanting to make him feel good. But if she was faking it, she was doing a fine job. His tiny spark of self-belief took deeper root.

***

Waiting at the restaurant for Catherine, Aiden was nervous. He expected her to be condescending or privately appalled by this relative rising from the gutter, and worried she had agreed to meet only on the insistence of her father. Or maybe she was suspicious that Aiden would be after his money. He detected anxiety in his uncle, too, and wondered if he shared the same concerns.

But when he became aware of a woman standing in the entranceway, he felt an unexpected flush of relief and pleasure. Catherine made straight for their table, arms wide, a huge grin, brushing past her father to give Aiden a big hug.

"Where've you been all my life?" she said, kissing him on both cheeks. "God, you even look a bit like me." She held on to him so long, he wasn't sure where to put his hands, then slid into the seat opposite and summoned the waiter for a glass of wine. "Geez, you're real, a blood relative in the flesh. I can't believe Uncle Colin didn't fess up. What a dumbass family we are."

Steven put a hand on her arm. "I don't think—"

"Shit. Aiden Quinn," she said, punching him in the shoulder. "Tell me everything right from the beginning. Dad says you have heaps of talent. Holy bananas, I still can't believe this. You're so cute, too. I love you already."

Despite her high spirits throughout the lunch, Aiden kept expecting her to remember an appointment, an excuse to leave, or say she was too busy to go with them to the gallery. But none of that happened. Much later, she told him she'd been as excited and nervous as he was. "Don't forget," she said, "I was an only child, no other cousins, with two separated and reclusive parents."

It was impossible not to be swept up by her exuberance and directness. She made him feel he was someone worth meeting, someone who had an interesting life with points of view to share. She even asked if he had any kind of love interest, professing great delight that he was unattached. Too bad he didn't live in Toronto, she said— all her friends would be lined up. He didn't believe that for a moment, but found himself indulging in something missing for so long in his life: laughter. Catherine made him laugh. And she made her father laugh, often in exasperation, but with rolling eyes and shrugs of happy defeat.

As Aiden listened to their bantering and teasing, he had a hard time suffocating the simmering resentment of his father, whose procrastination had robbed him of the chance to be part of this family.

CHAPTER 12

At Penelope's experimental gallery in a trendy west end neighbourhood, Aiden felt like a stranger in a familiar land. The pieces on display inspired a deep sense of connection, yet made him gasp with admiration: gothic gone mad, futuristic horror, a blending of sound and video, CG fractals, and algorithmic art. He moved closer to one wall, fascinated by a long skinny painting of baseball caps with crude slogans, pegged to a laundry line. As he watched, the slogans changed. Digital icons on the floors and walls came alive when he scanned them with his phone. They pitched him into the centre of forests, coral reefs, and waterfalls, and trapped him in the path of an avalanche.

Penelope sashayed out of her office, as warm and welcoming as she'd been in Vancouver. "Told you you'd love it," she said. "Walk around. Enjoy."

Aiden sat on the bench in the centre of the main floor and felt he was witnessing the future. Here was a whole new world of art with fresh textures and materials, inviting and shocking, passive and interactive. Despite following a few contemporary artists online, he had never seen so much innovation all in one place. He longed to be part of it.

Upstairs, a series of small paintings cleverly echoed and played with revered masterpieces, like Vermeer's *Girl with a Pearl Earring* sporting a face full of tattoos.

"Penelope," Steven said. "This is sacrilege."

"They're an homage to the masters. Don't be so *old*. You've always embraced the modern approach."

"I bet Monet would love this." Aiden gestured to a painting of water lilies, their centres replete with masses of tiny phallic stamens. "He liked breaking rules."

"Guess I *am* old," Steven said.

"No, Steven, you're middle-aged," said Penelope. "Which means you've stalled. We all need a kick in the ass at our age." She kissed him on the cheek, leaving a purple lipstick mark she rubbed away. "Don't even *think* of arguing. I am always right."

"So what's the plan?" Steven asked. "Are you keeping this place? Is it permanent? How are you going to manage it from Vancouver?"

Penelope explained the gallery was a pilot project, an attempt to find young, undiscovered talent, particularly artists experimenting with new media. She might move it online and only exhibit a few times a year, or find a small bricks and mortar place for a permanent location.

Catherine seized Aiden's arm and ushered him downstairs. "Come on, let's leave these two middle-aged people. Penelope wants us to look at the new stuff she's considering."

A whimsical little man named Michael, a friend of Penelope's, settled them in front of a monitor in the back office and showed them how to access the files. They scrolled through, exclaiming, recoiling, drawing closer to the different approaches. Aiden could tell this work was the result of sweat and passion, of beginning, discarding and starting over, as he so often did.

He absorbed the energy and enthusiasm of Catherine at his side, and had a momentary "out of body" experience, trying to grasp that this vibrant, attractive woman with a great mop of auburn hair was actually his blood relative. He asked her if it was weird, having him around.

She swivelled on her chair to face him. The intense brightness of her eyes gave her a curious and challenging countenance. "Weird but cool. I love that you're here. I was an only child, and you're my only cousin. Hey, you're my ally. We can gang up on my dad."

"Guess you don't remember *my* dad?"

She knew him from photographs, she said, reminding Aiden she was only three when he died. "Does it bother you to talk about the past?"

"Only when I think what could have been. But, what's the point?"

She suggested they have dinner before he left, just the two of them, and swap stories of their traumatic childhoods. He worried Steven would be hurt if he was not included.

Catherine laughed. "Aiden, my dad is barely social. You must have figured that out by now. He'll be thrilled he doesn't have to go anywhere."

They continued scrolling through presentations of both established and hopeful artists, and stopped on a photograph of a spiral staircase.

"It's kind of *tromp l'œil*." Catherine peered closer. "Where would you step onto it?"

"Maybe here." Aiden pointed. "But it would be like you're going down, not up. You'd feel drunk, for sure. It's amazing."

Penelope strode in and draped her arms around their shoulders. "Isn't it fun? That's Maurice Durand. You should see the furniture he does. Chairs with only two legs, sofas that swallow you whole. I'm going to do an exclusive. He's young, outrageous and so charming. You'll meet him tonight."

"Tonight?" said Aiden and Catherine in unison.

"My husband's party. Steven didn't tell you? What an impossible creature he is. He probably forgot on purpose. Lots of wealthy art patrons. They love the chance to show off to each other. You *must* meet them."

"Not sure I belong with your jet set, Penelope," Catherine said.

Penelope gave a throaty laugh. "You sound like your father. Let me teach you a life lesson, you lovely young thing. Everywhere you go, you *belong*. Get that into your head, and no one will stand in your way.

Understood? Same goes for you, Aiden." She planted a kiss on both their cheeks.

The brush of her lips and the smell of her perfume made Aiden's skin prickle. Quite the package, this woman, he thought, while wondering for the first time in his life if he had the right clothes to wear to a fancy party of artists and art patrons.

"Where *is* my father anyway?" Catherine asked. "Still upstairs fretting?"

"He slipped off to have coffee with his agent. We'll pick him up there in an hour. Enough time to tell you everything I'm planning for this gallery. I need some youthful input."

As she outlined her plans, Penelope kept pausing, asking them what they thought, encouraging them both to be honest.

Aiden seized the opportunity to voice his ideas. "These days, there aren't many things that exist just for you to look at," he said. "Even reading ... you can highlight a word and get the definition from a whole bunch of different dictionaries. You can click on embedded links to learn where the ideas came from. In some stories, you can even choose your ending. Everything's more and more interactive. Art and design should be the same way."

Penelope listened attentively. He wondered again if she was for real, or if this rapt attention was part of her game.

***

A few hours later, as they maneuvered through the chaos of downtown, Aiden could tell Steven was attending the party tonight under sufferance. Catherine had told him her father was useless at social gatherings, having the personality of an English bulldog. Now, he lagged behind, getting honked at by impatient drivers and yelled at by cyclists.

"Careful, Dad," Catherine called out. "Stay with the tour."

Aiden envied them their playful exasperation with each other. He'd never had that kind of relationship with anyone. His friends from work were sports fans and fake macho, and his quietness and artistic ways made him a bit of an outsider. He could often sense them shrugging or rolling their eyes behind him.

Penelope shared some gossip about the guests, separating them into those with "serious coin" and a genuine interest in art, and the pretenders who were desperate to prove they were living successfully.

As they reached the imposing condo on the lake, and a deferential concierge ushered them into a cavernous lobby, Aiden felt a flutter of nerves and hoped his black jeans and linen shirt would pass muster.

The door to the penthouse suite opened to laughter, the clatter of plates and a chorus of welcome. The hallway was jammed with people pressed against the wall, clutching their wine glasses in hands raised above their shoulders. Penelope wove through the crowd, introducing Catherine and Aiden. Most of the guests knew or recognized Steven and asked what direction his work was taking now and whether he had a show coming up.

"Do they own all this art?" Aiden asked Catherine. "The Lena Zielinska over there. Jesus. It must be worth more than the whole condo."

She shrugged, saying Penelope had oodles of money, and if he wheedled his way into her favour, he'd be set for life. "That's her husband. Vassilis. Come on, I'll introduce you."

Aiden followed her discreet point to the window. A man in a cream jacket with thick, iron-grey hair stood tall, one hand on his hip, the other cradling a cocktail, studying the sparkling frenzy of the city beneath him. He looked for all the world as though he were surveying his own property.

He turned, offering Aiden his hand, and introduced himself.

"Pleased to meet you. I'm Aid—"

Vassilis smiled, revealing a mouthful of perfect teeth. "The long-lost nephew of Steven Farrow, our famous painter. Enjoy yourself. My rich friends will want to meet you. Make them buy your paintings." He turned and was gone.

Aiden found himself alone in the high-pitched excitement of the room, everyone embracing and air-kissing around him. Climbing onto an empty barstool, he watched Steven being passed from one effervescent group of art lovers to another, all proclaiming their impressive credentials and private collections. He felt a surge of affection for his uncle—probably the only person in the room who did not give a fig about the social impression he made. Aiden doubted he himself could ever fit, or even make a dent, in this giddy world of sycophants. Artists are reclusive, he thought. They all have to act out of character to make a living.

Penelope was perched on the edge of a couch, listening to an elderly man, hands clasped under her chin. One black satin shoe hung loose from her foot. She caught his eye.

"Aiden, come and meet Sergei and his wife, Tanya. They are huge supporters of young artists. Show them your work."

Cowed by the Norval Morrisseau and Lawren Harris on the wall behind them, he considered pretending he hadn't heard. But there was no escape. Penelope took his phone and did the scrolling, stopping to comment on a few pieces, heartily agreeing with her guests' compliments. A few others joined the little group, leaning over Sergei's shoulder to peer at the phone. They asked him questions. When he answered, talking about a subject he knew and loved so dearly, his shyness gradually faded. He could scarcely believe these wealthy art lovers admired his talent, and prayed they did not quietly despise it.

CHAPTER 13

Catherine clinked her wine glass with his. "Our family, Aiden, is all screwed up. Welcome aboard."

They were on the upper terrace of a trendy, noisy, Italian trattoria in midtown Toronto, with hefty green canopied umbrellas, potted plants and fat candles. Aiden was not a wine drinker but felt obliged to share the bottle. Beer would simply not fit.

His cousin was full of barely contained energy, tapping her fingers on the table or dragging a stray auburn curl behind her ear. He admired the smooth, tanned skin beneath her off-the-shoulder white T-shirt, surprised he could smother a strong sexual desire with the even more intoxicating thought of kinship. It was an unfamiliar sensation, so intense, he was sure his confused excitement showed on his face. He sorted through the strange lettuce leaves on his plate, and tried to spear what he learned were pomegranate arils with his fork.

Catherine talked a little about her parents, admitting to being her father's girl. Her mother, now remarried, suffered from agoraphobia and was unwilling to leave the house for more than grocery shopping. They rarely saw each other.

"And *your* mother?" She gave him a quizzical look bordering on challenging, then reached over to pinch his arm. "Sorry, I know it's a difficult subject, but there's only us."

He told her Dorothy had devoted her life to raising him. *He* was her job, she'd said, and the other things she did—cashier at the drug store, answering phones for a telecom company—simply paid bills and put food on the table. He surprised himself with how easily all this fell from his tongue. *Dorothy* was his mother. Even when Catherine, after getting into the second bottle of wine, waded into the loss of his father, and asked how his mom had coped with it all, he lied with no hesitation. He explained how Dorothy had told him all about it when he was older, how devastated she was, waiting all night for Colin to arrive, telling Aiden he would have loved his dad like she did. Catherine gave him a curious gaze, as though she wasn't buying this touching story. With a theatrical sigh, she pronounced the two brothers, Colin and her father, to have been cut from the same cloth, and how it was such a pity everyone was scared of the truth.

She looked at him for a long few moments. "Dad told you my Aunt Amy—your dad's wife—knew about you, right? Women always know. How Uncle Colin could have an affair and a child and not think his wife had a clue … I mean, get real. When he died, the family more or less fell apart. I'm the only one who stays in touch with Aunt Amy."

The tangled web saying came into Aiden's head. Maybe Maggie and Amy knew his whereabouts through Catherine, he thought, his mind racing. Maybe Catherine knew about Maggie and was confused when he called his mother Dorothy. Or maybe Amy said nothing about Maggie. He found these speculations exhausting. If ever there was a time to confess, this was it. He looked at his food, not sure what expression he should assume. Here he was, guilty of exactly what irritated Catherine: hiding the truth. But the repercussions of honesty were too messy to contemplate. He didn't want to think, much less talk, about Maggie.

Catherine was still giving him that skeptical look. "So." She pushed her appetizer plate to the side. "You're going to Morocco. How fucking amazing."

He leapt at this, grateful for the change of subject. "I haven't been officially approved. I daren't believe it yet."

"Oh, bull. They'll adore you. You're meeting Mr. Sexy Pants himself tomorrow, I hear."

"I guess you mean Dominic? Do you know him?"

"Dad hasn't told you? Geez, what is it with men? They miss out all the important bits. He and I were engaged."

He must have looked shocked because she burst into a peel of laughter. "What a couple of idiots we were. How did it get that far? More secrets. *He* was in love with another woman, too, married to her now, which should have happened years earlier."

"No hard feelings?"

"None. We both dodged a bullet. Their third kid is on the way. *Three*, and one who's adopted. Lukas—another long story. You'll learn all about it when you go."

Now and then, Catherine flashed him a challenging look, and his sense of unreality grew stronger. He glanced at the growing lineup for a table and the crowd jostling at the bar. The people were roughly his age, maybe a few years older, talking loudly with brazen confidence. The women had short skirts, high heels and long eyelashes; the men wore pointy tan leather shoes and shiny navy blue jackets, their shirts open at the neck. The midtown after-work crowd, he thought, if there was still such a thing. Taylor Swift and Ariana Grande played in endless loops through speakers attached to light fixtures around the deck. The wine was making his head mushy. He ate mechanically, worrying whether his Visa could manage his share of the cost. Steven kept telling him not to fret about money, but only people with money said that.

Catherine topped up his glass again. The restaurant blurred and shifted sideways. He reached for the water instead.

"So your mom? She never met anyone else? She mourned your dad all those years and then died of cancer? I mean, sorry if it's painful but you know, that's like twenty-some years without a guy. Must have been hard."

Jesus. Not again. Aiden looked away, hoping she'd just drop it. In the end, it was none of her damned business.

Catherine leaned in closer, then abruptly drew back. "Never mind." She waved her arm and knocked her wine glass from the table. "Oh fuck," she said, making no move to retrieve it.

A waiter came over with napkins to soak up the spillage and replaced her glass. Those at nearby tables paused to observe the scene, but soon returned to their lively discussions.

Catherine took a long drink of water. "People shouldn't hold grudges. They only hurt themselves." She stared at him over her glass, as though wanting to make sure this sunk in.

Aiden nearly blurted out the truth, but knew he'd regret it. He wasn't sure how drunk *he* was, and didn't want to risk making more of a scene. Besides, he felt they should make a move to leave. Catherine insisted on paying, and the waiter had to help her with the machine.

After he saw her safely into the Uber, he walked unsteadily to the hotel, trying to replay the last part of their discussion. Throughout the dinner, he felt she was bracing to divulge something, or there was a silent accusation in the air she wanted to voice. He thought she might have been drinking all that wine to bolster her courage.

He undressed quickly, leaving his clothes scattered about, and fell clumsily into bed. Weeks ago, his uncle had said a lot of people's lives got messed up on the day his dad died. Every family has something to hide, he thought. He pulled the covers over his head and took comfort from the darkness, wondering if spilling secrets and learning hard truths were as liberating as people claimed, or whether some things were best left in the dark. Then he asked himself if that last thought was a weak attempt to justify his silence. He fell into a foggy, restive sleep before reaching any conclusion.

CHAPTER 14

The first thing Aiden noticed about Dominic was how people gave way to him, stepping aside to allow him to walk unimpeded. The hotel staff shrank back with deference, or retreated within hailing distance in the anticipation of being needed. Yet there was nothing ostentatious about the man, only the forgivable arrogance that comes from charm and well-honed self-confidence. A waitress he greeted blushed with confusion, a bellboy stammered his appreciation of a compliment.

Steven told him Dominic's family were wealthy, and Aiden tried to understand why this wealth was now obvious to him. Since he was a child, he took note of how people dressed, partly because the cheap, practical clothes he had to wear contrasted so poorly against those of other kids. The jacket Dominic wore was not particularly notable and his shoes had a few scuffs at the toe. Yet, somehow, the cut of the clothes, the slimline tailoring of pants, the way the shirt collar showed above the cream sweater, even the way the guy stood, shoulders back, eyes sweeping the whole room … all this spoke of understated wealth. And he had classic, enviable Mediterranean good looks: olive skin, dark deep-set eyes, a proud Arab nose that was slightly crooked, as though it had once been broken. And that hair—thick, long, unruly. A masterpiece of globe-trotting sensuality, Aiden thought. He understood the family would be going to Chile in a couple of weeks, so crossing oceans back and forth was obviously no big deal. Aiden was now acutely aware of his lanky frame, his lack of any muscular definition, his faded jeans and well-worn running shoes. He felt a heavy sinking in his gut. He was being considered for a role he had no idea how to play.

Dominic and his uncle embraced, holding on to each other for what seemed far longer than necessary. Steven beckoned Aiden over, and they went through the introductions, Dominic standing back to appraise him, then pulling him close for one of those long hugs.

"Welcome to the Darija, Aiden Quinn," he said. "*Incroyable.* The things life has in store for us. Just when we think the incredible story of our two families is spinning along more predictably, you step out from the shadows. Come, I've asked for Moroccan *meze* to be set up for us in one of the private rooms. We must talk and talk."

His English was flawless, albeit with a French accent that only underscored his charisma. The ensuing conversation over the constantly replenished small appetizer dishes, followed by bowls of sugared almonds, dates, figs and nuts, left Aiden in a daze. Whenever his glass of minted water was down a few sips, a young waitress emerged from behind the gold braided curtains with another refill.

"There are days when I regret we started this festival idea so quickly," Dominic said. "We could have waited a year, especially as we're off to Chile soon and we have the new hotels to worry about. But we can't afford to miss out on the new travel enthusiasm."

He explained he and his brother, Hadir, would be needed frequently at their other hotels. Zahra, their interior design consultant, an artist and designer in her own right, would be in charge of the festival arrangements in Fez. There were many people involved: event managers, travel and tourism reps, local artists and photographers, etc., etc. so there would likely be a fair amount of juggling of both schedules and egos.

Aiden drank a little wine but was conscious of the need to stay clear and focused, especially as the talk turned to his art and design skills, and the possible help he could give.

"Don't worry, Aiden," Dominic said. "Your job would be to help design websites and promotional material for our hotels. Zahra is our point person, and you'd be working with her guidance. But I know she can also use all the organizational help she can get. You certainly won't be bored."

"I've got to ask why you're even thinking of me for this," Aiden said, not ready to fully embrace the idea. "Like, what about the language? My French is pretty basic. I didn't make it past grade ten."

Dominic leaned back, clasping his hands behind his head, and looked up at the ceiling as though deep in thought. Aiden tried to guess his age … mid-thirties, perhaps, so nine, ten years older than him. One decade and a whole world of different experiences. What must it take, he wondered, to live in Morocco with a wife and family, to have so much money you fly to a different hemisphere for your vacation, to profess concern about various hotel properties you own? He knew such people roamed the world but had never imagined one of them would be sitting across from him, potentially offering him a job.

Dominic sat up and leaned close to him: "Do you believe in fate, Aiden?"

What? "I haven't ever thought about it."

"Well, let me tell you. It's real. A living, breathing force out there orchestrating the details of our lives. It separates people and it brings them together. Your uncle and I met through a weird twist of fate. We had no reason at all to cross paths, and yet we eventually learned we had a significant connection, a couple of overlapping and dramatic events in our pasts. It was the work of fate." He looked at Steven, as though for confirmation.

Steven shook his head. "I haven't bothered him with all the details. Too complicated."

Dominic laughed. "That's for sure. Well, Aiden, if you agree to come, you will meet one of those details—the young boy who came into my life right here in this city, just as you have. Lukas. He'll be ten this year. And don't worry about language. English has become the language of our business. Obviously the literature and the website will need to be in French and Arabic and other languages. All that will be taken care of."

"But how do you know I can do any of this?"

"I don't. But I trust you. Will you trust me?"

Both men looked at him with glasses raised and wide smiles, almost as though something they'd planned years ago was now predictably coming to pass, and there was no possible reason in the world for him to decline.

***

Later that evening, alone with his uncle, Aiden had second thoughts. He protested he could never live up to the expectations. Dominic was clearly successful and busy and was probably used to getting his way, snapping his fingers and having everything miraculously materializing. Aiden was worried about letting them down.

"Oh boy," Steven said. "Dominic would laugh out loud if he heard that. I know he comes across that way, but I assure you he's a bundle of nerves and insecurity. He has a natural charm, but he's not a natural businessman. Just has great ideas. To be honest, he's a little bit… wacko. He has an uncanny sense of something going on out there. His brother accuses him of being into psychic nonsense. Hadir is so different. Straightforward and logical."

"But how come he trusts me. He doesn't know the first thing about me?"

"He saw your work. He was very impressed. You saw that."

"But why me? Lots of people have the same skills."

Steven inhaled deeply and looked up at the ceiling, shaking his head. "Because he's convinced it was meant to be. I know it sounds cuckoo, but you'll understand eventually. You were *meant* to materialize, you were meant to play a role in his life. When we talked on the phone and I told him about you, I was building up to gracefully declining my own role in this festival, but he cut me off. He was astonished, delighted you had come into our lives. He said, 'Steven, I don't need you. I am clearly meant to be inviting your nephew, not you.'"

"Meant to be? Shit, I don't think I can buy into that. I mean, aren't you worried? I could turn out to be a huge disappointment. It would reflect on you. You don't believe in this fate thing, do you?"

"I never used to, Aiden. But far, far too many things have happened that defy any logical explanation. So, yes, in a way, I do. Just go for it. And if you need help, if you're feeling lost or insecure, go to Dominic's wife, Amina. She's a lovely person. You think *he's* something? Wait until you see her."

PART II—THE PHOTOGRAPH

CHAPTER 15

Three weeks later, when Dominic left the Riad Capella, the boutique hotel he and his brother, Hadir, owned in Fez, he was a happy man. He and his wife, Amina, their adopted nine-year-old son, Lukas, their daughter Rosa, now five, and son Raif, two, were headed to Chile. He had weighed the pros and cons of such a long trip, especially as the arts festival was looming, and Amina was three months pregnant. But he reasoned, if they didn't go now, it would be at least a year before another suitable time. The trip was primarily an early birthday gift for Lukas, who was destined to follow the great passion of his birth parents—their study and deep love of the night sky. The boy said it would be awesome to see the stars from Chile's Atacama desert one day, never dreaming it might be possible.

On the flight to Santiago, Raif asleep on his lap, Amina cradled against him, Dominic gazed through the window at the jagged, snow-capped peaks of the Andes mountains piercing the few frothy white clouds. He marvelled at what a lucky man he was. He'd spent his early twenties "seeking the constant high," as his brother put it, experimenting with drugs and drink and women, all the time lacking the courage to admit what he really wanted: the woman beside him. He was still astonished she agreed to marry him.

After checking on Lukas and Rosa across the aisle, engrossed in a video jigsaw puzzle, he drifted into sleep with a clear and peaceful mind. He had no clue that someone from a painful chapter of his past would slide into his world again, that his charmed life would be thrown into turmoil, and his daughter, Rosa, would be the cause of it.

***

They arrived late at night, very tired, and fell into bed with hardly a glance at the spectacular mountains looming in the near distance. The following morning, Dominic woke to find the place beside him empty. He leapt up, stumbling over his unpacked suitcase, and looked for his children in the adjoining room: they were not there. He checked his watch. It was later than he realized. Of course, he thought, they will all be at breakfast. He dressed hurriedly, feeling a strange anxiety, not bothering to wash or to comb his hair. After a few wrong turns, he found the dining area. There was no sign of them.

"Señor, your family is outside," a waiter called to him in English, giving him a puzzled look. "We have taken coffee to your wife. Your children are exploring the garden."

He followed the waiter to the terrace and stopped, stunned by the snowy mountains, reflected like a mirror in the azure blue of the lake at the edge of the property. And there was Amina on a lounge chair, the generous folds of her white cotton dress reaching the ground on either side. She was cradling a cappuccino and picking at a plate of raspberries and sliced orange wedges.

"Finally," she said. "I was going to send Lukas to check on you." She turned fully to face him and laughed. "Your hair. You look like a werewolf. Did you take a shower yet?"

"You should have woken me. I got a real scare, waking up with no one there."

"Silly man. Where could we be? We certainly wouldn't get far without you." She pulled him close for a kiss.

He nestled his face into her shoulder and stroked her belly. "I don't like not knowing where you are. Especially in a foreign country. And you being pregnant."

"Dominic." She put both hands on his shoulders and pushed him away to study his face. "What's wrong? I think you're shaking. You worry too much. The people here are so kind. When they knew I was pregnant, they shepherded me out here, brought food, and warned me not to stay in the sun too long. Look how absolutely beautiful it all is. One of the staff, a young man, Julian, I think, said they have lots of horses in the stables here. He's going to take us to see them later. He's with the children below, in the garden. They have a little sanctuary with a couple of guanacos, so cute. Go and see."

He walked along a trail leading to a walled garden flanked by great swaths of pink and purple lupins and yellow-flowered, spiky bushes. For a few minutes, he sat on a bench to watch his three children: Lukas, clutching Rosa's hand; Raif, stumbling around in a sandpit trying to catch a baby guanaco. He closed his eyes, filled with a relief he couldn't name, and wondered if he was suffering from the lingering effects of a frightening, but now forgotten, dream.

***

Four days later, after a short flight north to the Atacama Desert, Dominic stared through the window of his room at the vast, red sandy plains, still trying to quash that twist of fear curled tight in the pit of his stomach. His brother liked to remind him he'd been prone to unnecessary fear and imaginings since he was a child, blaming their mother's Roma blood. "I hope you're not reading those Tarot cards," Hadir would say, rolling his eyes. "Enough to send anyone off the rails." After a bad experience some years ago, Dominic stayed away from the cards but insisted that whenever he felt fretful, it was a sense of premonition. Something weird was happening that would eventually affect him. "Something weird is always happening somewhere," Hadir countered. Dominic knew there was no point arguing with his rational brother.

He had always wondered how they could be so different and yet so close. Hadir was the anchor in this life, the mainstay. He wished he were here now so he could listen to another lecture from him and try to dismiss the vague sense of premonition he was wrestling with.

The landscape through the window changed colour inch by inch with the rising sun: from charcoal to pale grey, from dull red to bright orange. One star held on, stubbornly bright on the far horizon. Venus, he thought. Planet of love, harmony, and feminine guile.

Amina and the younger children had stayed behind at the lodge. She insisted this part of the trip would be too much for her, but he suspected she wanted Lukas, who'd been looking forward to the stargazing for months, to have his undivided attention for a few days. She would relax, swim, have a massage, she said; there were plenty of people only too happy to help with Rosa and Raif.

Lukas was still fast asleep in the other bed. On his side table lay the notebook his father had been writing for him before he died. The boy had clung to this since it came to him five years ago. He was desperate to understand every densely written page of astronomical maps, ephemeris charts, Ancient Egyptian stories, and legends of the night sky. There was a great deal about karma and fate, concepts which Lukas's father, Karl Gustav, an astronomer and Egyptologist, clearly wanted his son to embrace. But much of it was still beyond the boy's grasp.

It was this notebook that prompted the family's trip to Chile. In it, Lukas had found a photograph of the stars taken in the southern hemisphere, and showed it to Dominic. His father had written a note beneath it: *Atacama, Chile. The best place on earth to see the night sky. You must go there one day.* When they told Lukas the trip was booked, he burst into tears, worrying it was surely too much money. His humility and never-ending appreciation for the privileged life he now led in Morocco made the family love him all the more. Dominic pushed aside any concern about spoiling him, believing that meeting the orphaned boy five years ago was part of a grand scheme, a catalyst for healing old wounds, and a channel to new love and new worlds.

Careful not to wake him, Dominic picked up the notebook. It fell open on the page with the photograph Karl had taken, close to where they were now. On the opposite page was an image of a hieroglyphic, with these words:

Thoth: a personification of fate in Ancient Egypt. The ibis-headed scribe records the weighing of the heart against the feather of Ma'at, at the end of a life.

Next to this was a picture of the planet Neptune and a list of facts: *ice giant, 4.495 billion km from sun, radius 24,622 km, 165 earth years to orbit sun.* Dominic skimmed over the other data. On the same page, he recognized the constellation glyph for Pisces, his birth sign. Beside it was an eight-pointed star with the hand-written word *Isfet. Neptune ruled by Pisces,* the notes continued, followed by: *Guilt is the heaviest of burdens, but the inability to forgive is heavier still. Ancient Egyptians believed that forgiveness liberates both the guilty and the wronged.*

He typed *Isfet* into his phone: *An Ancient Egyptian term for disorder and chaos.* As he had so many times in the past few years, Dominic wished his mother were still alive. She would understand how these seemingly random observations were connected. She taught him as a child to pay attention to the signs around him, the messages nature imparted to those who paid attention. One night, standing on a beach in France, where he was born, she told him to close his eyes and listen to the heave and pull of the turning tide, feel its silent, powerful energy, wise and deep, far beyond the understanding of man. Dominic was not a religious person, but was convinced a greater force was always at work, transcending our ambitions, our petty challenges, and disappointments.

He lay on the bed and stared at the ceiling for a while, thinking about forgiveness and trawling through his labyrinth of old, troubled memories. Then he eased himself back under the covers, hoping for another hour's sleep.

CHAPTER 16

The road from San Pedro petered out after an hour, and the jeep swerved and shuddered along rough, gravel pathways, deep into the Atacama Desert. In the pitch dark, the headlights illuminated a bare forty to fifty metres of the vast, red plains. Dominic was amazed at how Manuel, a Chilean astronomer and their guide for this evening's excursion, could drive with such confidence over a landscape with no clear markers, one hand on the wheel, the other punctuating his animated conversation.

Dominic wanted to text Amina, but there was no signal, and he realized she'd be in bed anyway. He was always tense when they were apart, but that did not explain the grip of unease he still couldn't shake.

The jeep lurched through a serious dip in the pathway; he braced himself against the dashboard.

"Not long now," said Manuel. "Is the boy alright?"

Dominic twisted in his seat. "Looks fine to me."

Lukas clutched the grab handle over the door. He grinned, thumbs up.

They veered off the path and joined other vehicles in a makeshift car park, flanked by giant, rocky hills. From the trunk, Manuel pulled out backpacks, a telescope, a tripod, hiking poles, and three nightlight bands that they strapped around their heads.

"Don't look up at the sky yet," he said. "Your headlamps will interfere with the view."

He told them they were heading up the hill to the left. They should stay close behind him and keep looking down. There was a stream to cross, and they must watch where they were treading. In the distance, other lights bobbed and weaved, fellow stargazers searching for a place to settle. Manuel helped Lukas cross the stream and, with much clambering over rocks and backsliding on steep sandy patches, they reached the summit of the hill.

"Let your eyes get adjusted to the dark," Manuel said, when they caught their breath. He unclasped their headbands and tossed them into his bag. "Ready? Now turn around."

Dominic and Lukas pivoted unsteadily in the soft sand and, in unison, let out a gasp, hands to their faces. The Milky Way soared above them, its countless stars clustered along a shimmering violet ribbon of sky. Constellations overlapped, vying for attention, so densely packed, they crowded out the blackness.

"Worth the drive, yes?" said Manuel. "Time to relax now." He left them and went to set up the telescope on a rocky promontory.

Dominic sank to the ground, lost in the dazzling splendour.

"Look," Lukas said. "The Southern Cross. See it? And Orion's upside down. He's diving headfirst. His sword is pointing the other way. In our desert, he stands nearly straight up."

As Dominic followed the boy's excited gestures, he felt a flush of pride. *Our desert.* Five years ago, with Amina, he had taken this boy to the top of a dune on the other side of the world, and asked him to live with them in Morocco, to grow up there, go to school there, be part of their family. He would never forget the wide-eyed incredulity he saw on Lukas's face, his lower lip trembling, his gush of tears. At the beginning, Dominic and Amina were Lukas's guardians, and he was their ward, but they chafed at these soulless words and moved quickly to adopt him formally. The boy had called them by their first names when they met, and they felt strongly that this should continue. They knew his parents, Karl and Rachel, were exceptional people, drawn together through a shared love of the stars and the desert. While they would raise Lukas as *if* he were their own, they would never presume to hold the same place in the boy's heart.

With his father's blond hair and angular, Germanic features, Lukas stood apart in Morocco, and curious people often asked the family to explain his connection to them. In his quiet, intuitive way, Lukas solved that when he was seven years old. He announced he would say Dominic and Amina were good friends of his parents, who had died. "I know you never met them," he said. "But if you had, you'd be their friends for sure." Amina had seized the boy, smothering him in her tight embrace, trying to stifle her tears.

Manuel joined them again and challenged Lukas to find Sagittarius. The boy scrambled to his feet. "You bet. It's my sign. And Saturn's in it. I'll find it for sure."

"Dominic, *mi amigo*." Manuel fished two plastic glasses from his backpack and pulled a flask from his vest pocket. "A toast? Santa Rita Floresta Cabernet Sauvignon. One of Chile's best." They clinked glasses. "*Por nuestro pequeño genio*." He raised his glass in Lukas's direction.

"I know what that means," Lukas called back. "Our little genius. No way."

"*Dios mìo*. How many languages does the boy speak?" Manuel laughed.

"*Not* Spanish. I guess he has a good ear. English, French, and pretty decent Arabic. We think he could be gifted, or maybe his brain is just wired differently. He's studying German now."

Manuel gave an appreciative whistle. "His father was Swiss, right? Swiss German. I attended a lecture he gave in Washington many years ago. Brilliant man. But … unconventional. He studied Egyptology too, as of course you would know, how Ancient Egyptians interpreted the stars. I heard he took people into the desert, read their future. Unusual for a scientist. How do you say? Far-fetched?" He shrugged. "Who knows? Might have been gossip."

"From what I've learned," Dominic said, irked by the insinuation Lukas's father was of dubious character, "he was a serious man, with an uncanny insight into—"

"I found it," Lukas yelled. "Easy. And I found the Trifid Nebula."

Manuel finished his glass of wine and joined the boy.

Dominic put on the jacket tied at his waist, and lay full length on the blanket, letting his thoughts wheel around with the shooting stars while his two companions chattered away about supernovas and galactic centres. For him, the allure of the night sky had nothing to do with cosmology and the complex mathematics that inspired the passion of astrophysicists like Manuel. It was a great mystery, filled with the myths and legends of ancient worlds, and old lessons to be learned. What lessons must *I* still learn, he wondered. He knew he was considered arrogant by some of the people he worked with, and this bothered him. He was easy-going and blessed with good looks, so perhaps he came across that way unwittingly. Now, staring at the grandeur of the universe, he felt small and insignificant.

"The Ancient Egyptians called Orion *Sah*," Lukas was saying.

"And I believe Sirius was important to them," Manuel added.

"It meant the flooding of the Nile was coming."

"Where did you learn all this?"

"Mostly from the notebook my dad left me. Some stuff I don't understand. Dominic's helping me a bit."

Dominic listened with one ear as Lukas told Manuel about the courses he was taking online, how maybe one day he'd go to the university in Zurich to study astronomy, as his father did. And he wanted to take a course on Egyptology, but knew it would be hard and he might have to wait until he was older. Dominic was proud of the boy's ambition but also sad that one day, he'd almost certainly leave to explore the world. He consoled himself with the belief that Lukas was becoming thoroughly Moroccan and, surely, like him, would always want to come home.

The stars spun and swirled in the deep purple sky, and he felt drawn like a magnet into their dazzling midst, lost in the labyrinth of galaxies. A gust of wind blew across him. He struggled to sit up, shivering, and thought he must have drifted into sleep. His body felt like a dead weight, as though it had been dropped abruptly from the sky. The twinge of anxiety grew sharper. He got to his feet, dusting the sand from his clothes, annoyed with himself for his inability to suffocate it. He took inventory of his life and found nothing wanting, nothing out of kilter. If there was a serious issue back home, Hadir would call him; if there was a problem with his family, the people at the lodge knew how to reach him.

The page he'd looked at in Lukas's notebook this morning floated into his mind. He tried to recall the details: something about the Egyptian god Thoth, and the symbols of Pisces and Neptune. He had learned a little about astronomy and Ancient Egypt since Lukas came into his life, but struggled to make sense of how the science and mythology were connected.

"Hey, you guys," he called over. "Where's Neptune these days?"

"Way over there," Lukas said, pointing. "Like, billions of kilometres. It's in Pisces, Dominic. Your sign. For about a year."

Dominic looked in the planet's general direction with a wry smile. "What do you want with me, Neptune?" he muttered.

∗∗∗

Manuel took them to two major observatories in the Atacama Desert, open to the public with professional connections. After three nights, they flew back to the lodge in Patagonia, where Dominic was relieved to find Amina and the children well and thoroughly enjoying their stay. They spent a few more days there, swimming, visiting the stables, taking trips to see guanacos and vicuna, flamingos and condors, enthralled by the lush landscapes of this land on the far side of the world, such a contrast to the hot, barren desert of their home.

Still, Dominic failed to convince himself that his unease was rooted in the worry of being apart. The pestering sense of premonition still gnawed at him, disturbing his sleep. No matter how assiduously he searched his feelings and memories, it eluded his grasp, skittering back to the dark corners of his mind.

CHAPTER 17

Gabi always enjoyed being in Chile. She loved the forests and glaciers, the steep steppes and broad plains of the Patagonian plateau, the endless march of the snowcapped Andes on the horizon. She spoke passable Spanish, and the owners of the estancia, who were business partners with Al Sayed, made her feel welcome and respected. The new horses they'd purchased from her family had arrived a week earlier. As was customary, Gabi was there to check their health and put them through their paces, making sure the Chileans were satisfied. She'd had several opportunities to ride, cantering along winding trails in deep woods, emerging into meadows that burst with yellow calafate and orange-red sundew. So many times, she pulled up the horse and turned in the saddle in awe, shielding her eyes to watch the Andean condors circling above, breathing deeply to fill her lungs with crisp mountain air.

But this time she was anxious to get home. Masoud's illness seemed to be worsening, and she was clinging to the hope that, finally, she would have good news to share.

On the last leg of her flight to Ouarzazate, her tentative optimism was crushed. First, a spasm, then a searing cramp made her hunch forward, her arms clenched around her stomach. She swore under her breath, grabbed her bag, and stumbled to the bathroom. And there it was: blood. Doubled over, biting on clenched fists, she fought the waves of pain without making a sound.

Back in her seat, she wept and seethed in angry silence, as she had every month for the last two years. She was not pregnant.

She waved a hand dismissively at the hovering flight attendant.

Gabi knew that she was the subject of speculation for everyone in the family in Egypt. With Masoud rarely being there, she felt her cousins looking at her with thinly veiled curiosity, dismissing her as they would an inconvenient spinster aunt, despite her dedication to the business. Her desire to eventually buy them out and take over hardened.

As for Masoud, she clung to the hope that a child would stop that faraway look in his eyes, the absence she felt even if he were sitting right beside her.

Before she left for this trip, her father made a crude speculation about his fertility, even suggesting her impulsive union could be undone. "You could marry one of those Chilean boys. There's a business merger for you. You even speak the language."

Al Sayed and the Chilean enterprise had collaborated for years, raising horses for breeding, racing and recreational riding. Her father was smiling, but there was censure in those dark eyes. The prestige and reputation of the business were his priorities, and Gabi knew her happiness was only ever a peripheral concern. She didn't respond, partly because she didn't want to give him the satisfaction, but also because she'd already indulged in the guilty contemplation of what he'd so callously suggested.

The cramps grew more intense, and her muffled groan brought the flight attendant again. That's the problem with a private jet, she thought … nothing private about it at all.

A couple of months ago, after another disappointment, she called her friend Sally who lived in Rabat. Sally questioned Gabi's mothering instincts and her worry about the future, knowing she already had plenty of money. "Hey, I've got to get the kid first," Gabi countered. "Then I'll love it to bits, I promise you." But Sally persisted. "You've told me your marriage isn't a bed of roses. A baby won't make it better. And your father is hardly going to turn mushy. Don't do it for the wrong reasons." Getting irritated now, Gabi reminded Sally she needed a child to help her run the place in the future. Never mind how much money she had now, she said, she'd be damned before she let her lazy-ass cousins end up in a better position. She confided that Masoud seemed to be giving up on his health and she hoped a child would change that. Sally murmured something sympathetic but Gabi could tell she was not convinced.

She took out a pocket mirror and rubbed at her smudged mascara with a tissue, alarmed by her swollen face and puffy eyes, and resentful, once again, that she'd inherited neither the sculpted sensuality of her father's Arab side, nor the blue-eyed cowgirl charm of her mother. Her looks were stuck in the middle: brown hair, a round face with barely discernible cheekbones, and a nose a shade too large. Her mother dismissed these lamentations. "You are an attractive woman, Gabriella, but you have to start believing that yourself, or it won't show."

How can I believe it, she thought now, when my husband barely pays attention to me?

Gabi's mother was more sympathetic to her needs. But she was a woman who had battled with guile and charm to hold her own in a man's world, and had a tendency to assume most problems could be overcome with a confident attitude.

The jet shuddered through turbulence, and another wave of cramps made Gabi clutch her stomach again. Every month, the pain grew worse, as though some cruel fertility Goddess were ratcheting up the punishment for her failure to conceive.

On her laptop, she distracted herself with emails. Julian, one of the half dozen or so "Chilean boys"—the numerous gaucho-type brothers and cousins who worked in the business in Patagonia—had sent the vet's bill for her to sign off on. Julian was fun. Unlike the others, he was not married and more of a loner. They called him Che because he was born and grew up in Argentina, and they made fun of his accent. But he could hold his own. He liked to tease Gabi and practice his English. Every time she went there ... once or twice a year ... he told her she should stay, they'd make a good team, they could start a business together. She was never sure what kind of a "team" he had in mind.

On this trip, late one afternoon, at the stables reserved for tourists, she was saddling a horse to ride, and became aware of him, propped against a stall, ankles crossed, stroking the horse who kept head-butting him. At the other end of the courtyard was a family, a mother and father, a boy about nine or ten, and two younger children. Their little girl ran along the stalls, reaching to stroke the horses' muzzles. Gabi asked the father if they wanted to ride but he said Julian had kindly brought them over just to look around and see the horses.

"Be careful on your ride, Gabi," Julian called out. "Two hours, it is dark. No moon tonight. You could be getting lost."

"I won't be gone *that* long." You can get lost, she thought, laughing under her breath.

"Let me take a photo. You send your husband. He misses you. No?"

She gave him her phone and indulged him with a few different poses.

"And one for me." He took out his own phone.

She shook her head, marveling at how flattery came so easily to Latin American men, but she posed once more, hoping he couldn't see her flush of pleasure. At least he enjoyed flirting with her, even if he was faking it.

"Thirty minutes to land," the pilot announced.

With the bitter realization there was no reason to avoid drinking any more, she asked the flight attendant for a glass of wine and scrolled through photos. The one Julian took was pretty good, she thought, the late afternoon light putting her face partly in shadow. Her riding gear was flattering, accentuating her waist and making her look slimmer than she was. She'd sent the best shot to Masoud with a text: *"Miss me?"*

There was no response. Maybe he hasn't seen it yet, she thought.

***

Masoud had seen it. At that same moment, on location for a film shoot in the Dadès Gorge in the High Atlas Mountains of southern Morocco, he was leaning against a pillar to support himself, zooming in and out of the photograph Gabi had sent, examining every detail of the background, his face a shock of pain and disbelief.

CHAPTER 18

Four weeks after her return from Chile, Gabi flew to Egypt and sat in the stark blue and white office of gynecologist Dr. Mona Morad at the American hospital in Cairo. At her mother's insistence, she had arranged for appointments and tests.

Endometriosis. She tried to absorb the explanations and advice of the doctor, but only one word sank in: *unlikely.* She was unlikely to get pregnant.

She remembered little of the ensuing discussion about pain medication and hormones and the more radical possibility of a hysterectomy. "Take it all out," she yelled at the doctor at one point. "I don't give a shit anymore." The doctor eased around the desk and placed her beautifully manicured hands on Gabi's shoulders, her red lips drawn in a sympathetic wince. She told her to take her time, think it through, and talk to her husband.

"Come," Gabi's mother said, ushering her out of the office. "I'll call the car. Let's get home, honey. We both need a drink."

On the journey to Al Sayed, Gabi's last store of resolute optimism drained away. The future felt dark and heavy, something to suffer rather than enjoy. She railed against the unfairness of life, this blow falling right on top of Masoud's illness.

"What the hell does all this mean to me now, Mom? My husband is sick, and I can't get pregnant. In this part of the world, I'm already considered old. What am I going to be in the future ... the embarrassing aunt, living in the farthest room of the compound, ignored at the end of the table during family dinners?"

"Don't be ridiculous, Gabriella. Your opinion will always count. As I'm sure you know, I make sure mine does."

How little we understand the dreams and challenges of our parents' lives, Gabi thought. But she was not convinced. Her uncle and cousins barely acknowledged her and refused to accept that she knew more about horses than any of them. On the few occasions the subject of inheritance came up, it was clear the other half of the family assumed they'd be calling the shots.

"Listen, honey," her mother said. "I know a child would make a difference to your life. You should think about adoption. What's so important about bloodlines? You need a child who will share your love of the business, who will help you carry it into the future, a child who will be on your side."

"I can't imagine Masoud getting into the subject of adoption. He's really sick, Mom. I wonder if he even cares. He never wants to talk about children. He could have come with me to the doctor."

"He flew out here with you, Gabi, and he's waiting for you now. He probably thought these matters are best left to women."

***

Gabi sat with Masoud on the terrace of the *mazraea*, above the family's rooms. The humid air from the day lingered. There was no movement in the date palms flanking the courtyard, no sound from the nearby stables. She caught sight of herself in the mirror set into one of the walls. Her hair was limp, her face distorted from angry tears. I'm such a downer, she thought. Masoud leaned toward her, elbows on his knees, and listened as she tried to summarize what the doctor said, the words feeling alien on her tongue. She searched for shock or pain in his face, but he stayed composed. In his soft voice, he told her it was a relief to finally understand why she suffered so much each month.

She tried to talk about adoption. The possibility had always been in the back of her mind, but she had clung to the desperate hope she would conceive, and had never given it serious consideration. Now it seemed imperative.

But Masoud steered her away. If she chose to have surgery, she'd need time to recover, he said. Then they would talk. She wanted him to show greater disappointment, so they could deal with it together, plan together. She couldn't understand his willingness to accept her cousins elbowing her off to the side one day, when it was *her* skill that kept the place going. It was clear to her now that Masoud's heart was in Morocco, not Egypt. His desire to run a horse-rearing and trading business had gone with the sale of his family's farm.

When she woke the next morning, it was a few seconds before her body's new reality pushed into her mind. Masoud was already up, working in the room next to the bedroom which he used as an office when he was here, no doubt telling the film crew in Ouarzazate he'd be home tomorrow. Through the open door, she could see the paperwork he'd brought with him spread out on the desk.

A text came from her mother. Prospective buyers from Saudi Arabia were arriving at noon, wanting to look at a pair of stud horses. Gabi texted back she wasn't up to entertaining, but her mother convinced her that keeping busy was the best medicine for the grief she was feeling.

"How did it go?" Masoud said, when she found him later in the rear stables checking the hoof injury of one of the horses.

"They're interested. They were more anxious to talk about their saker falcons. Dad did his hard sell, but they barely paid attention. They've invited me to a falconry tournament."

"You're good at reading people. Your father doesn't appreciate you enough."

"Nothing new there." She flopped onto a bench in the shade, kicking off her dress shoes.

When he finished with the horse, Masoud joined her. They talked for few minutes about her diagnosis, how she was feeling now. He put an arm around her shoulders, and they sat for a while in silence. As Gabi watched the changing light filter through the flame tree across the paddock, she became aware that Masoud was thumbing his phone with his free hand. He'd been checking it continually since her return from Chile. He would slide it away and perk up with feigned enthusiasm when she approached, or make a vague lighthearted comment.

"Something wrong?" she asked.

"I'm anxious to go home. There's a lot of work for this next project."

"Do you *have* to be there? Surely there's a lot you can do online?"

"We've had this discussion, Gabi. We're here whenever I don't have film work. And you can stay if you want. I'm not pushing you to go back. But I have to be on the set tomorrow."

When he limped back into the stable, using the cane, his breathing was laboured. She told him he was too thin, he should see the doctor in Cairo, the one her mother kept bugging him about. But he wouldn't hear of it, claiming he took enough drugs to kill an elephant, and there was nothing wrong with their doctor in Morocco.

Gabi saw no point in arguing. He was stubborn about his work and his health.

In the paddock, two horses chased each other, energized by the light breeze cutting through the heat of the day. Gabi checked her watch. She had enough time to ride before darkness fell. One of the horses, Rebelde, was her favourite. He was past his prime and no longer for sale. Her father kept threatening to put him down, but she and her mother had dissuaded him, thank heavens, reminding him they had far greater priorities.

"I'm going to ride," she said. "My last chance before we leave. I'll go and change."

When she returned, Masoud had collected Rebelde's tack. He walked with her to the paddock. They saddled the horse, and he checked the girth and bridle.

"He's excited," he said, as Gabi took up the reins. "Get him settled before you take off." He leaned on a tall storage crate by the fence to watch her.

She was irritated when the men in the family gave her instructions. She was born to ride, she kept telling them. Her mother went into labour while walking one of the stallions at her family's ranch in Alberta and gave birth to her right there in the paddock. Gabi liked to imagine the soft muzzle of the horse against her bloodied cheek, the curious look in his big dark eyes.

Sitting tall and straight, she wove Rebelde in figures of eight, tighter and tighter, using a gentle pull and release of the rein until he was finally calm.

Masoud left, telling her, as usual, not to ride too fast or stay out too long, reminding her they were leaving early in the morning. When she circled the paddock one last time, she caught sight of his phone on top of the crate and realized he'd forgotten it. She was about to call out to him but, glancing both ways, leaned over and scooped it into a pocket of her vest.

CHAPTER 19

Gabi kept Rebelde at a slow trot through the long rows of stables, the horses snorting and whinnying, sensing her approach. She rode by the offices and staff quarters, the shadows of the buildings lengthening in the late sun, and out through the thick columns of date palms. The guard waved and checked his watch as she passed through the gates.

Whenever she rode here in Egypt, she felt deeply content. It was the only time she could forget the challenges of the world she lived in, the unfairness of the family dynamics she was forced to deal with. Gaining the trust of a horse meant being totally in synch with the animal, respecting its greater power. Rebelde could be cantankerous and wilful, but never with her. Reaching the grassy fields, she pressed her heel lightly to his side, and he sprang into a fully stretched, loping canter, heading for open country and the endless desert sands. She listened for the rhythmic thud of his hooves, the slower, deeper cadence of his breathing, then gave him a longer rein, letting him stretch way forward, her calves locked around him. "Cruising altitude," she called it, believing if she were to let go of the reins and raise her arms in the air, they would surely fly.

Two crested larks circled high above her, dodging and weaving around each other. They fell silent and dipped low as though to check her out, then soared away, resuming their cheerful song. Rebelde was cantering as though he could reach the far side of the earth. She leaned forward and patted him. "You are my Egyptian prince," she whispered.

When the palms thinned and the grasses gave way to the desert, she pulled up. She would love to go on, but the soft sand placed too much stress on the horse's tendons. Shielding her eyes, she gazed over the dunes stretching to the horizon. In the distance, a train of camels walked sedately across a high sand bank, a Bedouin riding the first, the others roped behind him. She was fascinated by the lives of these proud, nomadic people who shunned the innovations of the modern world. Masoud said she was a romantic. The Bedouin life is hard, he claimed.

She moved Rebelde on towards the Nile. He was sweating and needed water.

When they reached the river, she slid off, loosened the girth, and guided the horse through the mounds of tamarisk and spiky thorn bushes into shade and cool water. He drank and pawed at the large glossy stones. Under a cluster of palms, she flattened the tall grasses and sat down to rest. Rebelde munched on succulents and herbs, one eye on the heron that landed close by on the marshy riverbank.

Staring at the black face of Masoud's phone, she hesitated for a second or two, then tapped open the home screen and swiped up. A photograph of a child appeared. Gabi's first thought was that it must be an attachment in a message, possibly from a friend. She checked. It was in *Photos*. The image was breaking apart as though it had been zoomed too close. The little girl was wearing a yellow dress with blue polka dots, staring straight at the camera, coy and mischievous. She looked vaguely familiar. Gabi noted the date. Six weeks ago. She thumbed through texts and messages, finding no clues. Her ability to read Arabic was weak, but as far as she could make out, there were no scary notes from doctors. She went to the browsing history and found sites on Ancient Egyptian anthropology, and one in English detailing the symptoms of worsening heart failure. This was a site she had also checked, fearing Masoud's condition was more serious than he admitted.

Leaning against the trunk of the tree, she gazed at the sky through its feathery leaves, and thought about the photo of the young girl, so out of place in a photo library filled mostly with Ancient Egyptian paraphernalia. She wondered if it could be a mistake, embedded from an internet search. But there was something about the girl she couldn't put a finger on.

The recollection came in a rush. She *had* seen her before. That family. At the stables in Patagonia. Husband, wife, two or three children. She'd asked them if they wanted to ride. The man said they only wanted to look around. Gabi strained her memory, sure now the girl was with them. Her father kept lifting her so she could snuggle her head against the horses.

She looked at the photo again and recognized the interlocking stones of the stable courtyard. But how would Masoud have this photo, she asked herself? It didn't make sense.

A dim memory wrestled to the front of her mind. Julian. He'd taken a few shots. Made her pose. She fumbled in her vest for her phone and found the photo he took, the one she'd sent to Masoud with *"miss me?"* texted beneath it. The family was in the background. The girl was a few steps behind Gabi, off to the side, facing the camera. On Masoud's phone, she tried to zoom out to see herself, but realized the photo had been cropped; only the girl was visible.

For long minutes, Gabi worked through possible explanations, almost convincing herself it was an accident. She stood, pocketed both phones, and brushed the sand and coarse shreds of *halfa* grass from her clothes.

When she rode in half an hour later, Masoud was emerging from one of the barns, leading an Egyptian Arabian mare recently shipped from South Africa. The horse had not travelled well and, for a few days, was lethargic and off her feed. Now, she pranced about, her head held high. That mare knows the smell of her true homeland, Gabi thought, the siren call of the desert.

She stayed behind the columns of date palms for a while, stroking Rebelde's neck, and watching her husband. The horse could smell the stable and was becoming impatient.

As they drew close, she held out the phone.

"Hey, I've been looking for that all afternoon," Masoud said.

She steeled herself to ask him about the girl, and opened her mouth to speak, but he had already moved away. "I didn't think you'd miss it for an hour or two," she called after him.

***

Later that evening, on the terrace outside their rooms, Gabi gazed over the rail at the tall, decorative obelisk in the centre of the courtyard below. She always thought it looked ostentatious, an insincere nod to the ancient past of the country. Generous mounds of *samwa* shrubs surrounded it, teeming with pale yellow flowers. The scent of jasmine blew from trees in giant, decorative concrete tubs.

Masoud sat at the table, going through film set drawings in a large binder. She fished the phone from her pocket, found the shot of her posing for Julian, and held it towards him.

"Do you remember this?"

He leaned forward for a better look, and she thought he hesitated for a fraction of a second. "Of course. You sent it me from Chile."

"Yes. I saw it on *your* phone. But it wasn't like this anymore. You'd zoomed in on the little girl. Cropped me out. Why?"

She hoped he would look confused, then laugh and say *Oh yes, I messed it up, I was trying to crop you closer, I wanted to print and frame it.* But he was silent.

"You shouldn't have taken my phone, and you certainly shouldn't have gone through it," he said, finally.

"Sorry. Didn't know you had anything to hide."

Another few long seconds dragged by.

"There was a family with that little girl," he said. "Did you speak to them?"

"What? Why are you asking me this?"

"Did you?"

"The man, yes."

"What language did he speak?"

Gabi cast her mind back. "Language? Shit. I don't know. Not Spanish. I think I asked him in English if they wanted to ride. They didn't."

"What were they doing there?"

"How would I know? Maybe they were with a trekking group, or maybe the stargazers, the ones who fly up to the Atacama. I have no idea."

"Did he have an accent? Could you tell where he came from?"

"What the fuck, Masoud? I don't remember. Look at me. Who is he?"

Masoud pushed back, his hands jammed against the edge of the table. "He's Moroccan. French Moroccan. His name is Dominic El Hassan."

"You *know* him? How can you tell from this photo? He's only half visible."

"We met. Once. He's hard to forget."

"So, what's the problem?" There was no sound but the rustle of leaves in the bushes. Even the whinnying of the horses in the stables fell silent. Gabi felt the world was holding its breath. "Masoud? What's all this about? Who's the girl?"

He looked up and met her eyes. "She may be my daughter."

The sun had gone, the day was shedding its light, and Gabi was cold. She looked at her husband, a man she thought she understood, and realized she didn't know him at all. He had a past he had not shared, and harboured secrets she dare not learn. The wind from the west made miniature sand tornadoes around the fences. She felt that same wind had lifted her, and she was staring at herself below, untethered from reality.

CHAPTER 20

After many long seconds, Masoud turned fully to face her. "Her mother's name is Amina. I knew her five years ago."

Gabi perched on the edge of one of the wicker chairs. "Who is she?"

"It's not important, Gabi. Nothing to do with us."

"Where does she live?"

"Why does it matter?"

"It matters to me."

"She's Moroccan. In Fez."

"How did you know her?" Her voice was light, empty.

Masoud closed the binder and pushed it aside. "Through my uncle. We only saw each other a few times."

"Long enough for her to get pregnant."

He said nothing. One side of her wanted to run inside, crawl into bed, and bury her head under the covers. But the other side pressed through, needing to question and probe, and learn every morsel of truth: why they didn't stay together, why he said the girl *may* be his daughter, why he didn't know for sure. He said only it was complicated, he hardly knew her, it was over, and they needed to get past this.

"Get past this? Just like that? You spend hours staring at that damned phone. You cut me out."

She flinched as the image of him doing this came into her head, the way he must have zoomed in. She imagined his dawning recognition, his fingers moving to Edit, Crop: Gabi cancelled. For so long she had tried to have a child with him, and now here he was, maybe already a father, the baby *she* needed granted effortlessly to another woman. She felt betrayed by her own body and now by her husband. A savage spear of jealousy immobilized her, making the few steps to the sliding door seem an insurmountable distance.

She asked him how they'd met, wanting answers even though she knew every answer would sharpen the pain. He kept saying it wasn't important and it didn't matter.

"If it doesn't matter, why shouldn't I know?"

He limped to the railing, keeping his back to her. "She got my name from my uncle. Da'ud … you know, the one who lives in Fez now. She wanted me to interpret a couple of hieroglyphic charts she'd been given. Gabi, please, it's not—"

"I deserve to know what happened."

He told her Amina learned something upsetting about her father, who'd died a few years before. He had stolen money from the El Hassan brothers. The resentment Gabi felt when he spoke the woman's name made it hard for her to absorb the details of what he said … something about Amina being shocked and humiliated because the family had been so kind to them, took them in when they were living on the streets.

"She panicked, wanted to run away." He still had his back to her, staring across the wide sweep of desert.

"And?"

"I took her to Cairo, to our farm. I was going to marry her." His shoulders shook. Gabi thought he might be crying. "They came, the brothers, to take her back. They claimed I only wanted the money. They knew it would make a difference to my family."

Oh, how history repeats itself, Gabi thought … money to bail out his family, a great reason to marry. "Were they right?"

"In the end, the money was irrelevant. But they didn't believe me. Neither did Amina. And it seems you don't either."

She noted the contempt in his voice. How dare *he* be contemptuous, she thought. "What happened then?"

"For God's sake, it's over. Gone. Finished. She married Dominic, the younger brother. I haven't heard from her since."

Gabi worked at a crease in her linen skirt, repeatedly rubbing her fingers over it, dismayed at how calloused her hands were from years of working with horses. She wanted to ask if he still loved this woman, but stopped, surprised to discover how much that mattered. It mattered, she concluded, because no man had loved *her*. If she had been truly loved, perhaps her other needs would have diminished to insignificance, like the fairy tales claimed … love conquers all. She was damned by plain looks and infertility. What would it be like, she wondered, to have one man want to rescue you and another leave his country to come and bring you home?

"The girl—what makes you think she could be yours?"

Masoud plucked red petals from the flowering star cluster shrub at his side, letting them fall to the ground. "She looks like me. And she's around the right age."

Gabi wanted to scream at his matter-of-fact tone, his apparent indifference to her distress.

She found the photograph on her phone again and studied the girl's face. "She could be the daughter of any man from this part of the world."

"Because we all look alike?"

She ignored the challenge. "There were other children there. I remember. At the ranch. You can see them in *this* photo, the one I sent you. Before you cropped us away. A toddler and an older boy in the background. The older one must be nine or ten. How come? Did she already have a child when you met her?"

He gave a closed-eye shake of the head, as though every question were painful.

"So, how could that be?"

Masoud shrugged. "No idea. A cousin, maybe."

"Even if the girl looks like you, it doesn't prove anything. How can you be sure?"

"I'm *not* sure. And anyway, what could I do?" He plucked more viciously at the flowers. "No matter what I think about the arrogant shit who thinks he's her father, I can't do that to Amina."

Gabi questioned where she ranked in this drama. He couldn't upset his old flame, but he had no problem upsetting his wife. She resorted to sarcasm, telling him she assumed he would delete the photo on his phone because there was surely no point in keeping it. He was furious with her challenge, telling her she should never have gone through his phone; he was sorry she found the shot, but that was on her.

Finally, the rage boiled over. She sprang from the chair, ran the full length of the terrace and down the stone steps to the courtyard. At the far end of the rows of stables, she slowed her pace, nodding curtly to the guard who called over, concerned all was well. She halted, out of breath and hunched over, coughing, fearing she might throw up. Taking deeper, slower breaths, she forced herself to a calmer state of mind, trying to rationalize that this was all in the past. The woman was married and had more children—if those in the photograph were indeed hers.

But, in the end, she knew this was not the reason for her fury. Her husband had lied to her, or lied by omission. And not only did this come to light right after her own devastating diagnosis, but he was so dismissive, not understanding or perhaps not even caring about the effect it would have on her. She worried again he was more seriously ill than he admitted, and that was why he didn't seem to care much about anything at all.

The lights on the property flickered to life. She checked her watch. They still had to pack for the flight back to Morocco tomorrow. She walked through the stables, lingering to pet the horses, taking comfort from the velvety touch of their noses, their low-pitched snorts of pleasure.

Back in their rooms, she found Masoud sorting through books on Ramses and various temples, a generous glass of wine at his side. She didn't have the energy to protest this. He obviously couldn't wait to immerse himself in the new project. Much of it was on location so she would barely see him for weeks. He'd be happy, preoccupied in the world he loved, where his opinion and advice were valued. These days, she often found him flicking through dense pages of hieroglyphics using a microscope, or examining huge whiteboards with an art director's ideas for staging or backdrops.

She stood on the threshold, imagining him rising to his feet, gathering her in his arms. They would stumble to the bedroom, make love with clumsy passion, laughing, racing to the end, the way they used to; then fall asleep and wake in each other's arms and start over, tenderly, with all the time in the world.

None of that happened. Masoud fell back to studying the papers, writing notes, and carefully turning each page.

She packed, took a sleeping pill, and slept until dawn.

***

On their flight home to Ouarzazate the next morning, Gabi experienced a strange detachment from everything she'd learned the day before, as though her anger and grief were emptied. Questions, protests, tears … all these were humiliating, beneath her, she thought. It wasn't as though this Amina woman was still around, a competitor.

She watched Masoud settle into his seat and caught his wince of pain as he reached for the seatbelt. This morning, he admitted there were days when every bone seemed to hurt, and he often shivered with sudden cold. She felt a surge of compassion and regretted subjecting him to such a painful inquisition yesterday, when his health should be her only concern.

She wished she could convince him to seek better medical care. There were so many new treatments for heart conditions; she could not understand his reluctance to explore them.

Her mind drifted to the little girl living in Fez with her happy family and, slowly, a new idea took root. From what she knew of the laws in this part of the world, Masoud could insist on a paternity test. If this child were indeed his, he could petition for joint custody or at least regular access. His daughter could spend the holidays with them, learn to ride, and grow to love the life at Al Sayed. And then, when she was older, she could make her own decisions about where she wanted to live. Gabi dwelled on this dream, giving it more detail and texture, willing it to life. This little girl in Fez could be her stepdaughter and the ticket to her future success.

She shared these thoughts with Masoud. "She could live with us, at least part of the time. It seems fated. Think about it. That this should happen right after I got that diagnosis. We were *meant* to find your child."

He took her hand. She was surprised, wondering if the anger had drained from him, too.

"Her mother would never agree to it. And *he* would never admit she could be mine. The child is surrounded by love. And wealth. Even approaching that family would be like walking on a minefield. Believe me, Gabi, you don't know what they are capable of. It would be a reckless gamble."

He told her how the two brothers had roughed up his uncle, Da'ud, to find out where Masoud had taken her. Dominic, now Amina's husband, apparently had to be physically restrained when they flew to Egypt and confronted Masoud. Gabi wondered again what it would be like to be the kind of woman a man would go to all this trouble to fight for.

He swivelled back in his seat and let out a sigh that made him cough. "Anyway," he said, "why would I pursue this? Who knows how long I have?"

She drew back. He had never spoken so plainly of his illness before. The word 'fatal' had lurked in the back of her mind for weeks, but she could never bear to confront it. Not only would she be denied a child, but she'd be a widow, not much better than a maiden aunt in the eyes of her family. She knew this sounded cold, even in her head, but she'd been thrust into the role of victim, picked on and bullied by the cruel turn of events, and felt she deserved better. Her friend Sally had delivered a rather cutting response when she told her about Masoud's illness. "I have to be honest, Gabi. You sound more worried about him running out of time to get you pregnant than you do about actually losing him." She tried to protest, but Sally knew her too well. "Guess that toxic family of yours has really fucked you up."

Why can't I want more, Gabi thought now, in self-defence? She wanted to challenge Masoud, tell him not to be so pessimistic, but she knew how tiring forced optimism can be for someone trying to deal with reality.

He cradled her head against his shoulder, the kind of tenderness they had not shared for months, and she listened with a deepening sadness to his shallow, laboured breaths.

∗∗∗

Back home in Ouarzazate, Gabi sat on the bed, her case open but unpacked beside her. The warm splendour of the room always calmed her: the pastel blues and yellows on the wall, the collage of patterned tiles she'd bought in Marrakech, tall clay pots of fiddle leaf she'd seized from a film crew who were going to discard them. Now, the depression and worthlessness she felt after her diagnosis flooded back. Her husband might have a daughter with another woman, and she, herself, could never have children. Putting all the financial and family issues aside, what was she there for? What was the point of her?

Many couples don't have children, she reasoned, but it never occurred to her she and Masoud might be among them. Their children would share their father's love of Egypt and its history; they would explore the world across the Atlantic that was also part of their heritage; they would develop business skills and participate in the successful future of Al Sayed. And they would learn to ride. Gabi understood the special relationship between children and horses, the sense of trust and empathy, and a tacit commitment to look out for each other. Now, it seemed so unfair that two people who grew up with horses, understood them and knew how to ride, would be denied the pleasure of passing on this love and these skills.

Checking Masoud was in his study, she opened her laptop and typed *Dominic El Hassan, Fez* into Google. The first link took her to the Riad Capella. Like most boutique hotels in Fez, it was in the walled medina, in a narrow alleyway not far from the Bab Boujloud, the famous blue gate. Browsing through the hotel's website gallery, she whistled with admiration over the inner courtyard, its ornately carved stone fountain, lemon trees, and elaborate Moroccan lanterns.

A photograph of the El Hassan brothers, Hadir and Dominic, came up next. They were standing in what was probably the reception area, a multicoloured mosaic mural behind them. Gabi lingered on this, not yet prepared to move to the photo registering on the edge of her vision. Hadir had the look of a serious man on serious business: trim beard, well-tailored jacket, burgundy tie. Dominic, the more attractive of the two, was unruly, his dark hair a good two inches past his collar, an open-neck lilac shirt. She recognized him as the man she had briefly met at the stables in the lodge in Patagonia. He looked impatient with this photography session, as though he were trying to stifle a laugh. It was hard to imagine him as the kind of man who would want to physically attack a quiet, gentle person like Masoud.

She swiped to the photograph of their wives, Sophie and Amina. There she was, the young, beautiful Amina El Hassan, long dark hair swept to one side, dark eyes with that classic, enchanting combination: seductive, yet unattainable. Gabi stared her down, fighting an intense burn of resentment. "You probably think you have it all," she whispered. "Well, think again."

She pulled out her phone and called Sally in Rabat. A mad, crazy, beautiful idea had formed in her head. She needed an alibi.

PART III—THE CHAOS OF ISFET

CHAPTER 21

When Aiden arrived at the Riad Capella in Fez, Morocco, jet-lagged and disoriented after nearly sixteen hours of flying with two stops, he was treated to the traditional reception of family and staff in the courtyard. Steven had warned him about this, but he felt unsteady, almost giddy, as he walked through the heavy wooden door in a narrow alleyway deep in the medina, through to the high vaulted atrium. On all sides, countless hanging lanterns lit the Moorish archways and colonnades with flickering, golden light. By the fountain in the centre, the family and staff stood in a semi-circle. Dominic ushered Aiden from one person to the next, each welcoming him in English, French, or Arabic, hands to the chest, a slight bow, a clasping of his shoulders or a big hug.

He was completely tongue-tied when Amina stepped forward. She had such quiet beauty, a soft voice, and eyes that could pierce a man's soul. He noticed she was pregnant, but she had none of the awkwardness of a pregnant woman. If anything, it added to her grace. Unable to meet her eyes, he focused on the long sheath of hair that hung forward over her shoulder, and muttered some sort of "thank you," feeling like a clumsy schoolboy. Dominic lifted up their daughter, Rosa, to greet him. She gave him a shy, playful kiss, then buried her head in her father's shoulder. Next to Amina was Hadir, Dominic's older brother who introduced himself as "the head of the household" and then winced from the playful cuff on the back of the head from his wife, Sophie. Sophie looked like a Spanish dancer, Aiden thought, with high cheekbones, dark hair pulled severely back. They both drew him into a big hug. Dominic nudged him along to at least a dozen members of staff. Finally, feeling increasingly lightheaded, he reached the end of the line. There stood a young boy, conspicuous by his pale features and long fair hair.

"I'm Lukas," said the boy, grinning. "I'm the last one because I'm the most important. I'm the one who's going to take care of you."

Before Aiden could thank him, a bellboy seized his two bags and disappeared, and the welcoming committee melted away. Dominic took him to a small room off the courtyard, and urged him to help himself to the dates, nuts, fresh figs and sugared almonds that were laid out on a coffee table. Aiden sank onto a low couch. A waiter materialized at his side, held a silver pot of mint tea at a great height and let it fall in a steady stream into his glass. With each sip, the stress of the journey melted away. Dominic insisted he put up his feet and relax, assuring him they would not even think about the work he'd be doing until he was over jet lag and settled in. They talked for a few minutes about his journey, what his uncle Steven was up to. Aiden wondered if there was something other than tea in the little orange and purple beaded glass. When he spoke, his words seemed to leave his mouth and hang for an instant before falling into place in the sentence. All the colours and textures around him—the blaze of Dominic's yellow kaftan, the deep red of the embroidered drapes hanging across the entrance to the room, the soft velvet of the turquoise cushion at his side—competed for his attention. He hoped whatever he was saying was coherent.

Lukas appeared in the doorway.

"Aha," Dominic said, getting to his feet. "Your guide is at your service. I'm leaving you in great hands. See you at breakfast."

"I've got your room key," Lukas said. "Your bags are there, and our chef gave me some food to put in the fridge in case you get hungry. And there's tea, and wine and water. And I think beer. Come on, I'll show you."

Aiden followed him up a steep curving flight of stone steps and along a corridor that overlooked the lush courtyard below. Lukas pointed out different areas of the hotel as they climbed. He learned his room was one floor up, in the same area as the rest of the family. Hotel guests were on the opposite side and on the third level.

"Ta da," the boy said, opening the door at the far end. "Hope you like it."

The room was painted in a soft yellow ochre, tall wrought iron lamps on the walls giving it a golden due. The enormous bed had big fat pillows competing for space along the headboard and a richly embroidered red and purple throw draped across the bottom.

Under the window was a small desk and an elaborate, carved wooden chair. And next to this, making Aiden stare in disbelief, was an easel and a stack of art supplies.

"Dominic called Steven and asked him what to buy," Lukas explained. "I went with him. We hope it's all the right kind of stuff. Dominic said he hopes there's room to paint here, but if it's not too hot, you can take it up on the roof terrace. I'll help you. He said you'll be … I forget … oh yes, 'artist in residence.' I think that's what he called it."

Aiden was almost numb with gratitude. "Geez, Lukas. This is all too much. Such a lot of trouble. I can't believe you did this. Thank you." He resolved to talk to Dominic in the morning and insist on reimbursing him.

Lukas took him to the marble and granite ensuite bathroom, two tall yellow candles on the vanity, an elaborate Moroccan-style mirror over the sink. He turned the taps on and off and showed him how to work the shower, saying it was sometimes weird and you had to wait for the water to get going.

When Lukas eventually left, explaining where to meet for breakfast, Aiden threw off his clothes and fell into bed, his head submerged in the soft pillows. On the opposite wall was a large, framed photograph of the *Festival of Fantasia*, Berber horsemen in full gallop, rifles raised. The horses, manes flowing, nostrils flared, charged towards him. Somewhere, a stick of incense burned. He tried to identify the scent … sandalwood, perhaps …and that was his last thought before drifting into a long, deep sleep.

In the following days, with the help of Lukas, he learned his way around the hotel, who all the staff were, when and where he could eat. The young boy was a delightful companion, an enigma, Aiden thought … a curious mixture of wide-eyed boyish curiosity and the wisdom and insight of a much older person.

Dinners were often a full family event, and he was awed by the animated conversation around the table. It covered so many topics—from travel and tourism to arts and literature, to business and politics. This was a cosmopolitan world he had no experience with. Discussion of the exploits of Hadir and Sophie's twin boys in New York and comments like "that meeting in Athens," or "our Sicilian friends maintain that …," or "the Parisians would never agree to it," left him grappling for a foothold, desperate to add something intelligent. But the family always rescued him, asking him what this or that was like in Canada, and gave him a chance to air his own knowledge and points of view. He was embarrassed that they all switched to English for him and made the odd attempt to employ his limited French. But they told him not to worry. Much of their business was in English, and they often found themselves speaking it to each other, without being conscious of it.

***

One week after his arrival, settled and ready to start, Aiden sat on a large, canopied lounging bed on the roof terrace of the hotel. The paperwork for the Moroccan Festival of Arts was scattered around him, and Zahra, the interior décor maven he was working with, sat at his side. Zahra scrolled through various sites on her iPad, making suggestions, asking Aiden's opinion and generally brainstorming ideas with him. Despite the darkening orange sky, the heat of the day lingered, and Aiden continually wiped beads of sweat from his forehead.

"We'll pack up now," Zahra said. "I don't want to overwhelm you. You've barely arrived."

She suggested they start on the website tomorrow at her office, which doubled as a small gallery, showcasing the artists and interior designers she represented.

He assured Zahra he was anxious to get started. Like everyone, she had gone out of her way to help him adjust and feel at home. She was the principal interior designer of this hotel and many others in the city and would be involved in the development of much of the material for the festival. He guessed she was in her late fifties, well established, well connected. If he wished to earn his stripes here, he needed to convince Zahra and his hosts he could work independently.

One morning, Lukas took him to the food market, walking him up and down the rows of stalls overflowing with every imaginable fruit and vegetable, some he didn't recognize. And the spices: pyramids of turmeric, cumin, saffron, cinnamon and bright blue pepper. He stood in awe, taking photographs, overwhelmed with the smell of sizzling lamb and garlic on firepits, fresh bread, vanilla, lemon and sugar. The boy had developed a liking for him, often seeking him out to see if he needed anything. Although Aiden had limited experience with young kids, he was certain they were interested in little beyond their immediate selves. This child had an adult mind in his young body. With grey eyes, pale skin and long blond hair, he was a walking paradox, totally out of place in this exotic Middle Eastern locale. Yet, somehow, he blended in as though this was the perfect and only place for him to be. It seemed strange and unsettling to Aiden that he should be here with a young boy who had also come from another world. The two of them were connected in such a convoluted way, and this added to the odd feeling of detachment he felt, as though he were watching his new life from outside himself.

At the market, Lukas kept laughing, urging him along, telling him there was much more to see. They sat at a little café where the boy was obviously well known, and where the hosts plied them with mint tea, a national obsession, and sweet, gooey ghoriba cookies. Lukas astonished him with what sounded like fluent Arabic, but the boy insisted he was still learning.

"These cookies are Amina's favourites," he announced. "She says this is where they make them best. I'm going to buy some for her."

"Let me pay for them. I'd like to. You've all been so kind."

Lukas made him ask for the cookies in Arabic, to the delight and general amusement of the little crowd around them.

Aiden secretly hoped the cookies would allow him to spend more than three minutes in Amina's company. She seemed older than him, although she didn't look to be more than mid-twenties. She had a mystical aura about her as though she could read minds. The last time he'd felt this uncomfortable flutter in his chest was at school with a crush on his gym teacher. So far, *everyone* he'd seen in this country was attractive—the family, the guests, the people on the street. And the staff, from Henri, the tall, imperious chef, to Farouk, the lowest-ranked bellboy ... all shared dark, well-defined features and a beguiling aura of sensuality. There was an exotic and mysterious nature to whatever he looked at. Nothing had any ring of familiarity. He resolved to find a way to paint it.

CHAPTER 22

On a day when there was no school, Lukas persuaded Amina they should take Aiden and Rosa to the Merenid tombs, the ruins of a necropolis on a hill north of Fez, overlooking the medina. Sophie said she would join them, claiming it would take both women to keep an eye on the children. Dominic had left with his brother to visit one of their other hotels.

The day passed in a haze of pure pleasure for Aiden. They made slow progress walking through the narrow, cobbled alleyways to where the cars were housed. Merchants and shopkeepers kept stopping to greet them, asking about the health and welfare of the family, the progress of the festival arrangements and more. They welcomed Aiden like an old friend. Five-year-old Rosa was a favourite in the neighbourhood, many of the women scooping her into a big hug. She had a certain shyness about her, turning her head away and putting a thumb in her mouth, but Aiden could see it was an endearing act. Even turned away, she looked coy, those dark eyes fluttering over to her admirers.

A young man at a clothing store suggested, tongue in cheek, that Aiden should be more Moroccan. He persuaded him to buy a bright blue Tuareg Berber scarf, which Amina and Sophie artfully arranged around his neck, and a pair of handmade *babouches*—red leather slippers, with intricate multicoloured stitching. In Arabic, what sounded like a heated argument about price ensued between Amina and the merchant, but eventually the man smiled and asked Aiden for a sum Amina approved.

Outside the store, she laughed. "It's all part of the game. They enjoy it. But if you had been alone, he would not have budged from his original offer. Even Dominic falls for his bluster. My husband is impatient, as you probably know. He would rather pay twice what something is worth, just to get away."

My husband, Aiden thought, with a flare of envy. He wondered what it must take to earn the love of such a woman.

When they finally reached the car, Rosa insisted on sitting between Lukas and Aiden.

"*Aiden est aussi mon ami*," she said to Lukas, who grinned and rolled his eyes.

Amina turned to look at Aiden. "You're her friend too, she says." Then she mouthed the word "Jealous."

Aiden marvelled at the closeness and magnetism of this family he had stumbled into. They had a sense of exclusivity about them, as though they existed on a different plane. Their intimacy was often tactile—a rub of the shoulder, a squeeze of the hand, a stroke of the cheek. Steven had told him bits and pieces of their history, how Amina and her father had been taken in by them when they were destitute and how Dominic had eventually come to his senses, realizing how much he was in love with her. And then, how Lukas, who lost his parents at such a young age, ended up here. He knew Lukas's mother was the art critic Steven had a relationship with, but his uncle did not go into detail, saying it was all too complicated.

Aiden thought he could stay forever in this small part of a parallel universe, suspended in time, with colours and sounds, scents and tastes that didn't exist in the one he came from.

When they arrived at the Merenid tombs, Sophie suggested she stay with the children and Amina could take Aiden for a short walk on the trails.

Little was known about these arched brick and stucco tombs, Amina told him, as they headed for a gravel pathway circling the site. They were a necropolis for the Merenids who ruled Morocco in the fifteenth century and were now a popular tourist attraction.

She checked her watch. "The sun will go down in about thirty minutes and you'll hear the calls to prayer all over the medina. It's quite magical. People ask me why our family stays here. Dominic and Hadir and Sophie were born in France, as you know, and I was born in Egypt. But none of us can imagine leaving. This place has captured our soul."

Aiden could barely process anything she said, totally flustered at being alone with her. He took photographs and kept stealing sideways glances. She had a shawl over her shoulders, but her forearms were uncovered, and he longed to touch their smooth, tanned skin.

On a narrow trail, she stopped and turned back to face him, nearly causing him to stumble. "Are you sure you'll be comfortable here, Aiden? It's a lot of responsibility to throw on you. It seems very impetuous of Dominic to have spirited you away from your home like this. But so typical of him."

Aiden worried the family may now be regretting his arrival, perhaps thinking he could be more of a liability than an asset. He hastened to assure her he and Zahra had already made good progress.

"With all the work to be done, you are a gift from the gods," she said. "I hope you'll be happy here." She placed a hand on his shoulder, and he prayed the flush of heat did not show on his face.

As they walked back to the others, she told him Dominic and Hadir would be out of town a great deal in the coming weeks, dealing with the restoration of two other hotels the family had taken over. They would handle festival issues remotely when possible. She and Sophie would always be available, but as she was sure he could imagine, running a hotel was a full-time business with not only day-to-day organizational and staffing issues, but also the occasional troublesome guest.

"What I'm saying, Aiden, is you might feel isolated at times, and left to fend for yourself. Don't hesitate to go to our chef, Henri if you ever need urgent help or advice. He knows everyone in town. And I think you'll find Lukas a great companion."

He told her Lukas had already taken him to the market, and what a great kid he was and how everyone seemed to know him.

"The two of you have a lot in common. It's lovely to see this connection."

They rejoined the others and walked to a viewing point as the sun sank behind the medina. The *Maghrib* call to prayer reverberated from minaret to minaret, carried by the wind toward to Atlas Mountains.

As they watched, Aiden became aware of the clicking of a camera shutter and turned to see a woman standing behind them, higher on the hill. She was in western dress, jeans and a T-shirt, a big straw hat with dark glasses propped on top. When she caught his look, she pointed to the sunset. "Beautiful, isn't it?" she said, in English, returning to her shot-taking. He thought she sounded American and was tempted to tell her about the festival and how she could enter her photos. But Rosa was restless now. Amina said they should start for home, suggesting they stop for lemonade and ice cream at a café not too far from here.

At this café, when Lukas took Rosa to the ice cream counter to help her choose one, Amina turned to Aiden, dropping her voice. "Dominic and Hadir are in Chefchaouen, as you know. They'll be in touch to let you know a good time to join them. It's an amazing city. The Blue Pearl, we call it. A big draw for artists and photographers." She hesitated. "How would you feel about taking Lukas with you? He misses Dominic and he adores you. I don't think he'd be any trouble. As long as you feel comfortable, I mean—"

"I'd love to. Lukas is terrific. No trouble at all."

"*Alors, merveilleux,*" Sophie said. "It will give Amina a break too."

Lukas was thrilled. They would go on the weekend, Amina told him, provided he made sure his homework was done first. Lukas hugged her and came around the table to give Aiden a hug, too. He was a jumble of contradictions, Aiden thought, on the one hand a savvy young man, on the other a little boy yearning for love and approval. He knew that feeling so well.

Aiden's scarf had slipped from its knot, and Amina leaned over to fix it for him. He thought he'd faint from the closeness of her, the soft sheen of her skin inches from his face. The smell of her jasmine perfume lingered after she'd settled back into her chair. He inhaled deeply, closing his eyes for a moment. When he opened them, he caught Sophie looking at him, a smile on her face just shy of laughter.

CHAPTER 23

On some mornings, Aiden rose at sunrise and painted in the low light at the window, wanting to capture the shadows receding over the honeycomb of roof tops, or the sun squeezing around the corner of an alleyway below him. A fruit seller usually set up her stand there. Once, the early sun, like a searchlight, caught a basket of lemons, making them shine like a lantern in the darkness.

He would pack up by eight a.m. and, after a quick breakfast, walk to Zahra's office in a little square close to the famous and much-photographed blue gate. The area attracted visitors because it had a tourist information centre and several places to get a snack. It was a popular drop off point for taxis and tour buses that had no access to the medina. Other than the odd long weekend in the U.S. with friends, Aiden had never left Canada and now, on his daily walk through the medina, he found himself constantly muttering *holy shit* and *what the fuck*. This old walled part of the city was as magical and bewildering as Steven had described, infusing each of his five senses with totally unfamiliar sensations.

On the ground floor of her studio, painted bright blue and orange, Zahra displayed examples of the work of local artists and sculptors, and a few furniture designers who sourced leather from the local tanneries. The pieces were not for sale but to tempt further enquiry. She did a brisk business with local hoteliers and homeowners, as well as travellers who wanted items shipped to their home countries. It was a natural location to advertise Fez's role in the upcoming Festival, and encourage tourists to participate and spread the word.

This morning, Aiden skipped breakfast and stopped at a café for a coffee and pastry to watch the unfolding of the day. Everyone around him was busy: a butcher sharpened his knives on a large whetstone, a woman used a long, hooked pole to hang fabric on overhead clotheslines, young boys loaded wooden trays with bread rolls, ready for delivery. Next to where he sat, in the shade of an old, twisted olive tree, a donkey stood patiently as its owner loaded baskets on both sides with apples, onions and carrots. The sun nudged higher, turning the sky to a pale orange.

Aiden thought about how much his life had changed since that visit to the lawyer's office where he saw his father's portrait in a magazine. A few months ago, he was grieving Dorothy's passing and felt listless and lonely. His girlfriend, who had left in such a rage, did not try to reconnect. His job was dead-end, and the future stretched before him murky and unwelcoming, with nothing to get excited about. Now he felt he'd been put through a time tunnel, emerging as a new person, one with a family and a skill that was recognized. He was living in a country he'd never thought about, with people he'd never heard of. When he woke each morning to the *fajr* call to prayer, it always took him a minute or two to realize where he was and that it wasn't a crazy dream.

On the phone yesterday, Steven sounded concerned for him. "Sure you're okay, Aiden? I don't want you to feel obliged to stay if you're not comfortable." He assured his uncle he was happy, everyone was terrific, and he enjoyed the work. "I just feel kind of stunned all the time. It's almost too much to take in. And now I'm going to that blue city, Chef-something. More mind-blowing stuff." Steven made him promise to call if there was anything he needed or, he added, clearly embarrassed, "even if you just want to talk."

Signalling to the waiter he'd like a refill of the thick Turkish coffee he'd grown to love, Aiden contemplated what his life might be like after this. Perhaps, he thought, one of the people Steven introduced him to in Toronto would indeed follow up and help him. His uncle's two friends, Nigel and Philippe, had been enthusiastic about his work and insisted he spend time with them in Toronto on his return. He tried to convince himself he wouldn't have to wake from this dream and go back to a soulless IT firm on the other side of the world. He'd taken a leave of absence and, in any case, had no guarantee the job would still be there when he got home.

From his jeans pocket, he withdrew a crumpled piece of paper. His friend, Dave, had promised to check his apartment from time to time and forward any important mail.

This was another letter from Maggie.

I was so sad not to hear from you in Toronto. I guess you're back out west again now. I don't expect you to forgive me, Aiden. I only want to see you for a minute or two. I'm your mom. You have to understand how strong that is. You're always with me, always here in my heart.

He left the café. With only a quick stab of guilt, he dropped the scrunched up letter into the trash can under the tree and walked the remaining few streets to Zahra's studio. He was thankful that, so far, Maggie had not discovered his email or cell number.

In the past two weeks, key players responsible for the overall planning of the festival had issued directives and guidelines for the development of online and printed material to promote the events. With this, Aiden had almost completed the new sections of the websites for the family's hotels. He and Zahra now turned their attention to general posters and handout literature about Fez, Chefchaouen and Marrakech, suggesting ideal places to paint and photograph in each city, and QR code links to participating hotels.

Around lunchtime, Lukas showed up. There was no school today, and he was filling in time, running errands for Amina. Later, he would collect Rosa from her play school, which he loved to do when their schedules allowed. Zahra put him to work unpacking boxes and putting items on display. Aiden had asked Zahra once why Lukas didn't hang around with friends in his free time. She claimed he saw his friends all day at school and would often visit with them on weekends, but she was sure he enjoyed adult company too. "He's wise beyond his years," she said. "You should hear the things he comes up with. Quite the little philosopher. And I can tell he loves being with you, especially now Dominic's away." Aiden felt a brief flush of pride hearing this, realizing this is what it must be like to be a big brother, as his father was to his uncle, Steven.

A young Middle Eastern couple came in and admired the mosaic tiles Lukas was arranging. Obviously assuming from the boy's fairness that he was not a local, they asked him in broken English if they could pick one up for a closer look. They stepped back in amazement when he answered in Arabic, handing them a tile. He made speaking Darija, the Moroccan dialect, seem effortless. Aiden doubted he could master it, but resolved to make more of an effort.

His attention was drawn to a woman outside who looked like a tourist, reading the poster about the festival they had put in the window. She had a camera hanging from her neck and this jogged his memory. He was sure it was the same woman he'd seen at the Merenid tombs.

He half rose from his chair. "Can I help you?"

She didn't seem to have heard so he went outside to join her. "I think I saw you the other day at the tombs," he said. "Are you interested in the festival? You must get some great shots with that Leica."

"Actually I'm just visiting a friend." She hesitated. "I think I recognized the family you were with up there, the El Hassans. My friend knows them. Are you staying at their hotel?" She glanced into the store and took a few steps farther away. "Sorry, we're in the direct sun here. Could we move to the shade?"

Aiden suggested they go inside, but she declined, saying she could see they were busy and didn't want to get in the way. He gave her one of the cards he'd designed and filled her in on why he was here in Fez. Checking her watch, she apologized, saying her friend was expecting her soon, and she must dash. She took a shot of the festival poster, promised to think about participating, and began to walk away.

Aiden called after her. "Hey… I didn't get your name."

"Nancy," she called back. "Thanks for the info."

Back inside, Aiden relayed the conversation to Zahra. "Interesting. But we will probably have more appeal to tourist groups. It's something for them to talk about together. People visiting local friends have a different mindset. Where was she from?"

"I didn't ask. U.S. probably."

Zahra suggested he finish for the day and go have lunch with Lukas. They were waiting for more information from the tourism rep and couldn't proceed without it. He was reluctant to leave, never wanting to take time off, but she promised to email him with updates. He could catch up tonight at the hotel if he was anxious, she said. She pointed to a nearby café, a tiny window in a wall with two rickety iron tables outside that would be easy to miss, claiming they served the best harira, the classic Moroccan spicy bean soup, in the city.

While they ate, Lukas showed him maps of the night sky for the coming weeks, and pointed out different constellations. He wondered if Aiden could go with him and Dominic on one of their overnight desert trips to look at the stars.

"Dominic's too busy now, though," he said. "We'd have to wait until the festival is ready. Will you still be here?"

Aiden wasn't sure how long he'd be staying. He was tempted to offer to rent a car and take Lukas himself, but doubted the family would approve of such a journey. It could be dangerous, and he had no driving experience here. He remembered all the promises Maggie had made about different trips—Wonderland or the Science Centre or Niagara Falls. He looked forward to them, bracing for the inevitable disappointment, but still felt so forlorn when they never materialized. Maggie always forgot, or was out, or said she didn't have the money.

He promised Lukas he would talk to Dominic about it.

After lunch, they walked to Rosa's play school, not far from the hotel, and waited at the gated entrance. When high-pitched squeals signalled the imminent arrival of the children, Lukas pushed his way through the crowd. In a couple of minutes, he reemerged with Rosa, and they began the fifteen-minute walk home.

As they drew closer to the hotel, Aiden had the unnerving feeling they were being followed. He looked behind and along the narrow alleyways off to the side, but concluded he must have imagined it.

Rosa swung herself back and forth between Lukas and him, chattering nonstop about the events of her day. He tried to remember if he'd ever been this carefree in his childhood, then chided himself for these "poor-me" thoughts. Dorothy had worked hard to make him feel safe and happy. He concluded that only money made anyone carefree.

He smiled at Rosa. Five years old, he thought, in a perfect life with a perfect family, and not a care in the world.

CHAPTER 24

On the morning Aiden was leaving with Lukas for Chefchaouen, Rosa made a point of sitting next to him at breakfast. She liked to practice her English with him, but as far as he could tell, she was close to fluent. He was amazed at the number of languages this family spoke without any apparent effort.

She tugged his sleeve. "How do you do?" she said.

"I'm just fine, thank you. How are you?" he replied.

"I'm very fine." Giggling, she hid her face against Lukas, sitting on her other side.

"I want to go to the blue city with you," she said, making a pouty face. "Mama says I can't. Papa would let me."

"I've told you, Rosa," Amina said. "There's a lot of work to do there, and you'd be a real nuisance. No matter how much your Papa loves you, he would not want you there."

"When I'm older, I'm going to marry Lukas. He'll take me anywhere I want," Rosa said.

They all burst out laughing. Lukas was embarrassed.

"Lukas is your brother," Sophie said.

"Not really," Rosa put on her coy look again.

Amina and Sophie exchanged a bewildered stare.

"Heaven knows how children learn the things they do these days," Sophie said. "Listen to your Aunt Sophie, Rosa. You've got at least two decades before you even *think* about marrying anyone. Got that?" She repeated it in French. "Right, Lukas?" she added.

"I'm not getting married," Lukas said. "Aiden's not married."

Sophie winked at him. "Men should not marry young. They take longer to grow up."

"With our husbands away, we are lucky to have two handsome young men at our table," said Amina. The slow smile she gave him seemed to take forever to creep across her lips and draw her face into a beguiling look of amusement. He swore the temperature in the room shot up a few degrees. Was she mocking him, teasing him, he wondered, or was this her natural way?

She topped up his coffee and asked the waiter to bring more. "Dominic told me you'd like to join them on one of their stargazing desert trips when things have calmed down a little."

"Guess it depends on how long I'm here," Aiden said.

"Don't worry about that," Amina laughed. "We may never let you go. You will love the desert. It's magical. It knows all our secrets."

"You go there, too?" Aiden asked.

"Sometimes I join them. It's where Dominic asked me to marry him."

The words were a deft slice of a knife to his heart.

"At least a dozen young men on our staff are still nursing their broken hearts," Sophie said, getting up to leave.

Aiden assumed this was directed at him and bristled at the thought that the two women might be making fun of him.

"Don't listen to her, Aiden." Amina leaned over to squeeze his hand, and he swore she let her fingers clasp his a few seconds longer than would seem appropriate. Then he dismissed that as wishful thinking. Regardless, his hand was frozen in place; he couldn't move a muscle.

Up in his room, getting ready for the drive, Aiden stared at his reflection in the long mirror: an average Canadian guy, average looks, enduring the torment of infatuation with a mysterious Middle Eastern woman. And this woman, he reminded himself, was married to a good-looking cosmopolitan, wealthy man who would likely slit his throat if he glanced at her the wrong way.

"You are truly pathetic," he said to the mirror. "Get over it."

Lukas was at the door, knocking. "Coming," he said. He grabbed his backpack and headed out, resolving to "get over it."

***

When he and Lukas strolled together around Chefchaouen, Aiden was unsure whether to be in awe of the astonishing 'Blue Pearl', its walls and roofs, doors and steps painted in innumerable shades of blue, or whether to stop short of full appreciation because of the somewhat contrived appeal to tourists. The local people had certainly clued in to what constituted the "perfect shot." Some were conspicuously dressed in local costume, with bowls of oranges and lemons on red tablecloths outside their doors; others were selling artfully arranged scarves and kaftans in bright, contrasting colours. On the famous "flowerpot" lane, groups of tourists stood in turn to take shots of red and yellow tubs of flowers on every step, and close-ups of coloured pots anchored to the walls, overflowing with fat orange marigolds.

It would be natural for the locals to get tired of tourists and tired of the blue, he thought, but there was an almost eerie quietness, a reverence among the visitors. There were no particularly famous sites here; the whole town was a "must see," so ambling around and lingering over lunch in the many elaborately decorated restaurants was the best way to fill a day.

The riad Dominic and Hadir had purchased was halfway up a steep flight of steps, which they felt was part of its appeal. Local boys anxious for tips would be delighted to help with luggage. Once again, Aiden fell back on his "holy shit," exclamations, blown away by the pale blue, black-studded door, flanked on both sides by intricately patterned motifs. It was quainter than the Riad Capella but just as comfortable and welcoming. The door opened into a dark, cool hallway dotted with terracotta floor lanterns. His room was simple, cream and yellow, a bistro table and chairs in the corner, a bench under a window looking over a tiny interior courtyard.

He enjoyed a steaming tagine of spiced, aromatic chicken and vegetables with Lukas and the two brothers on the rooftop, admiring the sweeping views of the Rif mountains.

"You can see how photographers are attracted to Chaouen," Dominic said, using the more common Moroccan variation of the name. "For the festival entries, we can expect a load of shots of the same streets, the same perfect little compositions. In some ways, it will make selection easier. We can reject all the clichés and hopefully find something unusual, surprising."

They agreed that, with Lukas, Aiden would spend the next day exploring the less frequented parts of town, taking photographs and finding material for the festival literature and websites. In the evening, their driver, Bachar, would take them to the lookout point that was, according to Hadir, *"assez formidable"* when the sun went down.

***

"Pretty formidable" was about right, Aiden thought now, gazing from the lookout point at the city below him, gold and shimmering in the dying sun, its blue medina nestled under the far hills. His mind drifted to his own city on the other side of the world. He loved the expansiveness of the views of Vancouver from Grouse Mountain, endless coastline, dense rainforests, and nonstop views over the Pacific. The wild beauty inspired people to raise their arms and pivot, feeling liberated, almost powerful. Looking westward, the heart could soar to the far horizon with the sinking sun, happy to be swallowed into the giant maw of the ocean. He thought of Canada as a young, new-world country, a teenager flexing its muscles. He had never been to Europe or anywhere overseas, so had no concept of "the old world," only what he learned second hand. It was hard to nail an apt description of Morocco. The country was more than old. It was timeworn, with a past full of fables and fairytales, the kind of history you absorb rather than read about. He wanted to capture this in the visual approach to the website and, especially, the design of the pictorial book that would eventually be produced. Nothing should be predictable. He resolved to take another look at the work he'd already done, concluding it was not yet good enough.

Lukas sat on a low brick wall at the edge of their lookout spot, craning his neck. "We won't see many stars from here, maybe a bit later." He opened his phone and showed Aiden the constellations overhead now, some Aiden had never heard of: Apus, Draco, Ophiuchus, and then a more well-known one, Scorpio, with its giant red superstar, Antares, near the centre.

"Your dad was an astronomer, right?"

"I think he was kind of famous. He was at the university in Cairo. He knew lots of stuff about Ancient Egypt, like how they looked at the stars. That part wasn't really astronomy."

"Astrology then?"

"Sort of. Most people don't get it. They think astrology is star signs. My dad wrote in the notebook that astronomy and astrology were the same thing. So there's, like, the science, but then there's a kind of force that makes everything happen in a special way."

"Do you believe that?"

"You can feel it. Sometimes it's in things and sometimes it's in people. You have to watch and listen for it."

Aiden felt the hairs on the back of his neck rise and worried, for a mad moment, that the boy had supernatural tendencies.

"What about your mom, Rachel? Did she believe in it?"

"For sure. I only have bits of memory of her. She let me stay up late and sit on the terrace to look at the stars."

Dominic believed Lukas had an uncanny sixth sense, like he was some kind of agent of fate, drawing people to him and making their lives coalesce. Aiden couldn't get his head around that, but had to admit there must have been a few weird things going on here. He'd learned his uncle and Dominic and the five-year-old Lukas all met in Toronto by a strange coincidence and discovered some overlapping connections from the past. They were in Fez together when Catherine was supposed to marry Dominic.

"Some things happen just to make other things happen."

"Why did you say that?" Aiden had the unsettling feeling the kid had read his thoughts.

Lukas shrugged. "My dad wrote about it. Like, people get upset if something is bad or wrong but then a good thing happens *because* of that."

Yikes, Aiden thought, blowing out his breath. He went back to gazing over the rooftops of Chefchaouen, watching the patches of light and colour change shape and texture like a kaleidoscope beneath the darkening sky. There was little noise, only the distant hum of traffic and the occasional gust of wind from the mountains. He checked his watch. One of the calls to prayer would soon begin. Lukas had taught him all the names and the times, but he couldn't keep them straight.

"I never knew my father either," Aiden said. "I was two, so I have no memories. My Uncle Steven says he was a great guy, so I guess that's good to know."

"Your dad died in the accident," Lukas said.

Aiden thought it odd he said "the" accident. "You know about that?"

"Dominic told me. My mom was there. In another car."

What? Aiden thought he must have missed the bus on this one. "Another car?" he said, playing for time.

"There was a deer in the road. But she was okay. The accident wasn't anybody's fault."

Aiden wondered why his uncle hadn't mentioned this but decided the whole thing was a probably a painful memory he'd rather forget. *Curiouser and curiouser.* He smiled to himself, remembering how Dorothy used to like saying this when life got confusing.

"It's kind of why we're here together," Lukas said, surprising him again with his apparent mind-reading. "That force. You don't have control. You think you do, but it's planned already."

"You mean like predestination?"

"Kind of like a path you have to follow. If you take another one, it brings you back to the one you're supposed to be on."

Well, that would be one neat way to explain it all, Aiden thought, wondering if he was the only person who didn't believe in all that stuff. He walked to the edge of the lookout point. The muezzins' voices rose high into the night air, reverberating across the landscape and sending a few chills down his spine. Lukas was still engrossed in his phone. Obviously, the boy was used to all this now, he thought.

They walked down the slope to the main road. Lukas texted Bachar to let him know they'd started back and would meet him at the bottom of the hill.

"I'm sorry your mom died too," the boy said. "Amina is kind of my mom. I really love her and Dominic. They're the best people in the whole world. But a real mom is a strong feeling, as well. I think mine's here. She knows about you. Maybe she brought you here."

Aiden felt drunk and walked closer to the wall on the side of the pathway, concerned he might stumble. Lukas said astonishing things like this with such a matter-of-fact tone, clearly believing they were perfectly feasible. The last echoes of the call to pray drifted over the town, and his feeling of being in a parallel universe grew even stronger. He swallowed hard and thought the most important thing now was to get back to the hotel, have a beer, and go to bed. Maybe when he woke up tomorrow, everything would make sense.

"Well, I'm glad I'm here," he said finally.

Lukas high-fived him and ran ahead down the rest of the slope.

***

They arrived home late the following day. On one of the alleyways near the hotel they saw in the distance a woman who looked like a tourist abruptly change direction, knock into someone and spill several items from her bag. People stopped and helped her retrieve them. As Aiden and Lukas drew closer to where this had happened, Lukas scooped something from the ground.

"Look," he said. "It's a business card of our hotel."

Aiden thought nothing of it at the time.

CHAPTER 25

Dominic woke early. It promised to be another perfect day. He raised himself on one elbow and gazed at Amina's face, half lit in the yellow glow of the nightlight. He missed her when they were apart, no matter for how short a time. The classic beauty of her features was more deeply rooted with each passing year, he thought, as though time paused only to etch a few laugh lines, then scurried away to work on others. Even during her pregnancies, she looked ethereal, the long skirts and scarves she favoured drifting around her body, making her movements seem effortless.

In his bed under the window, their two-year-old son, Raif, clutched a soft blue teddy bear to his chest. Knowing he would not fall back to sleep, Dominic rose and edged open the door to the room where Lukas and Rosa slept soundly. Amina tried to encourage Rosa to have her own room now, but she threw a tantrum and would not be pried away from her brother. Whenever possible, on his way home from school, Lukas picked her up from the daycare centre. He carried her bunny-eared backpack and held her hand. Amina treasured the photo on her bedside table: the two of them in the narrow alleyway to the hotel, half in shadow, the sun catching Lukas's blond hair, Rosa gazing at him with sisterly adoration.

After breakfast, on his way out to run errands, Dominic took a quick look around the lobby, to see if there were any guests he should greet personally. He made a point of glancing through the reservation list each night to check for loyal customers and develop a sense for the kind of people the Riad Capella attracted. At the fountain, a small group of tourists waited for their guide, and a few business travellers checked phones or pecked away at laptops.

A woman seated alone on one of the cushioned benches in the colonnade flanking the courtyard caught his eye. A wealthy tourist, he thought, noting the expensive camera and Hermès scarf. He didn't think she was a guest and concluded she must be waiting for someone. He smiled in her direction, but she drew the scarf across her face and turned away.

Dominic loved any excuse to meander through the Fez medina. He soaked in the noise and bustle of the day … shopkeepers replenishing goods on their trestle tables, waiters carrying the ubiquitous trays of mint tea his countrymen adored. He greeted merchants and accepted an invitation to drink a Turkish coffee and exchange news of friends and family. The sun crept into the narrow alleyways and squeezed through crowded, mudbrick buildings, as though seeking him out. Closing his eyes, he basked in its mellow warmth, breathing in scents of vanilla from the nearby bakery and orange blossom from the flower seller on the corner.

Stopping in the Aïn-Allou souk to collect a wall hanging he'd ordered from his friend, Youssef, he admired the wide range of leather merchandise on display. On the counter, out of place among the distinctly Moroccan craftsmanship, was a selection of miniature Ancient Egyptian paraphernalia, including a stand of silver cartouches. One of these drew his eye: a woman kneeling, her arms and wings stretched wide, an ostrich feather on her head. He remembered a reference to the feather of Ma'at in Lukas's notebook, when he'd glanced through it one morning on their trip to the Atacama Desert.

"Is that the Goddess Ma'at?" he asked Youssef.

"Well done. That's her. Justice. Cosmic harmony."

"Why do you have these Ancient Egyptian things here?"

"Because they sell. Maybe the tourists forget what country they're in. Ma'at is the daughter of Ra, married to Thoth, God of Wisdom, counterpoint to Isfet—chaos and injustice."

"You *know* this? Did you study it?"

Youssef laughed and slapped Dominic's arm. "I'm reading the note that came with it. It's hand-crafted, sterling silver. Buy it for your beautiful wife. She is a Goddess too, no?"

Dominic grinned, folding his arms. "I never see you without giving you more money than I planned."

Youssef was already dropping the pendant into a small green silk bag. "What do they say? 'If you have much, give of your wealth; if you have little, give of your heart.' You will always have a full wallet, my friend, *Insha'Allah.*"

On his way home, Lukas called, asking when Dominic would be back. Concerned by the pitch of the boy's voice, he told him he was only two streets away, naming the well-known carpet store in the neighbourhood. He picked up his pace.

"Is something wrong, Lukas?" His thoughts went immediately to Amina.

"Rosa's talking about a woman at her school. Kind of weird. I'll come and meet you."

A few minutes later, he saw the boy hurrying along the narrow street towards him, side-stepping donkeys and carts, barrels of vegetables and other obstacles.

"So what's up?" Dominic asked him.

Lukas explained how, when he arrived at Rosa's playschool, he saw a woman crouched next to Rosa on the other side of the railing. "When I called out to Rosa, she walked away."

"Was she one of the moms?"

The boy frowned. "Maybe. But I've never seen her. Rosa said she was stroking her arm, and she took a photo of her. Maybe it's okay. I don't know. Amina's in a meeting. I didn't want to bother her."

"A photo?" Dominic picked up the bags he'd let slip to the ground. "I'm sure we must know her. I'll check it out."

Despite rationalizing this was almost certainly nothing to be concerned about, Dominic felt once again that sharp twist of anxiety he'd hoped he was rid of. At the hotel, he hurried up the spiral stone steps to the family's wing, opened the door to their rooms, and gathered his daughter in his arms.

"Lukas said you met a lady at the school. Do you know her name?"

Rosa shook her head. "She said I was very pretty and very cute."

"And so you are. What did she look like? Do you remember, Lukas?"

Lukas said he didn't see her well enough. She was wearing white jeans and a coloured scarf around her head, not a hijab. She kept pulling it across her face. "She wasn't Moroccan. She was maybe a tourist."

Dominic remembered the woman he saw in the lobby this morning. He left the children and went to check the guest register, but found no female travelling alone. The woman in the lobby was probably waiting for a guest, he concluded.

He extricated Amina from the meeting and told her about Lukas's concern. She steadied herself against a column of one of the arches in the courtyard, her other hand cradling her swollen belly. "I'm sure there's a simple explanation. He's so protective of Rosa. It's probably one of the mothers. But she took a photo. I don't like that. I'll call the teacher."

Up in their room, she questioned her daughter, learned nothing more and went into the bedroom to make the call.

"Apparently," she said, coming back, "many of the children are picked up by different family members or friends—all authorized, of course. This woman was either one of those or more probably a tourist passing by. The teacher claims Americans, in particular, are friendly, always telling kids they're cute or 'such a honey.' Some of them take photographs. Obviously they don't give a thought to how intrusive this is."

Dominic leaned against the windowsill and tried to breathe more slowly. He gazed at the buildings tumbling over the hillside, the tall stands of cypress trees darkening against the late sun. The *Asr* call to prayer struck up from the minaret of the Mosque of al-Qarawiyyin, the first to start each *salat*. Within seconds, echoes from mosques across the medina rang out through the hot evening air.

"Can I have an ice cream now?" Rosa said.

All is well, Dominic told himself, all is well.

CHAPTER 26

With much of the structure and visual theme of the festival materials approved, Aiden was able to work increasingly from the hotel, either in his room or in a shady spot on the roof terrace. But, anxious to continue exploring the medina, he offered to pick up groceries for Henri some mornings. Depending on school schedules, Lukas and Rosa liked to go with him.

The kitchen was a good size, despite this being a boutique hotel. Henri was very much in charge, barking orders to his hapless assistants who, he claimed with a wink, rarely got anything right. As Henri energetically chopped bunches of parsley and coriander, he listed from memory what he needed. Aiden took notes on his phone.

Amina dropped by to remind the kitchen staff that a large group of tourism reps from Rabat would be joining them for dinner that night. Henri muttered something in French and made a slicing motion across his neck with the ominous-looking knife.

"When I first came to live here," Amina told Aiden. "Henri went with me to the market and taught me how to bargain. I was young and naïve, and some of the merchants took advantage of this. But Henri put them in their place, and they never tried again. He's a formidable presence in Fez. But Lukas will help you in the market if you run into trouble."

As always, when Amina was close, Aiden didn't know where to rest his eyes. He tried to look at her, pay attention, but could never meet that hypnotic gaze. Even as she spoke about such mundane things as the price of onions and the freshness of herbs in one store vs. another, it was as though she were some mythological siren, drawing him to his inevitable peril.

"Aiden?" she said. "I was saying you should get more cash from the safe. Most vendors still prefer it."

He assured her he'd do this. She floated away.

He was aware that the systematic chopping on the big wooden board had ceased. When he turned back to Henri, the chef was appraising him, arms crossed. Aiden couldn't tell if he was annoyed or trying not to laugh.

"*Mon pauvre ami*," Henri said, shaking his head. "She is but a beautiful fantasy."

"What? Sorry?"

"A mesmerizing creature, *n'est ce pas?*"

Aiden raised both hands in protest. "Look, I wouldn't want you to …. I mean, I have no thought of—"

"But a man can dream, and a great many men have shared that dream. No harm in that."

"No way. I mean, I wouldn't want Dominic to get the wrong—"

"Why not? Sadly, in the eyes of his lovely wife, the lucky man has no competition. None. It wouldn't hurt for him to worry from time to time. Keep him on his toes, *non?*"

"Please, Henri, Dominic is a good friend."

Henri drew the "sealed lips" sign with his thumb and forefinger and shooed him out to where Lukas and Rosa were waiting.

Fuck, Aiden thought, realizing he needed to get better control of himself.

The early sun was still low enough to cast long shadows throughout the medina. There was a liveliness and energy among the vendors as they set up their trestle tables, piling them high with pots and pans, clothing and tableware. They called out to each other, laughing and joking, and chastised their young children who were getting in the way. From experience, Aiden knew in a couple of hours the sun would burn more fiercely, nudging around corners, causing people to slow down, their voices at a lower pitch. As the day wore on, they would splash water from the drinking fountain on their faces and seek the shade.

Rosa clung to his hand, stopping to ask for sweets or cookies from indulgent merchants. She chattered away in French and Arabic until Lukas told her it was rude, and she should be speaking English with Aiden here.

"Don't worry, Lukas. I hope I'll pick up a few words and phrases by the end of my visit."

An hour later, laden with bags, Aiden was checking Henri's list when he felt a tug on his sleeve.

"That's her," Rosa said. "The lady who came to my school."

Aiden had heard about the "strange lady" from Lukas. He looked up. Rosa was pointing to a woman across the aisle, packing her purchases into a sling bag. "That lady in the big hat? I know her. Hey, Nancy?" he called out. She did not react at first. "Hello," he called again.

She turned, looking startled, as Aiden ushered both children over to her.

"Hey there," he said, extending his hand. "Aiden Quinn. We met the other day outside the studio where I'm working on the arts festival."

She hesitated for a second. "Right. Of course. How are you?"

"Good, good." He introduced Lukas and Rosa. "Rosa said you were at her school yesterday. Is that right? Was it you she saw?"

"Hi Rosa. Yes, I was there. Fancy you remembering me. I walked there with my friend,. She was meeting with one of the teachers. She has a daughter about your age she wants to enrol. What a small world."

They talked for a few minutes about the festival and Fez, and discovered they were both Canadian. She asked if he came regularly to the market. Two or three times a week, he said, whenever Lukas's school schedule allowed.

"Lukas is helping me with the language. Guess I should try to manage but he's great company." He turned to Lukas, who was standing back a few steps with a curious look on his face. He was staring at Nancy, rather brazenly, Aiden thought. "Aren't you, Lukas?" he said, nudging him.

Lukas looked down, finally smiling.

"Maybe we could have a coffee," Nancy said. "You can give me some pointers about my photography before I leave. I'm going home at the end of the week."

He told her he couldn't today … maybe the day after tomorrow. He explained Dominic and his brother would be out of town, and he and Lukas would likely bring Rosa to the market again to give her busy mom a break. They arranged a time, and she gave him the name of a good café.

"Be sure to bring Rosa," Nancy said. "My friend may join us. She'll bring her daughter. They have the best *msemen* with honey dipping at that café."

***

At dinner, before the two brothers left on business again, Aiden told them about his meeting with Nancy and was surprised at the sheer relief around the table.

Dominic closed his eyes and inhaled for long seconds before letting out a long sigh. "Thank God," he said. "It's one of those things that nag you. I've tried to reason I'm being over-protective, but then, as a parent, I guess there's no such thing, is there?"

"I thought there'd be a reasonable explanation," Amina said, sinking back into her chair. She pinched Rosa's cheek. "See how you make us all worry because you're so cute."

Hadir raised his glass and clinked it with his wife's and Dominic's. "Here's to all of us staying safe and well."

"That means you two men, too," said Sophie. "No speeding along those desert roads just because we're not there to nag you. That last fine was a small fortune."

The conversation turned to what needed to be done at the family's new, and as yet unfinished, hotel in Marrakech, where the brothers were headed. Aiden was pleased his little encounter with Nancy had contributed to the good spirits around the table. Only Lukas was quiet, concentrating on his food. Aiden caught his eye and mouthed "okay?" The boy nodded but still looked perturbed about something. Who knows, Aiden thought, what goes on in the minds of nine-year-old boys, especially this one. Back home, he had little exposure to children, but Lukas certainly didn't fit any of the preconceived ideas he had about what makes them tick.

"So, Aiden," Dominic said, pushing back his chair. "We're setting off early and likely won't see you tomorrow. Are you sure you've got everything you need? You'll probably get that new material from the sponsors soon. If you need help, just call." He clasped Aiden's shoulders. "Once more we leave our family in your excellent hands."

CHAPTER 27

Aiden would always struggle to connect his memories of the next day to the reality of actually being there. They were like scenes from a movie, the vignettes sweeping through his mind amorphous and remote. Even the overwhelming panic eventually lost definition.

When he arrived at the café with Lukas and Rosa, Nancy was already there. She was seated at a round table by the window, with a view of the street so she could look out for her friend who, she said, would be a few minutes late. He remembered a strong smell of coffee and pastries fresh from the oven, and the hustle of customers, some seated, some lining up to order. He remembered sounds: the cries of street vendors, the hammering of a shoemaker next door, the repetitive rhythm of *Gnawa* music from a speaker high on the wall. It was ten a.m., and the sun was already fierce, reflecting off large copper pots in the store across the narrow street.

Nancy ordered coffee, chebakia, fekkas, and apple juice for the children. She suggested Aiden and Lukas wait for the food at the counter. She'd stay with Rosa, saving the seats, and watching for her friend who had texted she was two minutes away.

The little café was crowded now. Aiden edged his way through with the tray, worried he'd get knocked and the drinks would spill. He asked Lukas to find more napkins.

When they got back to the table, Nancy and Rosa were gone.

Two elderly men were sitting in their chairs. Aiden wondered if he'd ended up on the wrong side of the café. No, he thought, they were right here at the window overlooking the little street, right by the door. But Nancy's sunhat and glasses were not on the table. Rosa's bunny-eared backpack was not under the chair.

The men said something he didn't understand.

"Do you speak English?" he said. "A friend was here. With a little girl."

"No here. No one here. You can sit. Enough space."

"Maybe they moved," Aiden said to Lukas, who stood behind him with a fistful of napkins, his face white. "Maybe they went to the bathroom."

Aiden put the tray down and walked from table to table, expecting any second to hear his name, to hear Rosa's laugh or feel her tug at his sleeve. He felt untethered from this time and place. If he began to imagine the worst, then the worst would happen. But if he held on to this moment, when everything was normal, then it would stay that way. Rosa would appear somewhere in the café or come in from the street. Yes, that's it, he thought, they've stepped out to meet Nancy's friend. They're outside. He dashed to the door and scanned the crowds in both directions. Nothing. His ears were ringing, and he had the sensation of floundering underwater, desperate for air. He wanted it to be an hour from now, tomorrow, next week, when Rosa would have surfaced, unharmed. Instead, each heavy, empty second stretched to eternity.

He pushed back inside where Lukas was still clutching the napkins, his lower lip drooped, his eyes wide.

"Lukas." It came out as a hoarse cry. "Tell them, ask them, everybody. A woman, a little girl. Ask if they've seen them."

The little café fell silent when Lukas shouted in French. The customers looked at each other in consternation. A woman called from the back, pointing through the window.

Aiden gripped Lukas's shoulder. "What's she saying? What does she mean?"

"She said she saw my mom and my sister leaving when she came in. Hurrying away." He shouted back to her. "*Elle n'est pas ma maman.* She's not my mom. Oh God, please help."

Noise and commotion broke the silence, everyone crowding around them, questions, exclamations: *wasn't she a friend? maybe she will phone; perhaps there was an emergency; I'm sure they'll be back any moment.* A customer called for water and made Lukas sit on a chair.

The seconds ticked on. People walked by the window, talking to each other. Aiden wanted to scream at them. *Stop, stop, stop. How can you pretend this is a normal day?* He took out his phone but he was shivering, his hands shaking. He didn't know what to do with it. He wanted only to be gone, blacked out, for this to be a nightmare he would wake from.

The phone rang, making him jump and almost drop it. Amina.

"Aiden. Where are you? Where is Rosa?"

He stared at the phone. *What?* He couldn't form any words.

"What's happening? Say something," Amina pleaded. "Where is Rosa? Where is Lukas?"

Lukas grabbed the phone. *"Elle a disparu.* They've gone. *Ce n'est pas possible.* We have to call the police."

Aiden heard the fury in Amina's voice. "No. No police. Get back here. Both of you. Right now. Don't stop. Don't talk to anyone. Do you understand? Leave. Now."

They ran. The people from the café stared, some calling after them. They ran through tiny narrow alleyways, across little squares, weaving past donkeys and carts, colliding with vendors who cursed and shook their fists.

When they pushed open the heavy door of the hotel, Amina was right behind it. In a frantic whisper, she told them to stay quiet, to get upstairs to Aiden's room. She kept looking over her shoulder, her breath coming in short gasps. Aiden fumbled with the key.

Once inside, Amina pulled a folded sheet of paper from the pocket of her skirt. "This came. A messenger boy delivered it. Read it."

Rosa is safe. She knows I'm a friend. Nothing bad is going to happen. I don't want money. This is between you and me, Amina. A matter for two women. I know your husband is out of town. I know what he's capable of. If you tell him, or anyone else, or get the police involved, things will get ugly and complicated. I will be in touch soon and tell you what I need. It's very simple.

He turned the paper over. There was nothing else. No signature.

"*Nothing bad is going to happen?*" Amina yelled. "What does that mean? Where were you? Who saw you? Were you with her? Is she mad? Who is this woman? Is she the one you were meeting, the Canadian, the photographer woman?"

They went through every encounter, every recollection, talking over each other: Lukas seeing her at the school, the exchange at the Merenid tombs, Aiden meeting her outside Zahra's store, the chance encounter in the market. Aiden could hear another person talking for him, one who kept saying inane things like "It can't be, I don't believe it, I'm sorry, I'm sorry, it's all my fault," one who kept pacing, went to the bathroom and threw up. The real person was someone else: cold and lifeless, retreating to the farthest chair in the room. He stared at his feet and willed the floor to open and swallow him.

"I knew it. I knew she was weird," Lukas said. "What does she want? What's going to happen to Rosa?" He sat on the bed, his hands clenched together in his lap. "Why can't we call Dominic and Hadir? They have to come home, help find her."

Aiden prayed Amina would heed the caution in the woman's note and not do this. The thought of Dominic filled him with dread. He remembered what he'd said about leaving the family in good hands. And now Aiden had allowed his baby girl to be taken right from under his nose. The humiliation burned through his whole body.

"Don't you know anything about her, Aiden?" Amina said, her voice rising. "Did she fill out a form for the festival, or was that a ruse too? *Is* she Canadian? Do you know the name of her friend who was coming, the one whose daughter is at Rosa's school? Is her friend Moroccan? Is she even real? You must know something. Anything."

Aiden knew he would do whatever it took to make this right, to find Rosa, anything and everything to wipe away Amina's disbelief, her borderline contempt.

"I gave her my card. She didn't text back. She didn't confirm. It was so quick, so casual. Just, 'let's grab a coffee.' She seemed nice. God, this can't be happening."

For a good half an hour they trawled through memories, trying to connect Nancy with a person, an event, a circumstance that would explain what was going on. Amina paced, stopping to hold on to the frame of the bed, or lean against the chest of drawers to support herself.

"She must know us somehow," she said. "How the hell does she know Dominic is out of town?"

Aiden thought back to the brief conversation in the market. He had a vague memory of mentioning this, saying something about looking after Rosa to give her mom a break. Jesus, why would he say that, he thought, punching the wall in frustration.

"And what about that comment—knowing what he's capable of?" Amina continued. "What on earth could that mean? If she's here visiting a friend, how would she—"

"I remember now."

They spun around. Lukas stood with his back to them, facing the photograph on the wall, the *Festival of Fantasia,* the Berber horsemen.

"I remember who she is," he said. "I knew it was weird. She was in Chile. At the lodge. The stables. There was a woman there. It's her."

"In *Chile?*" Amina cried. "How could that be?"

"She was talking to that man, Julian, the one who took us to see the horses."

Amina drew back from him. "*What?* That woman lived there. Didn't she? Or worked there. What are you saying, Lukas?"

"I knew I'd seen her before. I couldn't remember. For sure it was her. She was getting a horse ready, putting on his saddle."

"But why would she be here, in Morocco? What could she want with us?"

Aiden seized on this, desperate to get his mind going, his limbs working, anything to break through the helplessness. "Let me call them, those people in Chile."

Lukas was still staring at the photo on the wall, transfixed, his pale grey eyes narrowed. "Chile is four hours behind us."

Amina struggled to stand but faltered. Aiden steadied her, catching the scent of jasmine, wanting to fall at her feet and beg forgiveness.

"Go down to Dominic's office," she said. "He will have taken his laptop, but the files might be on the desktop. The trip. The lodge in Patagonia." She put a hand to her forehead. "God, the password … one of the drawers on the left, I think. A sticky note. Don't tell anyone Lukas and I are up here. We *must* keep this quiet. If someone asks what you're doing, say it's work for the festival."

"Shouldn't we get Sophie?"

She shook her head fiercely. "She won't be back till late. Tell *no one.*"

Aiden flew down the stairs. The lobby was crowded with guests checking out, bellboys carrying luggage and directing people to their rooms. He hurried to the offices, not making eye contact with anyone. As he rifled through the drawers looking for something resembling a password, he was aware of a portrait on the wall of an alcove opposite the desk. Amina. It must be the one his uncle painted, he thought. He swore those dark eyes bored into him with sad reproach. Finally, he found a green Post-it note with a series of letters and numbers. Forcing himself to slow down, he tapped these in and let out a long breath when the screen came to life. He typed *Chile* into 'search' and a folder appeared. After a frantic scroll through the files, he found what looked like an invoice from a lodge and wrote the telephone number down. Hurrying back, he prayed Lukas was right, no matter how far-fetched it seemed. He wanted something concrete to hang on to.

Amina sat at the little desk near the window by the side of his easel. The painting he had started was still propped on it. He had the sickening feeling the painting would never be finished now. He tried to imagine what it could eventually look like, willing that completion in his mind, knowing, if it were finished, it would mean Rosa had been found. Amina had an unsettling aura of calmness, but with such pent-up rage he feared she'd explode any moment, fall to pieces. He held his breath while she punched in the number.

Speaking in English, she introduced herself, said her family had visited there, and they needed to get in touch with a woman called Nancy who worked at the stables. She had to repeat this, saying it in different ways.

She covered the phone with her hand. "He doesn't speak much English. He said there's no woman at the stables."

"It's still early there. Maybe he's not the regular person," Lukas said.

She put the phone on speaker. "She was there when Julian took us to see the horses. Julian. Can I speak to Julian?"

"Julian? You mean Che? No woman with horses. Nobody is Nancy. When you came?"

"April."

A long pause. They heard him call over to another person. "Ah, *si*. Maybe Egypt woman. She bring horses from her father."

"Egypt? The woman we're looking for speaks English. She might be Canadian."

"Si, si. Maybe she. She ride. Very good riding. Her family with big ranch. Al Sayed. You call later. Talk to Che. He knows."

Amina raised her voice. "I'm calling from Morocco. Please find him. *Muy importante*."

The man told her to wait. He wasn't sure if Julian was there.

Lukas tapped Al Sayed into Google. "It's a horse place. A huge stable. Training and breeding. What is he saying?"

Aiden sank into a chair, felled by the growing weight of helplessness.

"Did she say anything about Egypt?" Amina said. "About riding? Think, Aiden." She doubled over and began to cry.

Lukas flung his arms around her. Aiden remembered the time he found Dorothy weeping in the kitchen and had done the same thing, desperate to make her sadness go away. He would have been roughly the same age as Lukas. And in both cases, the woman they wanted to comfort was *not* their mother, but a woman who had rescued them. He turned away.

"Señora?"

"Yes, yes." Amina held the phone closer.

"This is Julian. You are from El Hassan family, right? I remember you. Your husband and son, they go to Atacama I think. There is nobody called Nancy here. So sorry."

"But the woman, the one who was riding that day?"

"From Al Sayed you mean? She brought horses here. Her name isn't Nancy. She is Gabriella Burhan."

Amina asked him to repeat, then spell the last name. Her face changed, the fear behind her eyes becoming confusion, then dawning recognition, then disbelief. She took the phone off speaker and moved to the far wall. She asked questions: did he know anything about the woman's family, was she married, where did she live, could she be in Fez? Aiden couldn't hear the answers clearly, only the frustration in her voice and the change in tone of Julian's, which sounded like a growing unwillingness to give further information.

When she hung up, her hand was shaking. She put the phone down slowly, as though it were fragile, and stared into the middle distance, her body wound up like a coiled spring.

"Does he know where Rosa is?" Lukas said. "Does he know the woman?"

"I need a minute." She waved both hands at Lukas. He shrank back, clearly not used to this kind of dismissal. She paced to the window and back, sat down, then stood up again.

She pivoted and faced Lukas. "Here's what you must do." She placed both hands on his shoulders. "Get Rosa's little case. Put some of her clothes in it, a warm sweater, her favourite toys. Don't talk to anyone. Not a soul."

"But where—?"

"Do it, Lukas."

When he left, she spoke to Aiden in a rush. "I don't know this woman, whatever her name is. But I know her husband. I'm sure of it. I'm going to call that place in Egypt. Al Sayed. If she and her husband live in Morocco, I think I know where. I'll find out. It's a long drive. I have to leave right now. I'll tell the nanny I'm away tonight. She's to keep Raif with her. Please stay with Lukas. Don't let him out of your sight for a single second. Do you understand?"

She moved toward the door.

"Whoa. Wait. Stop. Where are you going? You're not going anywhere on your own." Aiden was shocked by the authority in his voice, his sudden firm decision that, if necessary, he would stop her leaving by force. He could not handle a second more of this day if she took off and he were left alone. "Who are these people?" He blocked the door.

She looked like a trapped animal, weighing her chances of fleeing. "It doesn't matter. Just … years ago, I knew him. Something happened. I had to get away. He took me to Egypt. But he had another agenda. There's no time to go into it. Get out of my way, Aiden. I have to go."

"Amina, are you crazy? This sounds bad. We have to call—"

"No." Her vehemence astonished him. "Dominic cannot know. They met once. Dominic nearly killed him. This would drive him over the edge. Something could happen to Rosa."

"I'm not staying here, Amina. No way. And we're not leaving Lukas. He'd go crazy with worry. If you're going, we're all going."

He couldn't tell if she was resigned or relieved, but he didn't care. "What about Sophie?" he said. "We can't leave without telling her."

"When she gets in, she'll go straight to bed. She won't know we're gone. Let me go. I have to pack things, I have to make that call. If you're serious, get ready, get Lukas ready. Don't tell him anything. Five minutes. That's all you've got."

"Amina, stop. These people …. what do they have to do with Rosa?"

"Maybe nothing. Maybe everything. Please… not now. Get moving."

CHAPTER 28

Gabi had not reckoned on discovering someone like Aiden. At first, he was a clear obstacle to the plans she was formulating on her journey to Fez, but then he proved to be an asset. Sitting with Rosa asleep on the seat beside her, driving as fast as she dared southbound on the N9, she congratulated herself on her quick thinking.

What helped the whole idea was Masoud's preoccupation with his new project and the fact he was out of town for nearly a month. She told him she was going to stay with Sally in Rabat for a week or two. At first, he balked at the idea of her driving there alone, wondering why she wouldn't fly. But she reminded him she'd taken her car all over the country and she enjoyed driving. Depending on where she and Sally decided to go, the car might be useful. Eventually, he was reassured.

She explained to Sally she had lied to Masoud; she needed to go to Fez, but couldn't tell him why. Sally was skeptical, even wondering if Gabi had a lover there, but did not press for details. At her suggestion, Gabi turned off the location sharing on her phone, but she doubted Masoud would call.

She stayed in a hotel near the Blue Gate, within walking distance of the Riad Capella. It proved to be so easy to stroll into the lush lobby, tell the bellboy she was waiting for a friend, and they might have lunch there, order a mint tea and sit back to observe. Her ability to speak Arabic was an asset. They assumed she was an expat and didn't bother her with tourist brochures or ask if she needed a sightseeing guide.

Dominic was the first member of the family she saw. He sauntered through the lobby, casting his eyes around as though eager to bestow fragments of his magnanimous presence on others. He approached two businessmen, clasped their shoulders and summoned a bellboy to help them. And then that strange boy, the one she could just make out in the background of the photo from Chile. He had run down the curved stone steps leading off the courtyard, stopped near the bottom and given her a fleeting, curious glance. But he was in a hurry, gone in a flash.

She hung around the hotel for two days, blending in easily with tourists who were waiting for each other and for guides, or guests planning to have lunch at the restaurant. At one point she struck up a conversation with a group of Americans so any passing staff would assume she was a part of their group.

She never intended to take the girl. The vague plans in her head as she began the journey did not go this far. She wanted only to get a closer look at the life of this lucky, perfect family, and find a way to approach Amina. She planned to tell her who she was, tell her about Masoud's illness. The question of his daughter's parentage may never have entered Dominic's mind, but surely Amina, in quiet moments, would have thought back and wondered … or worried. Gabi would reason with her, plead, maybe even threaten. All she wanted was a paternity test. Dominic need never know, and Masoud *deserved* to know. Gabi had done her homework on legal and custodial rights in this part of the world … she had leverage.

She went to the hotel the next day filled with new resolve. Rather than announce her presence and ask for Amina, she retreated to a bench, partially hidden by a palm tree in the colonnade, to go through her planned approach. She picked up a brochure about an upcoming arts festival and pretended to be engrossed. The hotel was busy. Clusters of suitcases stood neatly under the arches, people checked in, oohing and aahing at the décor, bellboys flitted about with trays of tea. On the far side of the courtyard, near the entrance to the restaurant, a woman matching the photo on the website on Gabi's phone came into view, hair swept back and pinned on one side, dark eyes in a finely sculpted face.

Gabi had to stop the startled cry lodged in her throat. It was Amina, the woman her husband had loved, may still love. And Amina was pregnant. This woman, who was blessed with a daughter, and the toddler Gabi remembered from Chile, and the strange blond boy … here she was, pregnant with yet another child. For a minute or two, Gabi sat rigid with anger at the unfairness of life, how this woman could be given beauty, a happy marriage, and children to love, when Gabi had none of these things. Like her husband, Amina walked with the confidence of belonging. This was her home, her business, her family, this precious bubble of French Moroccan life where she was valued and untouchable. Amina came within a few feet of her, chatting to one of the hotel staff. She rested a hand on one of the columns. Gabi stared at the slender fingers, the finely manicured nails polished a deep red, the heavy copper bangle at her wrist … no callouses, no bitten nails, no evidence of anything but a pampered life. In that instant, Gabi knew Amina would give her no more than a few fleeting seconds of her time. She imagined the consternation on her face, the memories of Masoud flooding back, and then the scorn, the call to the desk, to security, or Dominic, to get Gabi thrown out. She remembered what Masoud had said: "You don't know what this family is capable of."

Her nerve failed her, and she knew, unless she gave up right then, she would need a more drastic plan.

Earlier, she had overheard two bellboys talking about the family going to the Merenid Tombs. Her Arabic was weak, but she caught the word *lyoum* – today—and decided, on a whim, to go there herself, hoping "family" might include the little girl.

She took her camera, always an easy way to appear occupied and non-threatening, but after an hour of scouring the site, she concluded she must have misunderstood, or they had changed their plans. As she climbed a slope, preparing to return to her car, the blond boy appeared on the path leading to the main arch. He was with a young man, Caucasian, mid-twenties, she would guess. And, behind them, Amina and a woman she recognized as Sophie from the website gallery, Amina's sister-in-law. A little, curly-haired girl hop-skipped between them, chattering away to herself. Gabi's heart beat faster, and beads of sweat ran down her neck. *That was her.* She angled her sunhat over her face and turned onto another pathway.

She watched them for over an hour, grateful there were several other sightseers there, and she did not draw attention. That child, she thought, could be my stepdaughter …she may belong to me as much as she belongs to that woman's husband. She tried to imagine grabbing the girl and running to her car, but knew that would never work. The three adults would rush to the child's aid, along with any number of tourists. When the young man and Amina peeled off, she was tempted to act, but caution got the better of her.

Twenty minutes later, as the sun started its descent and visitors gathered in a favoured vantage point to take photographs, the young guy saw her and spoke. She made some innocuous remark about the view, wondering who the hell he could be, how he was connected to the family and whether she had to factor him into her half-formed plans.

That night, unable to sleep, images of the family hovered at the edge of her mind. They all looked happy, busy, normal, not a care in the world, secure in their present lives and in their future. Impenetrable. But she had planned to be here at least a couple of weeks, returning a day or two before Masoud, so there was plenty of time. She'd follow them for a few days, find out if and where the girl went to school, figure out their comings and goings, and exactly what her next move should be.

As she lay staring at the ceiling, she had the sensation of not belonging in her own body. These arms and legs, this unbeautiful creature was walking and talking at the command of an independent, spiteful mind, one fueled by resentment and humiliation. What happened to the young woman, she wondered, the one who had grown up in the Rockies with a love of horses, who thought she would live and work with them, and have a normal, happily married life? Her father had wrought this twisted soul, she believed. He could have recognized her contribution to the business, made her a partner right now, and made his precious nephews answer to her. And what of her mother, she thought … in the end, she was a willing accomplice, equally to blame.

Her phone pinged. She thought it could be Masoud, out in some bleak desert landscape, missing her. But it was Sally. *You okay? Don't want to interfere but let me know.*

She curled up on her side, drew her knees to her chest, and texted back: *Just fine. Talk later.* She felt a malicious hand squeezing her heart out to dry.

The next day, reluctant to enter the Riad Capella for fear of being recognized, she decided to hang around in the little streets leading to it. That's where she spotted the young blond boy. He had a bag slung over his shoulder and was checking what looked like a list.

She followed him to Zahra's store.

She was only momentarily flustered when Aiden came out to talk to her. She made the quick decision to give him a false name, the first that came into her head. In the crowded medina, it was easy to follow him and the blond boy and discover the kindergarten. She watched the parents and siblings and caregivers as they called out to the children, hugged them, and ushered them away, and realized there was no way she could capture the girl from here. There were far too many enquiring eyes and, she thought with a quick look around, no doubt a security guard or two close by.

She went back the next day, wearing a long veil that covered her hair and most of her face, and managed to get the girl's attention. She took a quick photo and reached for her hand, feeling the smoothness of the child's skin and the quick tug as she pulled away. The girl had a wary look in her eyes, both hands hooked under the straps of her pink backpack. She rose up on her toes to search the crowd. A moment later, she must have seen a blond boy. "Rosa," he shouted, his voice a little anxious. The girl beamed as he ran to her side. Gabi melted into the pressing crowd.

Rosa. So that was her name, Masoud's daughter.

She turned to look at Rosa now, still sleeping, curled up awkwardly on the seat beside her, clasping a soft blue bunny from her knapsack. "Well, Rosa," she said under her breath. "You don't have to worry. Your life will get better and better. And so will mine."

The rest was so easy. The "accidental" meeting in the market, hearing the name Nancy and not making the connection at first. She had planned only to follow and observe them, but there they were, Aiden and Lukas and Rosa, right in front of her, a real stroke of luck. She even learned the two brothers who ran the hotel were to be out of town. A gift. It had come to her in a flash, the idea of getting together over coffee on the pretense of wanting to learn more about the festival. He was so naïve, this Aiden, so trusting.

An hour into the drive, as they left the city behind them, Gabi felt the first bolts of fear. She could never turn back, never undo this. She had taken a child from her family. If things did not go the way she hoped, there would be serious consequences. She could lose everything. She clutched the steering wheel and had a fleeting instinct to turn off, drop Rosa somewhere—a police station maybe, and head for the airport in Casablanca. She always carried her passport. She could take a flight home, her real home across the Atlantic, leave this barren part of the world forever, shed the sand and dirt, the disappointment, the shame. Her mother would miss her. Her father would miss the work she did. As for her husband—she was never able to read his mind, never knew his true feelings.

But no, she reasoned. *They* had taken a child from her father. Masoud was her father, and she, Gabi, was her stepmother … a different kind of mother, but one who still counted, one who had been denied a meaningful role in the child's life. All she wanted was to prove this, get a paternity test to settle the matter. She had done nothing wrong. The child was unharmed, she would be cared for, nothing bad would happen to her. Masoud would come home to his wife and daughter. The rest, how it would all be managed … all that was for tomorrow and the next day. Everyone involved would see reason, realize the potential legal case for joint custody she and Masoud had. The family would not want a scandal. They would cooperate.

She pushed her foot down a little harder on the accelerator, barely registering the desert villages, mosques, and vast sandy plains as they flashed by.

Rosa stirred but did not wake. She had been excited at first, anxious to go to the store down the street, the one with even better pastries and ice creams. She believed the call Gabi pretended to take from Amina, "her friend," Amina claiming she was picking up Aiden and Lukas, and they would all meet at Gabi's home. Back in the car, Gabi gave Rosa a tablet with lots of photographs of horses and some of her young nephews riding in the paddock.

"You like horses, right Rosa?" she said. "This summer, you'll get to see them, and meet your cousins. Would you like to learn to ride? I will teach you. You'll be really good rider, I can tell. Those young boys are your cousins. I bet you'll be better than them."

"My cousins are in America," the girl said. "They're twins. They belong to Aunt Sophie and Uncle Hadir. They love me a lot. They always bring me presents when they come home."

It was a long drive and Rosa fidgeted constantly, wanting to speak to Lukas, wanting to see her mother, saying she had to pee, she was hungry, thirsty, asking over and over again where they were going, why weren't Aiden and Lukas with them, when would they get home. A lot of the time she spoke French, which Gabi did not understand. Gabi encouraged her to speak English. She kept reassuring her she'd see her family soon.

After a long period of silence, Rosa threw a tantrum, kicking at the car door and screaming for Gabi to stop. Gabi pulled up to a small restaurant on the roadside and bought a snack that they ate at a tiny table, under an umbrella.

She pretended to call Amina. "She's a little restless, Amina. We've stopped for a few minutes. Yes, we'll see you all tonight. Yes, I'll tell her that." She turned to Rosa "*Maman* wants you to be good, not to make any fuss."

Rosa reached for the phone. "I want to talk to *maman*. Please let me."

"Not right now. She's busy. You'll see her soon."

Back in the car, Rosa fell asleep again and did not wake until they were passing the turn off for Marrakech. She twisted back and pointed through the window to the highway sign. "Marrakech. That's where my papa is. With Uncle Hadir. I want to see him. He can come with us. Please, please. Let me see my papa."

"For sure, Rosa, but not now. Just a little while longer, and we'll be home."

CHAPTER 29

For Aiden, sitting in the passenger seat beside Amina, the journey was sheer torture—Meknes, Khemisset, Rabat, Casablanca, Settat, deserts and mountains and endless rocky plains, names infused with history, places to see and feel and touch. But now those places were in the way. He wanted them gone, miles behind them. The only town that mattered was one he could barely pronounce: Ouarzazate. That's where Rosa would be, Amina was convinced. Nearly eight hours away.

Amina had called Al Sayed asking for Masoud Burhan, the man she was sure was the woman's husband. She was told he was "back in Morocco," and may not be visiting Al Sayed again for a few months. She asked to be "reminded" of his address in Ouarzazate.

"Who are these people and what do they want with Rosa?" Aiden asked as soon as they were underway.

She put a finger to her lips and nodded toward Lukas in the back.

He wanted to clutch her tightly, kiss the fear from her eyes. Fixing his own eyes on the horizon, across the vast, unforgiving plains of the desert, he fantasized about what it would be like to rescue Rosa, bring her back safely to the arms of her family. He rocked back and forth, berating himself for letting all this happen. Amina gently tapped his hand, a soothing gesture that filled him with even more remorse. He thought he would melt from the heat of those fingers.

She tried to silence Lukas's persistent questions by saying the woman was not going to hurt Rosa, but there was no way she would wait for her call. She wanted to meet her face to face.

"Is it something like before, like when you were lost in Egypt?" he asked.

Amina drew in her breath and muttered what sounded to Aiden like a curse. "There's nothing you can hide from that child," she whispered. "No. It will be alright, I promise."

When Lukas fell asleep, she kept her voice low and told Aiden a little of what had happened five years ago, how she'd fled with Masoud to his family farm near Cairo. Dominic and Hadir learned it was a plot for his family to get her money. They flew to Cairo to confront him and bring her home.

"Obviously, we never stayed in touch. Masoud must have married this woman in the meantime. I bet they think Rosa is his child."

Aiden had consigned Dominic to a faraway compartment in his head, labelling him as an impossible combination: good-looking, smart, kind … and untouchable. Being jealous of him was a waste of energy. Now, learning there was once another man who had claimed Amina's affection was an unpleasant thought. He hated he guy.

"Wait a minute. Maybe she's taking Rosa to Egypt. She could be on her way to the airport right now," he said.

"She wouldn't get out of the country with her. And she has no idea *we* know who she is. She'd never dream we're only five hours behind her. Masoud probably still works for the film industry. She's taking Rosa to their home there."

He wished he could share her certainty. He tried to make her discuss what they would do when they got there, whether she intended to simply charge into the house, or call the police there first, or what. But she only lifted her shoulders slightly, hands gripping the wheel, looking straight ahead, clearly unwilling to think about that until they got there. With the look on her face, the savagery he could feel brewing, there was no point in arguing. Besides, he did not have any plan of his own to offer.

Now they knew more, he wished she would call Dominic, but a small part of him still wanted the little girl to be safe before he faced the inevitable wrath of her father. Over and over, he ran the scenes from the café through his mind. He was furious with himself for playing straight into that woman's hands ... that woman who told him her name was Nancy, staying with a friend, interested in the festival. *Lying fucking psycho.*

Lukas woke. He was agitated, moving from one side of the seat to the other, scrolling on his phone and telling them how far to the next town, where there was a gas station, where there might be traffic. Sometimes, he lay down and curled up tightly, burying his head in the bags and blankets on the back seat. Aiden couldn't imagine how a nine year old would process this kind of anxiety.

Once away from the complex signage of the towns, the roundabouts and crossovers, Aiden took over the driving, grateful to be able to help in any way. It was growing dark and only dim shapes of mountains could be seen on the western horizon, silhouetted against the last bloom of sinking light. Except for the occasional car, he couldn't see another soul in the vast, alien landscape. They had brought food and drinks and stopped only for hurried bathroom breaks.

Dismayed at the long road snaking ahead, the endless rows of highway lights growing shorter as they disappeared into the horizon, it seemed to Aiden the journey would never end. Sometimes Amina doubled over and wept softly, speaking French or Arabic, clenching and unclenching her fists. He wondered if she were praying, but none of the family appeared to be religious or of any particular faith. But then I'm praying now too, he thought. We all pray when we're desperate. He wanted to put an arm around her shoulder, but dreaded the thought she would flex and pull away.

Amina's phone pinged. A text. Dominic. "Please," Aiden mouthed at her, but she widened her eyes at him, shaking her head, and texted back.

"I told him I'm getting an early night." She turned off her phone.

A swell of panic went through Aiden with the thought of Dominic and Hadir being totally ignorant of all this. Here he was with this little family, alone in the middle of an unforgiving desert in an alien land, with no idea what was going to happen next.

He hoped Lukas was sleeping again, but a few minutes later the boy spoke.

"When's your birthday?" he asked.

"*What? My* birthday? July 24th."

"1999?"

"Yes. Why?"

Amina turned to him, looking confused.

"The same as Amina's," Lukas said.

Jesus, Aiden thought, could all this get any weirder?

"It's why you came. To Morocco. It happens sometimes, with the pathways."

Aiden looked at the boy's face in the rearview mirror. The faraway look in his eyes sent a cold flash across his shoulder blades.

"Lukas understands things the rest of us don't," Amina said. "He has the skills of his father." She drew in her breath. "There," she signalled through the window. "Ouarzazate. Next turn off."

CHAPTER 30

The house was like many others in the wealthy neighbourhood: orange-brown earthen walls decorated with geometric motifs, warm amber lights hanging from iron brackets, and Moorish archways flanking an upper balcony. The heavy steel entrance gate in the wall surrounding the property was open. They drove past slowly, peering for signs of life, and parked a few metres away.

"In her note, she wrote 'woman to woman,' something for the two of us to work out," Amina said. "I should go alone. You stay with—"

"No way," Lukas yelled. "Let me come. I want to get Rosa."

Aiden seized her arm. "Are you crazy? She's dangerous. And God knows what *he's* capable of. We don't even know if they're home. We're all going." He got out of the car before she could protest.

On the short walk to the house, Amina started to hurry. Aiden pulled her back.

"Slow down. There are people on the other side of the road. We mustn't draw attention. Act normally. We're friends, visiting … something like that. And stay behind me. Please."

They stepped through the gateway to a generous courtyard with spiky green plants in big iron tubs, two lounge chairs and several tall patio lanterns, all lit. An empty wine glass stood on the mosaic tiled table in the centre. In a narrow driveway off to the side stood an SUV, covered in desert dust. Aiden pointed to a canopied wooden door that looked like an entrance. He put his finger to his lips and, motioning for the other two to keep close to the walls, headed towards it. The door was heavy but gave way to his push.

They stood for a moment or two, listening. Aiden took shallow breaths, trying to still the rapid pace of his heart.

The short hallway in front of them led to a living room, dimly lit by a few wall lamps that threw the furniture into a confusion of light and shadow. Blinking and forcing himself to focus, Aiden made out a dining area on the far side with a large, heavy table and chairs. To the left of this was the entrance to a kitchen.

"Couscous," Lukas whispered. "I can smell it. Rosa loves it."

Raising both hands to make Amina and Lukas wait, Aiden tiptoed to the kitchen. He saw a bowl on the counter, half filled with what looked like chicken couscous. At its side were two used plates and an empty glass with a straw.

He came back to them, shaking his head. "No one in there."

"She's here. I know it." Lukas said.

Amina shushed him. She clutched Aiden's arm and gestured to the far side of the living room, where a wide stairway with a carved wooden railing curved up to the second level.

They moved to the foot of this staircase. Aiden caught the sound of a low voice and strained to hear better. Two voices. One of them was a child's. He widened his eyes and pointed up.

Amina gasped and stepped forward, knocking into a tall pedestal. The terracotta lantern on the top fell and smashed on the wooden floor. Lukas was about to cry out. Aiden clamped a hand over his mouth and pushed him and Amina into an alcove, out of sight of the upper floor. He begged them, in urgent whispers, to stay there; he would handle it.

He heard footsteps, scuffling, a door opening and banging shut, frantic instructions in a low voice in English... *it's alright, you'll be fine, do what I say.* Then silence.

"Who the hell is there?" The loud voice made him jump.

And there she was, leaning over the balustrade of the upper walkway. "*Nancy.*" He started up the stairs.

"Where's Rosa?" he shouted. "What have you done with her?"

She glared at him, clearly shocked. "What the *fuck* are *you* doing here? This is no business of yours. Get out. I'm calling the police. You're trespassing."

Aiden leapt the stairs two at a time, but Gabi stood at the top blocking his way. She looked taller and larger-framed than he remembered.

He heard a sound behind him, turned and saw Amina at the foot of the stairs.

"Please stay there, Amina," he called down. "She might hurt you. Don't come up."

Amina ignored him and started climbing. "Where is my daughter? What have you done with her?"

"I told you this was between us," Gabi yelled at her. "I said I'd call you. What the hell are you all doing here? How did you find out? If you've called anyone, I swear you'll—"

"*Maman.*" The pitiful cry made Aiden's blood freeze.

"Rosa, Rosa. It's okay. I'm here." Amina clasped the rail and climbed higher, crying out to her daughter in French. "*Maman* is here. We're taking you home."

A frantic banging started up at the end of the corridor. "*Maman, maman.*"

Aiden lunged at Gabi, shoving her back against the wall. "Have you locked her in? Are you crazy? You're sick, demented. What kind of person does this? This is kidnapping. Let her out. Now."

Amina made it to the top of the stairs. "I know who you are, and I know who your husband is. Let my daughter go. There will be no discussion, nothing, nothing, nothing."

More frantic banging. "*Maman, où-es tu?*" Rosa's cries grew desperate.

Amina elbowed past Aiden and Gabi and ran to the room where the banging was coming from. She wrenched at the door handle, twisting and pulling, then fell to her knees before it.

"Rosa, *habibti, je suis ici, tout ira bien.* Don't worry. We're taking you home." She turned to Gabi. "Give me the keys, you stupid woman."

Aiden leaned more heavily into Gabi, making her gasp for breath. "Where are the keys? Where's your husband? Hiding?"

"My husband is Rosa's father," Gabi twisted round and bit his arm.

"Fuck," Aiden yelled, wrenching his arm free. He gripped her around the neck with his other hand and pushed his full weight into her. "You crazy bitch,"

"She didn't tell you that, did she, the little tramp? My husband has rights. And so do I."

Aiden had never seen the kind of fury he saw in Amina's eyes, like that of a vicious animal broken free of its chain. She sprang to her feet and went for Gabi, twisting her hair and yanking out a great clump of it. Gabi screamed, a high-pitched shriek, that made Aiden recoil and nearly lose his grip. The two women hit and clawed each other in a frenzy, and nothing Aiden did made any difference. Terrified Amina would be seriously hurt, he released his hold on Gabi and wrested Amina away from her. Gabi headed for the stairs. Aiden grabbed her shirt and tore it from her shoulder, managing to jerk one of her arms and twist it behind her back. His surge of adrenaline was exhilarating. He felt a heady rush of power. He didn't care how much pain he was inflicting. He didn't care about anything except getting Rosa free and making this cruel, spiteful, lying bitch of a woman pay for what she'd done to all of them.

A voice below made him stop and look down. Lukas, rigid with shock. "Where is Rosa?"

"Lukas, move away, she's here, we're getting her. Stay there," Aiden yelled.

Amina was back at the locked door, wrenching at the handle, calling to her daughter on the other side. "Get the keys, Aiden, she must have them."

"Where is *your* precious husband?" Gabi screamed at her. "If you're so sure he's Rosa's father, why isn't he here? I'll tell you why. Because he knows the truth. He's a coward."

In his peripheral vision, Aiden saw Amina slump against the balustrade, keel over and sink to the floor, clutching at her stomach. Jesus Christ, he thought. *No, no, no. Don't let something happen to her, to the baby.*

Gabi coughed and spluttered. "You're not getting her that easily. You never told Masoud about her. She is his daughter, and we're going to get proof. Do you have any idea what this means, denying a man the right to see his child?"

She writhed and kicked to free herself from Aiden's tight grasp but he wouldn't let go. They staggered together toward the top of the stairs. Without thinking for more than a nano second, Aiden pushed her forward, holding her full weight over the stairway, and let go.

She seemed to fall in slow motion, her arms wheeling back, clutching at the emptiness. Her body shuddered down the long flight, her knees and elbows banging on every step. She screamed, a scream of fear and panic and pain, ending with the sickening thud of her head hitting the floor.

Maggie's face swam before him. Years ago, as he lay crumpled at the bottom of a flight of steps, she watched unsteadily from the top. He had tried to call for help but the breath had been punched from his chest and no sound would come from his mouth.

There was no sound now. The house was still. The silence pressed against him.

"Maman, *j'ai peur. Qu'est-ce qui se passe?*" The pitiful sob broke through.

Lukas leapt over Gabi's body and raced up the stairs.

Telling him to stand aside, Aiden threw his body against the locked door, kicking and punching at it, over and over, harder and harder, shouting for Rosa to keep clear. Finally two splintered panels gave way. He punched them through, reached for Rosa and dragged her up and out into the hallway. She and Lukas collapsed together into Amina's arms.

Amina let out a long, keening cry of joy and relief, hugging both children, the tears making her chest heave, her breath shallow and laboured. Gently, she moved Rosa away, checking her over, smoothing out her clothes, her hair, asking if she was okay, if anything hurt, kissing her again and again. They would soon see Papa, she said. They were all going home.

Aiden's body was cold, his legs like jelly. He leaned against the wall.

"Help me up, Aiden," Amina said. "I don't think I have the strength."

He moved unsteadily toward her, fearing his knees would buckle, took Rosa from her lap, and lifted Amina slowly to her feet. She leaned against him, the firm mound of her belly pressed into his waist, her face against his chest. Tears and beads of sweat dampened his shirt. Without thinking, he stroked her back, aching to take her somewhere safe and quiet, to cover her whole body with soft kisses.

"Are you hurt?" he whispered.

She stiffened and pulled away, saying she was fine, dizzy, that was all. Rosa was here, she was safe; that was all that mattered.

Rosa reached for his hand. "She pushed me in there when you came. I want to go home."

He leaned through the broken door to see inside the room, little more than a closet with floor-to-ceiling racks of wine.

"Is the woman dead?" Lukas said.

Aiden's mouth was dry. He walked slowly down the stairs, clutching the rail, dreading what he would find.

She was breathing. *Thank God, thank God.* One leg was twisted awkwardly beneath her; her left wrist lay at a strange angle. She stretched out, inching across the floor. He saw what she was trying to reach. Her phone. It must have dropped from her pocket as she fell. He kicked it farther away.

Amina came down with the children, still breathing heavily. "How badly hurt is she? We have to call an ambulance."

"He tried to kill me," Gabi said, her face contorted with pain, blood in her mouth.

Amina came to her side. "Where are you hurt? Can you sit up?"

"You don't give a shit. Leave me alone."

"Where is Masoud?" Amina said. "How long have you been stalking my family, following my little girl around? She has nothing to do with you. How would you even know about her?"

Gabi tried to raise her shoulders from the floor then lowered them again. Aiden thought she looked pitiful now, her shirt ripped, her hair in strands all over her face, one wrist possibly broken. He knew he should help her up or bring over a cushion, but couldn't find the compassion to do this. He hated the woman intensely and revelled in her pain.

"Masoud saw a photograph. From Chile. You were all in the background. As soon as he saw Rosa, he knew she was his daughter."

Gabi coughed, spitting out blood. She tried to move again but cried out in pain. She looked up at Aiden. "Jesus, you hurt me, you nearly killed me, you sicko." She turned to Amina. "My husband is a good man. He didn't want to push his case. He knows nothing of this."

"You expect me to believe that? You crazy, stupid people," Amina said. "You will both get locked up for this."

"Don't come over all innocent with me," Gabi spluttered. She managed to roll onto her side and push herself to a sitting position with one arm. "You're all just as guilty. We want a paternity test. That's our right. And we know what it will prove. Masoud told me you'd never agree. You're such a smug, self-righteous family."

"A *paternity test? Your right?* Are you mad? Rosa is Dominic's daughter. When he finds out, you'll wish you'd never been born. Both of you."

"My husband is a better man than yours will ever be. I did this. I did it for him. I'm proud of it. We will get the test done, and you'll be the one who has to beg to see her. You think you've got the upper hand now, but just wait. Wait until all this comes to light—your silence, your husband's complicity, keeping the truth from Rosa's legitimate father." Her voice gave way to a weak croak.

Amina leaned closer. "I don't believe he knows nothing. Where is he?" She grabbed a fistful of Gabi's hair. "Answer me or I'll rip another chunk of hair from your head."

Gabi laughed. "You're scared. And you should be. You broke into our home, and your friend here threw me down the stairs."

Amina stood, arched her back, and spat into Gabi's face.

Aiden put his hand on Amina's shoulder, easing her away. The adrenaline he felt earlier had seeped away. His brief role as saviour was executed and over, and the stark reality of their situation began to register.

He asked Gabi if she wanted water, but she swore at him. She pulled herself up to a sitting position and wiped her face with her shirt sleeve. Cradling one arm, she edged backwards to lean against a wall and tried to straighten her foot, yelping in pain. "Masoud will make you pay. We could have worked it out. But not now."

Aiden knew they should call for an ambulance and that, when the paramedics got here, they'd want the police involved. He looked around him, trying to slow his breathing and stop the shivering along the full length of his body. He felt disconnected again, as though watching himself, rather than actually being there. For the first time, he became fully aware of his surroundings. Clustered near a tall, narrow window that gave onto the courtyard were plants with shiny green leaves and cascades of star-shaped white flowers. A light breeze drifted by, carrying their musky scent. Prints of Ancient Egyptian themes hung on the walls. Photographs of horses were crowded together on the credenza opposite, some with ribbons pinned to their bridles, some with proud men at their side holding trophies.

The full weight of what he had done finally broke through. He locked eyes with Amina and sensed they were each trying to read the other's mind, weighing the wisdom of making a run for it. Rosa was quiet, delayed shock, he imagined. Lukas had her in a tight hug. The boy was looking toward the door, as though he, too, longed to run away.

"I guess we should call the police," Aiden said finally.

Amina pulled out her phone.

"Don't trouble yourselves," Gabi slurred. "Looks like they're already here."

Walking slowly through the doorway came two uniformed police officers. The first one halted, putting out an arm to stop his colleague. They both lowered their guns.

"I'm sorry," Lukas said, his voice faltering. "I called Dominic."

CHAPTER 31

In the police station, Aiden was separated from the others and left alone for more than an hour in an interrogation room with no distractions. There was nothing on the table in front of him, nothing on the walls. He learned later they had tried to separate Lukas, too, but Amina's fury and Rosa's deafening refusal to let go of her brother's hand put an end to that. Although Aiden's interrogator spoke English well, he brought in an interpreter, a woman, to make sure Aiden fully understood his obligations and the position he was in.

The position I am in, he repeated to himself. He felt like he'd fallen asleep and woken marooned in a sinister place where no one knew or gave a shit about him.

At one point, he asked if Gabi was okay, but they didn't answer that, or any of his other questions. The police officer was a short, heavy-set man whose lips smiled but whose eyes never changed expression. Aiden's only knowledge of police procedure came from TV crime series, and he wondered if he should ask for a lawyer.

"Why did you push Mrs. Burhan down the stairs? The child was safe then, you said."

Over and over, they made him recite the sequence of events.

"Goddamnit I've told you this. I didn't push her. She fell. She was still threatening all of us. I thought her husband might be there somewhere, ready to grab Rosa and take her away."

Sometimes, not even acknowledging his answers, they conferred with each other or left the room for a few minutes. He had no idea what was on their minds.

It all changed when the door opened well past midnight, and Hadir strode in. His stature, impeccable attire and air of authority filled Aiden with a relief so palpable he felt he would sink under its weight.

Hadir said something in Arabic to the two officials and beckoned to Aiden. "This is over. We're leaving."

The interrogators were on the point of protest, but must have realized they were no longer in control. In the corridor, Hadir told Aiden he'd thanked them for their prompt response and efficiency, and told them Dominic would be pressing charges. There was no reason to take any more of their time.

He ushered Aiden to the main reception area where the rest of the family were huddled together. Dominic took Rosa from his lap, handed her to Amina and stood before Aiden.

"I'll never forgive you for not calling me, for not stopping Amina from leaving. But thank God you insisted on going with her." His voice broke. "You helped to get my daughter back." To Aiden's great shock, Dominic pulled him into a tight embrace. "Remember what I told you in Toronto. About fate. Now you understand why I was so certain you should come to Morocco, why you were meant to be here."

"*Mon Dieu, j'en peux plus.* Enough," said Hadir. "Ignore him, Aiden. He gets all mystical when his emotions run high." He pulled Dominic away, squeezing his shoulders. "I've booked a hotel. We're all going straight to bed. Tomorrow, we'll leave after breakfast. You're coming with me, Aiden. I need a break from my high-octane brother." His phone rang and he pulled it from his pocket. "Aiieee, and from my wife."

***

On the way back to Fez the next day, Hadir told Aiden what he and Dominic had gone through when Lukas called. They were in the kitchen of the family's new riad in Marrakech. It was being renovated, and they were having heated discussions with the builder over the lack of progress. Dominic couldn't make out what Lukas was saying and had yelled at the workers to stop the noise. The boy was whispering, terrified of being overheard.

"The rest of us, the workers and I, we're standing there, waiting for him to finish the call. But Lukas hung up. Dominic's shouting his name, punching his number back. And then, you'll never believe it, Aiden. What does my brother do? He picks up a fucking hammer from the work bench and flings it full force into the opposite wall. A great gouge of plaster fell out and a framed picture crashed to the floor—glass shattering everywhere."

For a minute or two, they could barely believe what Lukas had told them, he said. Their instinct was to call Amina or Aiden himself, but they worried a call might trigger more hostility from the woman, or her husband, or accomplices, or whoever. They worried they might have been armed.

"I can smile now, but *mon Dieu*, the guy at the police who answered our call asked a million questions. I thought Dominic would start hurling furniture around any minute. I had to grab the phone from him. We were sick with worry and wanted to make sure the police would get to the house undetected—no lights and sirens, no guns blazing."

Even though they broke every speed limit, Hadir claimed it was the longest drive he'd ever endured. He thought Dominic would have a heart attack or pass out from anxiety. It was at least half an hour before they got a call from the police station in Ouarzazate, who put Amina on the phone.

Hadir encouraged Aiden to talk about his own experience, what they all went through. Aiden struggled with that. Despite a blissful sleep, the experience sat like a dead weight inside him. He doubted he was making much sense. But Hadir was a good listener, occasionally punching his arm or giving him an elbow nudge.

"You still look tense," he said. "Let it go. Nothing to worry about now."

"Rosa was in my care when she was taken. I'll never forgive myself."

"That evil bitch had been plotting this for days. She could have taken Rosa from the school entrance, or even the hotel itself. Rosa and Lukas often go out in the neighbourhood, just the two of them—never far, but still, they would have been vulnerable. Dominic will never tell you this, but having you there to help support Lukas was a blessing. If it had been Lukas alone, it would have killed the kid. He'd never have recovered."

The brothers had chosen to drive home directly north through the mountains, a longer route back to Fez but much more scenic and laid back. The highway drives for everyone the previous day had been so stressful, they were now looking forward to relaxing, stopping for lunch, indulging in the pleasure of relief and the luxury of time. It was also, Hadir said, an opportunity for Aiden to see a magnificent part of Morocco. He encouraged him to lean back in the comfortable reclining seat of the SUV, and relax.

It was the first opportunity they'd had to spend any meaningful time together, and Aiden realized how different the two brothers were. Both had an enviable air of confidence, but Hadir was definitely the businessman, almost statesmanlike. Zahra told him Dominic had the ideas, Hadir managed the money. Somehow they worked it out.

"Is it true that woman's husband wasn't involved?" Aiden asked. "Seems weird to me that he didn't know anything at all."

Hadir shrugged. "It's all in the hands of the police now." He gave a bark of laughter. "A paternity test. Now she's failed in her attempt to get one through Rosa and her husband, she's insisting that Dominic get it done. Can you imagine my brother ever agreeing to that?"

He gave Aiden a little more of the story of Masoud and Amina, how they'd met in Ouarzazate when she consulted him to have some ancient Egyptian charts read. Their meeting had been orchestrated by Masoud's uncle, another nasty character, who lived in Fez.

"It's a great place, Ouarzazate. Lots of film productions. I was really keen to invest in a hotel there, but Dominic wanted nothing to do with it. Said the place was cursed. Now he'll insist he was right, of course."

They talked for a while of other things, of Aiden's life in Canada, his work, what he hoped to do with his artistic talents. When they fell quiet, Aiden let his gaze drift across the vast landscapes unfolding before him … endless rolling sandy hills, acres of palm trees spread along the foothills of the Atlas mountains. He saw deep gorges with green rivers snaking through, and fields of low-growth shrub, dotted with sheep and goats. The small towns and villages all had mosques, their minarets rising tall through jumbles of orange and saffron coloured buildings with ornamental turrets or tall lambrequin archways. A painter's country, for sure, he thought.

Hadir coordinated a stop with the others for lunch at a tiny restaurant in one of these towns. They sat at a table outside on the street and ate pieces of lamb carved from a spit, with dates and slices of pomegranate. The two brothers spent several minutes texting and calling, catching up on abandoned business matters. Amina was completely engrossed with the children, barely touching her food.

Looking at this scene in this strange part of the world, Aiden felt his own life must be in another universe altogether. He couldn't believe that both places existed on the same planet.

After the meal, Dominic and his family left to take a short walk in the town and visit a merchant he knew. He squeezed Aiden's shoulder as he walked by, a gesture that filled Aiden with gratitude.

Hadir had a shisha pipe lit and invited him to share. Aiden declined, worrying he wouldn't get the hang of it. They discussed the final preparation for the festival launch gala, only a month away now. Aiden assured him his own work should be done in a week, two at the most.

Hadir narrowed his eyes. "Are you anxious to get home?"

This was a difficult question. Under the flawless deep blue of the sky, Aiden gazed along the narrow street. A few young boys were playing a kind of hopscotch, laughing and pushing each other over. A man leading a donkey stopped to chat to an elderly woman, laded with heavy baskets. No, he was not anxious. His life at home lacked colour. It was grey and white and steel, and there was a dreariness about it, despite, or perhaps because of the constant buzz of growth and innovation. Apart from the last two days, he'd been happy here. He stopped himself. *Happy* wasn't the right word. *Content* was closer. Day-to-day life was a joyous, chaotic hustle, yet there was a sense of peace and gentleness running at a deeper level.

But he couldn't stay. Morocco would always be a beautiful dream he had stumbled into for a while, and, as with all beautiful dreams, he knew he must eventually wake up. He flexed his shoulders and raised his arms above his head, feeling the need to stretch out, to live a bigger, fuller life.

"I don't want to outstay my welcome," he said. "Guess I should book my flight for the end of the month."

"What? You're staying for the festival party at the very least. When I spoke to him yesterday, your uncle said he's happy for you to take his place."

"My uncle? Yesterday?"

"Aiden … for hours on end, we worried whether you were dead or alive or in jail for attempted murder. You think we're not going to call your uncle?"

CHAPTER 32

When Gabi woke, only a few seconds of disorientation passed before she knew where she was. Not at home with her stepdaughter, eagerly awaiting the return of her husband as she had planned, but in a stark white hospital room, her wrist in a cast, her ankle strapped. On the table beside her was a tall glass of what looked like orange juice and a half-eaten sandwich.

As she stared at the ceiling in the little room, she let her good arm dangle over the side of the bed and flinched as she felt something leathery at the side of it. Leaning over, she saw a wide strap. She checked the other side and found another. Her breath came in short gasps. She wondered if all the beds were equipped this way, or whether she was in a special wing of the hospital, considered dangerously disturbed.

She pressed the button at her side and told the nurse who appeared that she wanted to get up. The nurse summoned the doctor.

"Get me out of here," she told the young doctor who helped raise her to a comfortable position. "I want to go home."

He told her they were waiting for the results of the CT scan to rule out concussion, that her whole body was badly bruised. Her wrist was fractured and her ankle badly twisted but stable. They wanted to be sure she could walk unassisted. "You will need to be driven home. Your husband has been informed."

"My husband? I made it clear he was not to be contacted. I was going to do that."

The doctor gave a half smile, a few muscles shy of a derisive snort. "That was not for us to decide, Mrs. Burhan. It is a police matter." His turned his back, scanned the file from the end of her bed, and left without another word.

A police matter. All she had done was take a child who was almost certainly her stepdaughter, on a little trip. Any other approach would have met with a brick wall of refusal. She was merely fighting to assert a fundamental right.

All the people she had seen, from the police and paramedics who came to the house, to the staff here at the hospital, had that same knowing look in their eyes: *sick, crazy, psychotic.* The doctor was the most judgmental. Last night, she overheard him speaking in Arabic to one of his minions, something about their priority being the little girl. They needed to make sure she and her poor mother, who was pregnant, were completely well.

Throughout her life she had struggled with having no recognized role in the lives of others. And now, her bold plan backfiring, she was condemned to this prison cell of a hospital room, sidelined once again. All the fawning attention had gone to that wretched, privileged family from Fez and their sycophantic hangers-on. To them, she was the villain, not the victim.

In her groggy half sleep, she convinced herself Masoud would understand. He'd be astonished and touched she'd gone to all this trouble, furious she was being treated so badly. Getting a paternity test would be even more critical now. When it was proven, all those righteously indignant accusers would have to back off. And even if they still considered what she did was wrong, they'd have to acknowledge the girl had four parents. And Gabi's rights would be no less than those of Dominic.

She comforted herself with the thought that, now he knew, Masoud would be here soon.

But he did not come. He called. She struggled to retrieve her phone from the side table and punch the green button with her good hand. There was a long pause before he spoke.

"Gabi, have you completely lost your senses?"

She flinched at his coldness and couldn't find breath for a moment. "Whoa. Hold on a minute. I did this for us. I wanted leverage. I had no intention of harming the girl. I didn't expect them to show up on my doorstep within hours. I still have no idea how the hell they knew who I was."

"You were recognized, Gabi. Somehow they connected you to the lodge in Patagonia. They got your name. They learned about Al Sayed. It all fell into place."

"Well aren't they just the clever people. Are you coming to get me out of here?"

"Your mother is coming. She's waiting for a call from the doctor."

"My *mother*? She's here? Are you serious?"

"Gabi, what the hell did you expect?" His breathing sounded laboured and he was obviously struggling to articulate. "Your father's with me at the police station. You can't begin to imagine what kind of a mood he's in."

The whole nightmare immediately took on an uglier dimension. "What do they want with my father? How does he even know? Did you tell him?"

He told her the police had tracked him down on the film shoot, ready to accuse him of being an accessory to kidnapping. If he had not called her father, they would have. Her parents took the jet. They were in Ouarzazate long before him.

"I was in the middle of the desert, remember? Miles from anywhere. The police brought me back. It took hours."

He said he had no choice but to tell her parents the whole story, how he'd been adamant about not pursuing this matter, but Gabi had taken things into her own hands.

She could hear only the ragged sound of her own breathing and thought for a second he had hung up on her. "Masoud?"

"You need to call your mother. Your father is too angry to think clearly."

She sank back onto the pillows and felt a growing sense of panic, realizing the futility and possible consequences of what she had done. She kept telling herself it wasn't her fault. She couldn't help being born a woman, couldn't help having a wretched medical condition. The fault lay with the misogynistic men in her stupid family, her weak husband, who had married her for money and was now dying. She was furious that the thought of a child did not give him a reason to fight harder. If nothing else, a daughter, even if they only had partial access, would be someone to love, to help him face whatever grim future lay ahead … a future Gabi had never bargained on.

She heard a sigh of frustration and what sounded like a police officer shouting instructions in the background of Masoud's call.

"Do you have any idea what this family could do to us, Gabi? They intend to charge you with kidnapping. Dominic won't rest until you're locked up. I warned you." His voice was weak, the anger in it had grown tired.

"Why are *they* talking about charging *me*? What about the guy who pushed me down the stairs? Why isn't he being charged?"

She heard his effort to take a deeper breath. "I can't talk to you anymore. I can't handle this on top of everything else."

"I don't want to see any of you. Tell my mother I'll take a fucking taxi home."

Wincing with pain, she curled into a fetal position and wept from the heavy, overwhelming sense of betrayal.

CHAPTER 33

It was the family's lawyer who oversaw Gabi's humiliating release from the hospital, having to sign a sheaf of forms while Gabi endured the thinly veiled condemnation of the officials. He had flown with her parents in the jet from Cairo to Ouarzazate the minute they'd heard the news. He accompanied her in the taxi to her home and said he'd be coming by to talk the next day.

Her father thanked him, yanked her overnight bag from the cab and strode into the house. Her mother ran out to give her a hug, protesting this was all too much and what was she thinking, but never mind, come in, come in, they would work it out.

"I haven't murdered anyone. Why are you even here?"

Her mother dropped her voice, said her father was very upset, worried for the safety of the whole family. They would talk about it over supper.

"They've called the Egyptian police," her father shouted from the doorway. "They're hanging around our property. A goddamned nightmare. Are you coming in or not?"

"Where's Masoud?" she asked.

Her mother said he was inside and not at all well.

Her father dumped her bag at the foot of the stairs and lit a cigarette. Gabi started to protest, but her mother shook her head and raised a cautionary hand. "Let him be," she mouthed, ushering Gabi into the living room.

Gabi couldn't stop her eyes from sliding up to the second floor, to the closet where she'd desperately pushed Rosa, its panels broken through, splinters no doubt still lying in the hall.

Masoud was slumped in a large armchair, looking even thinner than when she left, and dwarfed by the chair. She went over to him, but drew back when she saw the anger in his eyes.

"It wasn't supposed to be this way," she said. "I wanted to prove you're her father, I thought you'd be happy, you'd have something to fight for."

Her mother announced supper was ready and they should come to the table.

Masoud struggled to stand but resisted Gabi's help. He held on to the back of a sofa and limped to the nearest dining chair, avoiding her eyes.

"Can you imagine how this looks to the police?" her father said. "For all anyone knew, you could be working for one of those child porn merchants, the ones who go through photos and choose which little girl they're going to rape next."

Gabi felt a flush creeping up from her collar. She sat straighter in the chair. Her father's face, with its prominent jaw and hooked nose, was dark with suppressed anger.

"The best we can hope is they think you're having a breakdown," he said.

The bright colours of the inlaid tiles on the table fused into a frenzied kaleidoscope that made Gabi heave. The vein on her father's neck throbbed, and his face took on grotesque proportion. She became aware of her mother's fixed smile as she passed around the dishes of food with determined optimism, and felt a kind of stage fright, as though she had a critical speech to make, but couldn't remember her lines.

"Do I have no allies in this room?" she finally stammered. "Does no one give a damn about my feelings—me, the one who does most of the work and gets none of the glory? As for you, Masoud … isn't a daughter worth fighting for?"

"For God's sake, Gabi. Even if you take her wretched husband out of the picture, she is Amina's child. Amina is the one with all the rights. What were you thinking?"

"You should have gone through legal channels, Gabi," said her mother, pouring herself more wine. "We have good lawyers."

For the first time, Gabi noticed her mother seemed to have aged. Even with the makeup she was never without, her face was pale and drawn and there were shadows under her eyes.

"Lawyers take forever," Gabi said.

Her father scowled. "So let's just kidnap the girl and drive her seven hundred kilometres from her home because lawyers take too long. That's a better idea?"

"Perhaps you should tell them the circumstances, that Masoud is ill, that you have this condition," her mother suggested. "They might be more sympathetic if they know what you've been through." She turned to her husband. "It would be a plea from the heart. The husband, he's French, isn't he? Surely he'd understand."

Her father froze, the fork halfway to his mouth. "What in hell has that got to do with anything? Fucking French. They have no morals."

"He's French Moroccan. As if it matters," said Masoud. "He won't give a damn about anybody's emotional state."

"If he has any Arab blood in him," said her father, "he would do the honourable thing."

Masoud grimaced. "You mean get the test done? He'd never stoop so low."

"Everyone relax," said her mother. "We're meeting with the lawyer tomorrow."

"Do you know what I had to do to get you out of there, Gabi?" her father said, with his mouth full. "Has that even crossed your simple mind? I had to plead with that self-righteous French son of a bitch not to have you arrested, convince him you were sick, not a serious threat. If he gets his way, you'll be locked up. We are foreigners in this country, don't forget that. Masoud and I have assumed responsibility for you. You'd better not leave the house."

"Why not make me wear a hijab, take my car keys away, lock me in the bedroom?" The idea of her father and husband assuming responsibility for her, claiming she was sick, made her seethe with suppressed rage. She fought the threatening tears. She was damned if she would cry and make her father gloat with satisfaction.

Her mother put up both hands. "Stop. Enough. Gabi is home, everyone involved is safe and well. Masoud, you've had time to think …what do you believe we should do?"

Gabi slammed her good fist on the table. "Who is this *we*? I will handle the fallout."

"You will handle it?" her father bellowed. "How is that working so far?"

"Please, everyone, let's eat," her mother said, scooping more vegetables from the dish and holding the spoon aloft.

Masoud tried to speak, but Gabi's father raised his voice another octave. "I am trying to ask a question. Does she, do *any* of you understand what this could do to the reputation of our estate? Word can get around in a flash. People will think she's unstable. They will certainly hesitate to do business with us."

Gabi pushed the plate away, glaring at her father in disbelief.

"Ali. Stop," said Masoud. "Getting this angry is not going to help."

"Don't even try," Gabi said. "Dad only cares about his goddamned horse trading. This is not an international crisis. It's a dispute between two families. Maybe when *that* family thinks it through, they'll realize what we are asking is not unreasonable. And we have rights."

Masoud turned to face her. "They've had hours to think it through, Gabi. Getting their own lawyers involved and pressing charges *was* their response. Amina is pregnant. Dominic was ballistic, terrified about how this would affect her. And after what you've done, we have no moral, let alone legal grounds." The effort to speak made him fight for breath. "What did you expect?"

What did you expect? More than this, she thought, more than life as a bystander in the wrong country, wrong job, a body unfit for childbearing, making desperate attempts to secure her future and win the support of a man who had married the wrong woman, who was probably worried sick for the sake of his former lover. Even though there had been little more than mutual respect between them, the sound of Amina's name on her husband's lips sent a flare of jealousy through her.

Her parents spent the rest of the meal talking over each other, Masoud trying in vain to interrupt. Gabi listened in silence, incredulous not one of them offered her a sliver of sympathy.

"Shut up, all of you."

They looked at her warily, clearly braced for more trouble. She stood, scraping the chair. "Masoud, do you seriously not want your own child, our child? Does no one in this family care what she could mean to us, to me in the future?"

Masoud leaned over the table, his head in his hands. "Gabi, have you listened to anything I've said? And please stop this mad 'ownership' claim. She may *not* be my child."

"Don't you *want* to know?"

"I don't *need* to know. And I could never take her from her mother."

"You mustn't worry so much about the future," her mother said. "Your—"

"*I could never take her from her mother,*" Gabi affected Masoud's tone. "I guess that woman's feelings are way more important than mine." She brushed her mother's hand away. "I'm sorry, okay? Not that I tried, but that it turned into such a circus."

"If you are genuinely sorry, we will need to—" her father began.

"*You* will not need to do anything. *I* will talk to the lawyer tomorrow and go with him to the police." She backed away from the table, her breath coming in coarse, shallow gasps. "*You* can go home and save the business. No need to keep the jet waiting any longer. It's costing money."

She fled the room, ignoring her mother's protests, and ran upstairs. Cradling her painful wrist, she lay on the bed, trying to block the whole family from her mind.

In less than fifteen minutes, she heard a car pull up and rapid steps along the hallway. Her mother stood in the vaulted archway to the bedroom. "Sweetheart, we're going. You're doing the right thing. Both families must draw a line under this. Forgive and forget."

Gabi put her good arm across her face. She could not handle the pleading tiredness of her mother's voice.

"When it's blown over, you and Masoud must come and live with us," her mother pressed on. "He's not getting the right medical attention here. He needs to be seen at the American hospital. This whole business has turned him inside out. And you need to settle down now. I'm going to send you the name of the therapist you need to talk to."

"Mom. Stop. No fucking way."

"I'm sorry, Gabi, but your father promised. That family can still press charges. You need to reassure everyone, including the police. You have to put it behind you."

Gabi peered at her through swollen eyes. Her mother was incongruously trim and tidy, her streaked grey-blond hair clipped in a neat knot at the neck, her lipstick reapplied. Gabi felt wretched, ugly. She pushed her face into the pillows. "Leave me alone now."

She listened to the muttering and gruff talk of her father downstairs and her mother's parting advice to Masoud, furious that her desire for future happiness and prosperity had turned into the mortifying need to reassure everyone she was not a damaged, dangerous person.

She heard Masoud's limp on the stairs and moved to sit on the edge of the bed, straightening her clothes. He sat beside her and put an arm around her shoulder.

"I tried to protest, Gabi. I told the police you were fine, just badly upset. But you know your father, what he's like."

She felt the thinness of him, the tremor in his hands. All desire to fight drained from her.

"So now what? What about you? You promised to speak to the doctor again. Did you?"

He pulled away and cradled her good hand in both of his. "Doctors only tell you the truth when they absolutely have to."

She stared at his sandalled feet on the intricate grey and white pattern of the tiled floor. Outside, the desert wind rustled the wide, fanned leaves of the date palms, making their shadows flutter in a ghostly dance on the opposite wall. She knew what he was going to say next, but had no idea anymore how to react.

PART IV – THE FEATHER OF MA'AT

CHAPTER 34

Amina lay on her bed in the Riad Capella, propped up by cushions, cradling the sleeping Raif. Dominic, sitting on the chair beside her, kept leaning over to kiss them both. He was simultaneously distraught and forgiving about Amina's decision to drive across the country, not to call him, not to tell anyone else what was going on. She tried to convince him that everything looked different in retrospect. At the time, she had no idea what Gabi could do, how crazy she might be and whether she might harm Rosa.

"You're saying you didn't trust me not to do anything foolish," Dominic said.

She only smiled.

Hadir had hired a security guard to keep watch at the hotel. Sophie warned the staff there had been a few unpleasant incidents in the neighbourhood, and they should not let anyone in without a room or dinner reservation. Despite this, and the reassurance by the police in Ouarzazate that Gabi was under surveillance, and her husband had indeed not known anything about her plans, Dominic was still nervous.

"What was she thinking, that woman?" He got up and started pacing, running both hands through his hair. "Even when her nasty plot failed and she couldn't get a paternity test through her husband, she wanted to force me to take one."

"Rosa is yours," Amina whispered. "I knew it the night she was conceived. Please sit down."

Dominic sat down again and stroked her hair, wondering if she might now question that conviction and if it would matter to her. He'd been so astonished she agreed to marry him, to forgive his high-living and fooling around, that he'd shut down any thought of other men in her past.

What kind of star-crossed madness could be at work now, he wondered? He thought about the uncanny way the whole story had started: a photograph taken in Chile. *Chile*, of all places. That's why he'd had that ominous feeling over there, the sense of premonition. Once again, he was proved right. And Lukas, he thought, connecting the woman to the stables in Patagonia … unbelievable. He shuddered at what might have happened without that knowledge, what other mad ideas the woman was plotting.

In the car on their way home, Lukas had been obsessed by the idea of *Isfet*, the Ancient Egyptian concept of chaos, the flipside of harmony and order. His father, Karl, had written about it in detail in that notebook. The kid seemed to be convinced all this was unfolding at the whim of some malevolent force out there, and Dominic could easily believe he was right.

"When I think about what you went through in the past," he said, leaning over to kiss Amina again. "That same family, conniving to get your money, taking—"

"Stop, Dominic. He didn't know. Masoud didn't know what his wife was up to. He was on a film set a long way away. I don't believe he would be capable of something so cruel. If he'd known, he would have stopped her."

The police, she reminded him, believed him.

They talked for a while about Gabi, what could have prompted her maniacal idea, what state their marriage might be in, and whether she had a hidden agenda.

Dominic did not admit this, but he was worried Masoud might now decide to press his case, that this whole incident could have fired him up and he might take legal action to have the test conducted.

"What's supposed to happen next? What are the police saying?" Amina asked.

He told her about the latest conversation with the lawyers, that they would be in touch tomorrow. "*Their* lawyer will probably claim she's not in her right mind, not responsible."

He went and stood by the window. A thin shimmer of clouds with grey and purple bruises was lit brightly beneath by the dying sun. The sounds of the early evening—street hawkers, the clatter of donkey carts—had given way to the hush of the coming night. He thought what a fortunate man he was to live here in this beautiful ancient city, in the lovely hotel his grandfather had built, with a family any man would die for. The idea any of it could be vulnerable terrified him.

He turned to face his wife. "Did you love him? I never dared to ask you."

Amina looked away for a moment, and he swore his heart would stop dead from the fear of what she might say.

"He's not as bad a man as you believe," she said. "I hoped one day I would learn to love him."

"And you would have forgotten me."

"Every time you took up with another woman, I tried to forget you, and never succeeded."

You damned fool, he told himself, as he had so many times, you nearly lost her. *Well, my love, you're stuck with me now.* He returned to her side.

She placed his hand on her stomach. "This one will be as hot-headed as his father."

She gave him her long, slow smile, the one that made him feel her eyes were drilling into his soul. In the madness of his past, before he dared approach her, that smile would render him speechless, and he would have to turn away lest she see his confusion.

"Go check on Lukas and Rosa," she said. "I hope they're both asleep now."

He found Lukas reading in French from the star book he'd bought for Rosa. The boy flinched as the door opened and Dominic had the crazy thought, if the boy had a gun, he'd have reached for it. He hugged them both, fighting the tears of relief he still had trouble holding back.

He told Amina about Lukas's reaction. "He's only nine. Who knows how this has messed him up. Maybe we should get him to see a doctor. To be sure."

"Sophie says we must all get back to normal. Routine is soothing, especially to children."

Dominic smiled, thinking about Sophie's reaction as they all stumbled into the lobby of the Riad after their long drive home. She had stood like a matriarch, hands on hips, berating them at length for what they had done and not done, racing around the desert like the *jinn* possessed them. She threw her hands in the air and stamped her feet, then seized each one of them and burst into tears. Dominic always felt like a naughty schoolboy in the eyes of his sister-in-law, but this time she singled out her husband for her sharpest tirade of recrimination. "You are the eldest member of the family, but as ridiculous and irresponsible as all the others. You should have called me," she said. Hadir protested she'd have worried too much. "You'd have jumped in a car and given me yet another reason for heart failure." He took her in his arms, lifting her off her feet and hugging her until she couldn't get a breath. Dominic remembered watching the two of them in his younger years, before Amina, wondering if he would ever find such a love himself. He thanked God the family were so blessed.

He lay down beside his wife and discussed the arrangements he'd made to take Lukas and Aiden overnight to the desert next week. He wanted to postpone it, but Amina insisted, reminding him that everything should be as normal as possible. Lukas would be disappointed to miss a night he always looked forward to, and he was anxious to show it all to Aiden.

"It's so beautiful there," she said. "It will do you all good."

As he curled up against her and the sounds of the night outside fell away, he marvelled at her level-headedness amid all this emotional upheaval. The relief settled slowly through him. He would sleep well.

***

The official response from the Burhan's family lawyer came the next morning while they were having a late breakfast. Realizing the envelope the bellboy handed him had come special delivery, Dominic glanced at the sender's address and left the table. He didn't want to open it and spoil the camaraderie of his children who were clowning around with Aiden, nor interrupt the relaxed conversation between Amina and Sophie. And he didn't trust his ability to remain calm.

"Nothing," he signalled to Amina who looked up enquiringly.

He retreated to one of the rooms off the courtyard and sat for a minute pressing his hand into his chest, trying to slow his rapid heartbeat, then tore open the envelope. Inside was a legal document with a "cease and desist" guarantee, signed by both Gabriella and Masoud. It stipulated that no member of the Burhan family would initiate any further contact with any member of the El Hassan family. The covering letter from the lawyer stated Gabriella would receive a psychiatric evaluation and, based on the assurances herein provided, suggested it would be in the best interests of all parties for the El Hassans to sign the agreement, not press charges, and draw a line under the matter. Also attached, in "the spirit of goodwill," was a personal letter of apology from Gabriella's mother to Amina explaining, albeit not excusing, her daughter's actions.

Dominic held the envelope, his wife's name hand-written across the front, resisting the temptation to open it himself. He skimmed through the legal document again, impatient with the jargon, and became aware he was being watched. Amina stood on the threshold, a look of concern on her face he wished he could banish forever.

"Well, they're 'deeply sorry' apparently. All kinds of promises." He motioned for her to sit beside him.

She opened the personal letter, written in English, and they read it together.

Dear Amina,

I know I can never expect you to forgive Gabriella, but as a mother, I am asking for your understanding and begging you not to press charges.

I believe my daughter is deeply unhappy. She was recently diagnosed with endometriosis and can never have children of her own. For many reasons, she was devastated by this news.

I understand Masoud was once in love with you. When Gabriella found out about Rosa, and the possibility —

Dominic looked away, a wave of jealousy seizing him. Fragments of sentences swam before his eyes: *realized she acted irrationally …. wanted to bring some joy to his life … now seeking therapy to help her deal…*

Amina put the letter aside, rang for a bellboy and asked for a tray of tea to be brought. She tapped something into her phone.

"What else does she say?" Dominic said, still looking away.

Amina waited for the tea, then picked up the letter again. "Can you imagine what it must be like to be the mother of such a woman? On the one hand, a mother must forgive her child anything. That love is unconditional. On the other hand, what the child has done is unforgivable. Both their lives are marred forever."

"Not our concern, Amina. What does she want?"

"I looked up Masoud's illness. *Cardiac cachexia.* It's serious. Fatal. The mother writes *'You are blessed with the joys of a family life Masoud and Gabriella are denied. They both have so much to grieve, so much pain to handle.'* Dominic, if this Gabriella is unstable and her husband is dying, but we still insist she is charged, what good will it do? And what does that say about us? Her mother sounds like a kind person. It would kill her."

Dominic was suddenly tried. The high pitch of anxiety gripping him without mercy and then the intense euphoria of relief had left him drained, empty. He looked at his wife, wondering again how she could remain so calm when he himself was utterly exhausted. The unfinished work for the festival, the renovations at the hotel in Marrakech, matters at the forefront of his impatience a couple of days ago, seemed so trivial now. He doubted he'd ever find the energy to address them.

"You are always ready to believe the best of people," he said. "No wonder everyone loves you. Rosa is safe. We're all safe, *Dieu merci*. Maybe I've lost my appetite to fight. But I don't feel sorry for any one of them. They can all go to hell."

Amina said nothing, and he regretted his last comment, the cold echo of the words a stark contrast to her compassion.

CHAPTER 35

A week before Steven learned about the kidnapping and his nephew's involvement, he had other things on his mind. His daughter Catherine had texted him a few days earlier, asking when he could talk. He was on the point of responding he could 'talk' any time but there was a sense of gravitas about the word in the text that unsettled him. He called her.

"Wow. Quick on the draw today, Dad," she said. "I'm impressed."

"Yeah, yeah. What's up?"

A momentary hesitation, unusual for Catherine. "Have you spoken to Amy lately?"

"Your Aunt Amy? Why would I? Not since I called to tell her about Aiden."

"Get a drink and sit down."

He had been clearing up in his studio and now threw a paintbrush in the sink in frustration. He told Catherine to wait, then followed her instruction, hurrying downstairs, pouring a generous scotch and flopping into his favourite armchair.

"The woman who died in Vancouver General," Catherine said.

"Dorothy? Aiden's mother?"

"So here's the thing, Dad. I don't think she was his mother. His real mother is still alive."

"*No*," Steven said, more to himself than to his daughter, railing against yet another curveball in this twisted saga. "No fucking way."

"Yes way. You know I talk to Amy a lot. So a couple of months ago, I mentioned Aiden was going to Morocco. As you know, she doesn't give much of a shit about him. I mean, why would she? But she seemed interested in this and asked me a bit about it. Then she said something about life being strange and how his mother will be amazed. I forget exactly how she put it. So I said 'his mother, like, Dorothy? I thought she died.' Then Amy kind of stammered and said 'Of course. I was thinking how amazed she would have been.' Well there's no way that's what she said. And it was almost like she *knew* his mother. I mean, you don't talk about the *other woman* that way, not with the tone she used. There was no sarcasm or anything."

Steven tried to take all this in, realizing again he had no idea how women's minds worked, only that he could rarely follow any kind of logic. In his view, this was nothing more than a misunderstanding.

"Catherine, aren't you making too much of this? Maybe that's what she did mean."

"I tried to give her the benefit of the doubt, but then I had that dinner with Aiden in Toronto. Remember? I didn't ask him directly. I mean we'd barely met, and who knows how touchy he might have got. I asked him a couple of questions about his mom, and he was going on about her, how amazing she was, how sad that she died. It just didn't ring true."

"Jesus, Catherine. Can't you take anything on faith?"

"No. No one in our family tells the truth. Shifty eyes and barefaced lies. I've learned to pick them up a mile away."

Steven winced, realizing that he was probably included in the deceitful family condemnation. "And why are you telling me this now, months later?"

"Because I've done some research. I don't know what his real mother's name is, where she is or anything about her. But I'm sure she's alive. Dorothy, the one who died, was his aunt."

When they hung up, Steven let out a long monologue of bad language. After refilling his glass, he sank back into the chair and went through his options: find out more for himself, call Amy, confront Aiden, or forget the whole thing. The suspicions he'd had when he first met Aiden crept to the front of his head again and he wondered if he *had* been duped and this was some kind of scam. As he drank, the periphery of his vision beginning to blur, he tried to absorb the alarming idea that his brother's mistress, the ethereal woman he'd never known about, may not be conveniently dead, but living and breathing somewhere, and no doubt harbouring two decades of resentment.

And why, why, why, he wondered, would Aiden have lied about this? His mind flew from one possible reason to another. His mother could have abandoned him, or he could have run away, or perhaps it was an agreement between the mother and the aunt. Or perhaps his mother was unwell, or maybe Catherine had got something wrong. Who is this woman, and where is she, he kept asking himself, and why was Aiden keeping them apart?

By the time Natalie got home, he had a blinding headache from both the drink and the problem. He didn't tell her right away, believing that saying the words out loud would give them credibility. He clung to the hope that Catherine was mistaken.

But as he and Natalie lay in bed that night, listening to the soft rain on the skylight, he spilled the story.

She cradled his head on her shoulder. "Steven, stop getting all wound up. There is a reason for everything. Most people are doing the best they can to get through each day. They make good decisions, they make bad decisions. Talk to Aiden. More importantly, listen to him. And don't judge."

He pulled her close and fell into a deep sleep.

***

When he learned about the drama with Rosa and the eventual safe return of the family, all thoughts of Aiden's mysterious mother were stifled for a while. His nephew had been in danger. He was worried and proud, distraught and relieved all at the same time.

He answered the call from Aiden on the first ring.

"Jesus Christ almighty, Aiden. God knows what I've smoked and drunk in the last twenty four hours."

"I'm sorry," said the tired voice on the other end. "Seems I've been saying that a lot lately. I wish they hadn't called you. It turned out okay, and you'd have never needed to know."

"That's nonsense. I'd have been *very* upset if they hadn't called. I understand you were a real hero. Battering doors down, tossing the villain over the banister."

"Don't listen to Hadir. He makes it sound like some Mission Impossible thing. It was nothing like that," Aiden said. "But I was ready to kill the woman, that's for sure."

Steven was anxious for details, but he could tell Aiden was reluctant to get into it all. He backed off, telling him it could all wait for a long dinner once he was back home.

"There's a lot we need to talk about, Aiden," he said, gearing up for the question about Dorothy. But then his nerve failed him. The guy had been through a huge ordeal, he was no doubt going through a whole slew of different emotions. The mother thing could wait, too. Instead, he asked about the festival and how the work was progressing.

"They want me to stay for the gala," Aiden told him. "All kinds of big deal people. Not my thing. I mean, I'm proud of the work, but you know, I was just one of a ton of people involved. I don't want to feel like a hanger-on. But they're insisting."

Steven gave a rueful smile, realizing his nephew's aversion to full throttle social interaction ran in the family. But he told him not to be an idiot. If past experience were any indicator, the opening would be an extravaganza he shouldn't miss.

"Aiden, they have nothing but praise for you. They want you to be there. They still want *me* to fly over for the gala but I've got too much work here. And I'm afraid Philippe's not well."

He explained his friend's cancer had returned and he wanted to spend more time with him in Toronto. Aiden should stay, have fun, and represent the family. He told him not to mention Philippe's illness to the El Hassans, who knew him well. He didn't want to burden the family with sad news at such a happy time.

"I'm sorry about Philippe," Aiden said. "The best people get the rottenest luck."

There was a bitterness in Aiden's voice that Steven had not heard before. He wondered if his nephew were harbouring some kind of hurt or grievance.

The question came out of his mouth before he had time to check it. "Aiden, is there something we should talk about, something you haven't told me about the past?"

He heard the sound of a window being opened and faint voices from the street.

"Why are you saying that?" Aiden asked. His voice had turned suspicious.

Steven ran his tongue across his teeth. "Dorothy was your aunt, I think, not your mom."

A long silence. "Does it matter?"

"Of course it does."

"Well, Steven, I gotta say this. It's no concern of yours. It's history. It doesn't matter. Dorothy was the woman who took care of me, the woman I loved as a mom. She's the only mother I give a shit about."

Wow, Steven thought. What the hell does all that mean? "Can we at least talk about it when you're home?"

"Maybe."

Steven walked out to the deck. The sun was shafting through a break in the clouds. A huge Cooper's hawk circled above him, lazily riding the vortex, on the lookout for unsuspecting prey in the dense forest beneath. He thought about Natalie's comment, how most people are just doing their best to get through the day.

"Aiden," he said. "I guess we've all got secrets, a whole bunch of stuff that's hard to deal with. We'll talk only if you want to. Now take care of yourself, okay? Come home safely. We love you."

CHAPTER 36

Aiden leaned against the window frame and pocketed his phone. He watched the people in the narrow street below him, one man stooped forward with a huge sack of produce on his back, another dusting off copperware and setting it out for sale. A woman measured and cut fabric from dozens of colourful rolls stacked like breadsticks in the basket beside her. He wondered if their lives were simple or if they, too, grappled with the past, with secrets and resentments. They were poor, he thought, but always looked happy, ready with a greeting, a wish for a fine day, *Insha'Allah.*

How could he ever have hoped to keep the truth of his birth mother from his uncle, he wondered now? Everyone's life was open to scrutiny with a few deft clicks of the mouse. He hadn't bothered to ask how Steven found out. It didn't matter.

The most recently forwarded letter from Maggie lay crumpled at the edge of his desk. She'd learned he was in Morocco and begged to see him when he passed through Toronto on his return. With the perspective of distance, in a country so far from his home, Maggie had become even less important to him, and he regretted that he hadn't been honest with Steven right from the beginning. Lots of people grew up in unpleasant circumstances, some given up at birth, some abandoned, some, like Lukas, losing both their parents when they were so young. Maggie was more or less incidental to his life. Steven would probably have understood and let things be. Instead, the whole business had now assumed the pathos of melodrama.

He remembered what Lukas said when they were together that night in Chefchaouen … something about a real mom being a strong feeling, and how he was convinced his own was there somehow, and she'd brought Aiden to meet him. He had none of those feelings about Maggie. Perhaps for some women, motherhood was all consuming, inviolable. He had seen such feelings in action over the past few days, the fear and wrath in Amina's eyes, the ferocity with which she fought for her daughter, giving no thought to her personal safety.

"You think you're a mother," he muttered toward the crumpled letter, "but you have no idea what that means. You never fought for me."

He sat at his desk, tossed the letter in the bin and scrolled through his files on the festival. It seemed a lifetime ago he had last looked at them. The gala event was closing in and there were still a few last-minute adjustments to make to literature and websites. He looked over his work, indulging in a little self-congratulation. Both his designs for the festival and the painting he'd done on his own time had brought him such pleasure. Last week, on a whim, he'd asked Zahra for her professional opinion. She took his laptop to her desk and flipped through images of his earlier work in silence, sometimes lingering on one, sometimes swiping by in a second or two.

"You're very talented, Aiden," she said. "Some of this work is truly engaging. I bet I could stand in front of it for a long, long time, getting lost in it."

"But?"

She told him a few pieces felt restricted, as though something were gripping his hand at the wrist, and guiding it, forcing it to go in certain directions. "These are the directions you *think* it should go, not the ones the brush wants to go. In other words, you don't trust your heart, so you let your mind take over. Look …"

She opened his laptop again and pointed out the differences between what she called "expressive work" and what she felt was "confined."

"I guess I'm saying you should stop thinking." She gestured around the studio to the exhibits of the creative people she represented. "Do you believe any of these artists were thinking? I doubt it. They were only feeling. Sometimes with great passion, sometimes with sadness and introversion. When you look at what they've created, you feel the blood in their veins, the tears in their eyes."

He had left that day with new energy and resolve.

Now, as he began to get ready for dinner, his eye was caught by the photograph on the opposite wall, the Berber horsemen in full charge that had sparked Lukas's identification of Gabriella Burhan. He froze with a shock of remembered panic, still not quite able to believe it was over and, not only was his negligence overlooked but his modest role exaggerated and praised. He doubted he'd ever meet another family like the El Hassans.

There was a knock at his door. He opened it to find Rosa, her ankles crossed in her coy, little girl stance. She handed him a large file.

"This came for you from Zahra. *Maman* said *I* could bring it and give you a big kiss because you helped get me away from the bad lady."

He lifted her off the ground and buried his face in her hair. The kiss she planted on his cheek would have to be the proxy for the one he longed for from her mother. When he put her down, ruffling her hair, she giggled and ran off down the corridor as though the events of the past couple of days had glossed right over her.

On his way downstairs to dinner, his phone pinged. Catherine.

Geez. High drama in the desert. Dad was on supercharged freak out. Glad you're all ok. Saw Penelope the other day. Your work impressed those wacko clients at her party. She needs help with Toronto gallery — an arty-techie type. Asked me to tell you to go see her on your way home. Consider yourself told. Hope you're having fun. Miss you. AML.

The text had an enervating effect on him. Life here in Morocco was like a continual magic mushroom high. But the world he had left behind, the real world, was still there, less colourful but solid. And he had a family. Maybe there was a good place for him there after all, a place he could genuinely belong.

CHAPTER 37

Seeing Aiden and Lukas standing in the hotel lobby, packed and ready for a night in the desert, Dominic was struck once again by their strange connection. There were fifteen years between them, yet both had overlapping histories they knew little about. Both had dropped into his life from totally different worlds and played a life-changing role in his own. Providence, fate, whatever was at work here, Dominic would always be deeply grateful for its silent presence.

They rode in silence for a while, occasionally exclaiming at the spectacular views of the Atlas Mountains and the early stars blinking more fiercely through the growing darkness.

After a lot of soul searching, he and Amina signed the paperwork from the lawyers and agreed not to press charges in Rosa's abduction. Their lawyer said they were dealing with a very troubled family. Gabriella's father, one of the two owners of Al Sayed, was still curdling with rage over the "psychotic madness" of his daughter. He would likely never acknowledge it, but he was deeply grateful to the El Hassans, would ensure Gabriella received treatment, and hoped the matter would be forever closed.

Rosa, despite all her panic, was clearly seeing the whole traumatic incident as an adventure in which she played a starring role. Dominic was now more worried about Lukas and possible PTSD. He and Amina had talked it through with the boy, giving him a little more of the history, why it had happened, and suggesting Gabriella was not well. But Lukas said little, nodding wisely as though everything were unfolding as it should. Dominic told him he and Amina and Aiden were heroes, and he was proud of them all.

Sitting beside him now, his backpack between his knees, Lukas peered through the window at the sky. From time to time, he thumbed through an app on his mobile, his nimble fingers zooming in and out. Not only did he embrace the mystery and magic of the desert and the night sky, as his parents had, but clearly took great comfort from being here.

"A whole bunch of planets are lining up tonight," Lukas said. "Jupiter, Uranus, Mars, Saturn. I mean not perfect, but pretty close."

He chattered on, mostly to himself, occasionally holding up his mobile to show Aiden, who had insisted on taking the back seat, and describing the constellation he was examining.

There had always been something hard to pin down about the young boy, Dominic thought. On restless nights, checking on the children, he often found Lukas at the window, staring at the night sky as though he were in a trance. Anxious not to startle him, he would speak softly, coaxing him back to bed. And Lukas had an uncanny intuition, saying things that made people look askance. This morning, at breakfast, he interrupted a whispered discussion Amina was having with Sophie about the Burhan couple. "You know about messengers, right?" he said. "I think she was maybe a messenger …. a way for a good thing to happen." Sophie was astounded. "That woman and a 'good thing' don't belong in the same sentence, Lukas," she barked. Hadir confronted Dominic later to make sure he hadn't been messing with the boy's head, bothering him with all that "psychic business."

Dominic reminded Lukas of the comment now and asked what he meant.

Lukas scrunched up his face in thought. "It's like what I told Aiden. Sometimes people have to do things so that other things can happen. They may not even know about this other thing until later."

"Are you talking about fate?" Dominic asked.

"Probably fate's making them do it. My dad wrote you shouldn't get in its way."

Dominic wondered if he was getting in the way of something. He was no longer afraid or worried about his family, but his mind was not fully at ease.

After nearly two hours on the road, he took the familiar turn off through a group of giant rocks with a few argan trees that somehow sucked nourishment from the parched earth. The path was hard and rock-strewn for a couple of kilometres, but gave way to sand, and soon they had to stop and proceed on foot. They walked up a hill to a rocky outcrop with a flat place to settle, sharing the burden of the telescope, tripod, food, water and blankets.

Lukas switched on a small lamp and instructed a willing Aiden on how to set up the equipment, first lining up all the pieces on the blanket: the main body of the scope, tripod, lenses, mounting bracket, cables, filters, and more … wiping each with a cloth, taking care to keep them all free of sand. The boy was meticulous, as surely all astronomers and would-be astronomers needed to be, Dominic thought.

"Want to see this?" Lukas called out when the scope was all set up. "The Little Dipper's really clear. The bowl is right over Polaris. So cool."

Dominic shook his head. "You show Aiden. Do your thing."

He was happier lying on his back, letting his mind explore the dark cosmic canyons, wild with stars. Removed from the clutter of his life, he became aware of the insignificance of his physical self and this brought him a deep sense of fullness and peace. He could feel the faint stir of breeze across the sand and, if he concentrated and closed his eyes, he swore he could hear the low hum of the universe itself. Rolling his jacket under his head as a pillow, he let the darkness sink around him and felt the stirring of a force far greater than all of them. He had felt that same force as a child, standing on the edge of the ocean with his mother, a force that transcended cultures, continents, and the passage of years. He focussed on a single point of light, and felt his body lifting, weightless, yearning to soar heavenward and dance among the glittering spirals, hop-skipping from one constellation to another.

Shaking himself from these reveries, he looked over to Lukas, fiddling with the dials of the telescope, and Aiden gazing in awe at the violet luminescence of the Milky Way. Through the weaving of the countless paths of fate, the lives of the three of them under the stars tonight, the lives of the people they had loved in the past and would love in the future—all were meant to intersect, fuse inextricably together. It might be Lukas himself who was the alchemist, he thought, an apprentice to fate itself, bringing them together, carrying forward the spirit and beliefs of both his parents.

As he turned on his side for a different view, he felt something fall from his pocket. He moved his hand around in the sand and found the Goddess Ma'at cartouche pendant he'd bought for Amina from his friend Youssef, still in its green silk bag. He had completely forgotten about it. He knew little of the ancient Egyptian gods and goddesses, but the name of this one was beginning to feel significant in some way.

"Hey, Lukas, can I look at your notebook for a minute?"

His two companions came over to sit with him. He told them about the morning in the Atacama when he couldn't sleep and had found a page in the book with a picture of Thoth on it and a few lines about the goddess Ma'at underneath.

Lukas turned on his lantern and flicked through the notebook. It was thick, the pages crammed with information, and he took a while. "This must be it. Thoth is the guy who weighs your heart."

Dominic took it from him. "That's it. Weighs your heart against the feather of Ma'at."

"See the drawing here, eight arrows going a different way. That's chaos. It's the symbol. It's why my dad wrote 'Isfet' next to it. It's what

I was telling you about. Kind of what happened to us. Remember? So this goddess Ma'at, she's the opposite. Justice and truth my dad wrote."

In silence, Dominic read the sentence that struck him when he'd seen it in the notebook the first time. *Guilt is the heaviest of burdens, but the inability to forgive is heavier still.*

"How do you figure all this stuff out?" Aiden said, peering over their shoulders. "All those diagrams and star maps and hieroglyphics? They look so complicated."

Lukas told him about the course he was going to take on Ancient Egypt, designed for kids, but it was hard, and the teacher said it takes "years and years" to learn it all.

Dominic noted the reference to Neptune and Pisces in the margin.

"Back in Chile, you told me Neptune's in my birth sign," he said. "Is that supposed to mean something?"

Lukas drew circles in the sand with a small stick, and said his dad had written it was a time you faced up to things. He took the notebook from Dominic, turned the page and pointed to another entry. "And, see, when Neptune's in retrograde…it says here, it means regret, intro—" He stumbled. "Introspection. Does that mean looking backwards? Hey, Neptune's in retrograde now. Until December."

Dominic wondered if the astronomical and astrological bits and pieces made any real sense in the boy's mind. His father drew no distinction between science and mythology. Even his mother, Rachel, apparently a real skeptic at the beginning, became so convinced of Karl's esoteric beliefs that she ended up devoting her life to following them.

"Retrograde means going backwards, right?" Aiden said. "Not that I know a thing about any of this."

Lukas explained the planet wasn't really going backwards but looked like that from Earth, and said retrograde times were supposed to be important for looking back. He jumped to his feet and told

Aiden he'd show him how to find Neptune. It was right by Pegasus, and this was a good month to see it.

Aiden stood, hands on his hips, and craned his neck back to stare into the heavens. "Jesus. It's so amazing. I mean, it makes me feel so small, like I'm just a speck, totally lost in hundreds of universes. But, it's kind of neat. Not scary."

Dominic lay down on the sand again and gazed at the desert sky, feeling inextricably connected to the complex, magical world up there. He, Dominic El Hassan, was a tiny cog in a gigantic wheel, but he believed that what he did, how he led his life, still influenced the way things fell. He thought about the cosmic mythology that was supposed to be at work at this time, its encouragement to face and learn from the past, and felt an unexpected sadness sink through him. He wondered if he were riding too high on his luck and his beautiful life, and the mysterious forces of the universe were trying to tell him something.

A strong need to look more deeply into his soul took hold of him. He had the unsettling feeling that, when he did this, he would find a flawed human being with work to do.

CHAPTER 38

From the shade of a narrow alleyway off Nejarine Square, Dominic watched the activity in a store selling copper and brass jugs and other decorative items. The crusty old man who used to run it had died. A woman with a more customer-friendly disposition was now in charge. She had reduced the clutter and reorganized the display cases so there was room to move around and better appreciate the craftsmanship of the goods for sale.

Earlier, Dominic called to make sure a man named Da'ud Karaoui was still involved in the business and still living in the adjoining rooms at the back. The last time they met, five years ago, Dominic was with his brother, Hadir. They were forced to be "persuasive," as Hadir put it, to extract the information they needed: where this man's nephew, Masoud, had taken Amina.

Dominic did not warn Da'ud of his visit, fearing the man would refuse to see him, and believing he'd have a better chance of an audience if he arrived unexpectedly. He waited until the few browsing customers left the store.

"*As-Salaam-Alaikum.* I'm Dominic El Hassan," he said, approaching the man. "You may remember me. We met a few years ago."

Da'ud scrutinized him, then straightened up, his watery, sunken eyes struggling to focus. He had lost considerable weight, and his grey hair was lank and thin. There were food stains on his *gallabiyya.* "*Wa Alaikum as-salaam,*" he said, finally. "You are hard to forget."

"I hope you can spare a little time. I need to ask about your nephew, Masoud Burhan."

"I thought all that business was done with. What do you want with him now?"

"I need your perspective on something."

"My perspective? *Alalalah.* You take me for a fool?"

"Please. I mean no harm."

Da'ud let out a long breath and called over to the young woman. "Yasmin, bring us some tea." With a curt wave of his hand, he directed Dominic to the back room.

Not much had changed in that room over the last five years. The threadbare carpet, low sofas with scattered cushions, and the shelves of canopic jars were still there. Dominic did not care for mint tea but dared not decline when Yasmin brought the tray, for fear of being considered ill-mannered.

His host reclined on a sofa opposite. "I heard what happened. Not all of it. It was not my business. But you signed the agreement. It's hard to imagine what you could want with me."

"I want to know if he is truly seriously ill?"

"My nephew?"

Da'ud was obviously affronted, asking why Dominic would even question this. His nephew and wife were shortly moving to Egypt, he said, to Gabi's parents' estate, and he was planning to visit them. He understood Masoud would be going into a clinic or hospice soon.

Dominic muttered a few words of regret, but these were met with a cynical, doubting stare. He was determined to stay calm, reminding himself he was here to learn more about what happened five years ago, not to relive the rage he felt at the time, all so recently renewed. He chose one of the buttery *maamoul* cookies from the tea tray, took a bite, and brushed the flour dust from his jeans.

"Do you truly believe he's a good man?" he said.

Da'ud raised his hands in the air. "A better man than you, for certain. You cannot see beyond your jealous heart. He loved Amina. Her money was irrelevant in the end. And it was my idea, not his. I hoped it would help Masoud's family. I admitted that to you."

"Under threat."

Da'ud snorted. He leaned over, dragged a shisha pipe to the edge of the sofa, and went through the ritual of sprinkling tobacco, wrapping aluminum foil across the bowl, poking holes, lighting the charcoal tab … all without saying a word. When the water was bubbling, he took the hose and inhaled, making no move to share.

"Why did his family need the money?" Dominic asked. "They bred Arabian stallions. A lucrative business, from what I understand."

At first, Da'ud refused to explain but then appeared to have a change of heart, muttering it all happened a long time ago and hardly mattered now. Masoud's father, his own brother-in-law, was a crook, he claimed. Apparently, the wrong kind of people started coming to the property, uninvited. He got into brawls and spent a fortune paying them off, trying to stay alive.

"Did you notice Masoud had a limp?" he asked.

"A riding accident, Amina told me."

Da'ud gave a scornful laugh, claiming his nephew was a superb horseman, none finer. "He was beaten up trying to protect his father in a nasty fight. His father died. They broke Masoud's leg in two or three places. He could not walk for months, let alone ride."

For Dominic, the idea of Masoud falling from a horse had made him seem vulnerable, even weak. Learning he was an accomplished equestrian and had the guts to intervene in a serious fight put him in an enviable light that did not sit well.

"Why did he lie about it?" he asked.

"What a question. For the family's sake, of course. He withdrew into the world of Ancient Egypt, which he had loved since he was a child. He became a consultant to the film industry. You know this, I think."

"So you believe his affection for Amina was genuine?"

"Affection? He was deeply in love with your wife."

Dominic could see the spite behind the smile and could barely stop himself from grabbing the man and throwing him into the shelf of canopic jars.

"If it's true the family needed money, why was he prepared to give it up?" he said.

"A question of honour. Perhaps this would never occur to you."

Dominic reeled from the insult, one of the worst that could be levied in this part of the world. He pushed his glass of tea away and began to rise, intent on leaving with a stream of insults. But he had planned this visit for days and knew he would be furious with himself later if he let the old man rattle him.

"As I said, he went along with my idea," Da'ud continued, "but when he realized how much he loved Amina, the money was no longer important. He wouldn't have kept it."

"Things worked out for him though, didn't they? The Al Sayed ranch? Pretty wealthy family to marry into, from what I can gather. Another convenient set-up?"

"This is fine talk from a man who has never had to worry about money for a single day in his privileged life and who, for many years, felt free to squander it ostentatiously all over town."

Dominic was speechless with the audacity of this claim, but powerless to rebut it; it was true. He felt a sudden need for something stronger than mint tea. He took another cookie, realizing too late he'd already eaten half of them.

Da'ud stared at him for a few moments, as though trying to decide whether to throw him out, but relaxed back into the couch again. He asserted the marriage was convenient for both parties—she needed a husband and a child, he needed financial security for his family.

"But it seemed karma was at work," he concluded. "They were both punished for contriving to make a life they were clearly not destined for."

He had harsh words for Gabi's father, claiming the man loved his business more than his family, declaring they should all have been far more grateful to Masoud, a man who knew a great deal about Arabian stallions, and was always willing to help. He said the father should have turned over a sizeable chunk of his share to the two of them. It would have had no impact on the family fortune. Instead, their daughter grew up with intense resentment that turned vindictive and hurt a great many people.

"If you are questioning her state of mind, her intentions," he continued, "I have no doubt she regrets her journey to Fez and hopes never to set eyes on you or your wife, or anyone in your family ever again. As I did." He took another drag of the shisha pipe. "Are we done?"

Dominic resorted to pouring another glass of mint tea, struggling to sort out his feelings. "I need to think things through."

"You have a letter of contrition, and you have agreed to put the whole matter behind you. What more do you need?" Da'ud surveyed him through narrowed eyes, puffing at the shisha pipe. The sweet, earthy smell of apple and molasses tobacco filled the room. "Tell me about the boy," he said. "I believe his name is Lukas. He lives with you now, I hear. Strange how that worked. Fate, of course. The winds of fate will blow you half around the world and back, but somehow, you end up where you belong."

Dominic concluded they were past the acrimony. "That's what Lukas would say."

"It's what his father believed. I knew his parents well, as you may recall. Before I left Cairo to join my family here, I specialized in Ancient Egyptian artifacts. Karl would often consult me."

Dominic looked at him with new interest. Five years ago, he had dismissed this man as the conniving, manipulative force behind Amina's disappearance, suppressing any interest in his earlier life in

Cairo, his connections to Rachel and Karl. He wondered now what more the old man might be prepared to tell him.

"Lukas wants to be an astronomer," he said. "And he's enrolled in a course for kids on Egyptology."

"Ah. Karl would have known this, in that special way he had. I swear he could see into the future. He kept a notebook for the boy, miraculously saved from the fire that killed him. I assume the boy has this?"

"It never leaves his side."

"Difficult man, his father. Brilliant in his field. He and Rachel … ah, who knows … all so intense. Invoking Osiris out in the desert." He glanced at Dominic's virtually untouched glass of tea. "I don't drink alcohol, but I can have Yasmin bring you a glass of wine, if you wish."

From a childish sense of pride, Dominic declined. "I should be going."

As Da'ud led him back along the narrow corridor to the store, he stopped and reached for a leather bag on a shelf. Then, obviously changing his mind, he pushed it back and shuffled to the exit.

Out in the square, Dominic turned to thank him for his time, but the old man was gone.

***

That evening, the receptionist on duty at the hotel called Dominic to say a package had come for him. Because of the late hour and the new rule not to let anyone in who was not expected, the delivery boy had been told to wait outside in the alleyway.

Dominic eased open the door and saw the young boy under the yellow light of the overhead lamp. He looked harmless. The boy took the few dirhams tip and handed over a well-worn leather satchel. "It's from Mr. Da'ud Karaoui," he said, scampering off.

Inside the satchel was a note from Da'ud:

This was Karl's, another item untouched by the fire. I found those charts in it, the ones I gave you five years ago ... Amina's and the boy's. Who knows what direction fate would have taken without them? Insha'Allah, it is on its intended course. This satchel is of no use to me now. Give it to Lukas. One day, he might like to carry his books and papers in it, as his father did.

A light breeze skittered along the alleyway and brushed Dominic's face. His body shuddered as though from a surge of electricity. For a few moments, he was lost in time, far from this Moroccan city, and possessed, he was certain, by the vagrant spirit of the man who had owned this well-worn leather case, a man who would remain an enigma ... scientist, mystic, star reader, a man whose insight and prophesies, he was convinced, were still at work.

CHAPTER 39

There was no air-conditioning in the taxi Dominic took to the hospice in Cairo, and the heat through the open windows sapped all breath and energy. Rosa fidgeted on the seat beside him, beads of sweat on her face, her usually thick hair lank and lifeless. The city moved in shimmering slow motion; even the ubiquitous honking of horns lacked conviction. Their driver sighed at every red light, leaning on the wheel as though to sleep.

In the past two weeks, Dominic felt he had aged far beyond that span of time. His high spirits and energy flagged, and his impetuousness moved to a lower gear. But he was happier than ever, a quieter kind of happiness, more deeply rooted than the pleasures of his past, more resilient. Hadir commented on the change, with a little concern, claiming he had never seen his younger brother "thoughtful." Dominic assured him it was because his earlier, persistent anxiety had been put to rest. But it was much more than that. It was a sense of resolve that gained definition on the night he went into the desert with Lukas and Aiden, and became clearer after he met with the old man, Da'ud. He confessed these feelings to Amina one night as they gazed at the stars through the skylight in their bedroom. He told her what Lukas had said about Neptune, and what he felt he must now do.

The taxi ground to a halt again. A young barefoot girl on the sidewalk, not much older than Rosa, caught Dominic's eye. She wore a faded dress, too small for her. Her hair was dirty and tangled. She ran toward their car, thrusting out a sprig of jasmine. The driver yelled for her to move away, but Dominic stopped him, searching his pockets for a few piastres.

He held the jasmine to Rosa's nose. "Beautiful, isn't it?"

"It smells like *maman*."

Dominic cradled his daughter against him. *Maman.* He and Amina had agonized over this trip, knowing it was something he must do, but worrying for different reasons—Dominic, because the baby, due in three weeks, might come sooner; Amina, because she did not fully trust her husband's temper. In the end, she agreed because, with Rosa in his care, he would do nothing rash. When he left, he clasped his wife tightly to his side and assured her all would be well. But he could not dispel the fear behind her eyes.

The sealed envelope bearing the results of the paternity test was slim and light, but it sat as heavy as a stone in the inside pocket of his jacket.

He paid the taxi driver and found a bench in the shade of an acacia tree in the forecourt of the hospice, opposite a stone fountain. Pulling out his phone, he motioned for Rosa to climb up beside him and called Amina.

Everyone was fine, she told him, but everyone wanted him home. He heard the deep breath she took and knew what was coming. "Dominic, you don't have to do this."

"I do."

He passed the phone to Rosa, twisting his fingers through the limp curls of her hair and kissing the top of her head as she chattered away to her mother. Amina had told her it was an adventure, a trip with Papa to see a friend who was not feeling well. He watched the gentle pulse of the jets around the fountain and felt the burn of the Cairo sun through tiny gaps in the tree's dense canopy. Cairo, a city of secrets and myths, and ancient wisdom, clinging to the banks of the Nile. He had always been drawn to it, loving the chaos and clamour, the hospitality and kindness of its citizens.

Hadir challenged him the night before he left. "I can't believe this. You went ahead and got a paternity test? And you haven't read the results? What's going on?"

"Amina and I have discussed it. I'm sorry, Hadir. I will explain when I'm home."

"Don't tell me you've been reading those wretched Tarot cards again."

"I don't need to read them. I know. Intuitively."

"And what if you learn an unpleasant truth? You're prepared to risk your marriage for this *feeling* you have? Are you crazy?"

Dominic took a step closer to Hadir and pointed a finger at his chest. "*Nothing* risks my marriage. Nothing and no one will take me from my wife and children. I would kill for them."

"So why are you going *there*? To indulge some selfish need you harbour?"

"Stop, Hadir. When you talk this way, I know you don't trust me. You think I'm still the man I used to be, before Amina. That man has gone. Forever. I am *meant* to do this. I'm certain of it. I don't expect you to understand."

They had glared at each other for a few moments until Hadir pulled him into a hug. "For God's sake, brother, you have a family, a new baby boy coming. We all need you. Do what you have to and get back here quickly. And safely."

The *Asr* call to prayer began. Dominic gazed at the minaret of a nearby mosque, a smudged, yellow sky behind it, and thought about the long, long story that began in this city. Two people he never knew fell in love here; a love deep and complex, steeped in the lore of the desert and the mystery of the countless stars above it. What would they think of him, he asked himself, a stranger whose life had never touched theirs, destined to raise their son and carry on their story with its never-ending loops and splices, its sudden narrative shifts?

He glanced at his leather bracelet with the Roma wheel, the one he always wore when travelling, and thought about the series of coincidences that had thrust him from the shadows onto a long walk with fate. And now this strange new twist. If fate had indeed contrived to place him here, with this unbearable burden, he wondered what possible ending it could have in mind.

The lobby of the hospice had a hushed air: comfortable chairs, scattered rugs, and blinds at the windows angled to deflect the fierce sun. A few people sat in clusters, their voices low.

"I'm here to see Masoud Burhan," he told the receptionist.

"What is your relationship with the patient?"

He was unable to think of an answer.

A voice came from behind him, female, a strongly accented Arabic. "We are expecting this man. My son-in-law will see him." A woman stepped forward. "I'm Eleanor Mazhar, Gabriella's mother. I'm sorry you travelled so far. It was not necessary."

Eleanor Mazhar. So this was the mother of the woman who caused his family so much pain, he thought, the one who wrote the pleading letter to Amina. He was not sure what to expect, but certainly not this neat, contrite person, a scarf around her head, her face etched with fatigue and grief, who was unable to meet his eyes.

"It's okay to speak English." He stood for a moment, unsure of what to do next. "You will come with me to see him?"

She said Masoud preferred to see him alone, but asked that he let her know when he was leaving. Dominic's anger had long drained away and in this moment, he was flooded by the same sorrow so clearly engulfing this broken woman.

The receptionist suggested he leave his daughter in the children's playroom behind her, in the care of one of the staff. "Call me when you want her to join you. Mr. Burhan is in 205, second floor."

He took Rosa's picture book and Fun Phone from his bag and guided her to the playroom, telling her he was going to see the man now, and he wouldn't be long.

On the threshold of Room 205, he hesitated, one hand on the door frame. He could scarcely believe the frail, withered person on the bed was the same man he had confronted five years ago: the quiet

Egyptian with his gentle manners and soft voice. Back then, this man's composure and contriteness only fueled Dominic's rage. Now, Masoud's body was wasted: hollow cheeks, a yellowish hue to the skin, bony shoulders sinking into the heap of pillows on the angled bed. The white cotton robe he wore was loose and crumpled. A needle connected to a drip was taped to one of his hands.

Dominic tapped on the door. *"As-Salaam-Alaikum."*

Masoud's eyes flickered over. He whispered the response.

A curtain fluttered from the fan over the window. Dominic felt conspicuous by his evident health, his ability to stand tall and feel strong. "We meet only under the worst of circumstances," he said.

A faint smile passed over Masoud's lips. "You have always wanted to kill me."

"I was wrong. I know this now. Your uncle told me more."

"Da'ud? He saw you?"

"Reluctantly. I will never like or trust him, but I'm grateful for what he confided."

Masoud shook his head. "Why did you come? There's no point. I'm dying. There was never a point."

Dominic drew the envelope from his jacket and placed it on Masoud's chest.

Masoud lay still, his eyes unfocused. Grimacing with pain, he raised himself higher on the stack of pillows and looked at the envelope, his eyes widening. "It is still sealed."

"It's for you to open."

Masoud stared. "I thought you were here to show me proof. That *you* were her father. Put the final nail in my coffin."

"Of course, that's what you would think. I deserve no better."

"*I* did not ask for this." Masoud pushed the envelope away. It slid to the floor on the other side of the bed.

Dominic went to the window and gazed at the courtyard below, with its clipped hedges and frothy mounds of periwinkle. An elderly man was slumped forward in his wheelchair, drinking water from a bottle through a straw. Two nurses in blue hijabs stood at his side, one of them steadying his hand. He wondered what they must witness here in this sombre place, this last refuge of the dying, and whether they wept or took joy in the solace they were trained to give.

For the hundredth time, he thought about how he would react to the truth inside the envelope. With its seal intact, it held two possible stories. One meant the freedom from ever having to think of this again. *And the other?* He loved Rosa beyond words. He loved her as he loved her mother. He would lay his life down for either of them, even if the cold truth of the second possibility meant fate had skirted around him, pausing only to push him off the stage.

He looked at the dying man on the bed, those eyes filled with a torment Dominic could never imagine. Like him, this man would have spun out two different endings, weighing both in his failing heart.

As he searched in his pocket for a tissue to dab the sweat on his forehead, his fingers closed around the cartouche pendant Amina told him he should bring. He worried now it would seem frivolous. But he had promised.

"Amina wants me to give you this," he said. "She would have come herself, but she is pregnant. She cannot travel."

"Amina would have come?" Masoud coughed with the effort of speaking. "I don't believe it."

Dominic took the pendant from its green silk bag and held it up. "It's the Goddess Ma'at. You will know better than I what it means. Would you like to wear it?"

Masoud could barely raise his head for Dominic to put the braided leather cord around his neck. He gripped the pendant tightly, his knuckles white with the effort. "It means truth, karma. My weak heart will be weighed against the feather of Ma'at. Who knows…" he gave a brief, sardonic smile. "Maybe I'll make it to the Afterlife."

He fell silent for a while. Dominic thought he was sleeping, but then he stirred. "Please give me the envelope."

Dominic picked it up and handed it to him. For a few moments, Masoud pressed it to his chest. Then, with both hands, he held it high and ripped it in two.

"Wait, what are you doing?" Dominic cried, reaching for his arm.

Masoud pulled away. "You are her father," he said. "The only one who matters."

Dominic sank onto the chair at the side of the bed, stunned by the honour of this dying man and filled with remorse for the feelings he'd once harboured against him. It was a while before he could find voice to speak.

"I know you loved Amina," he said finally. "You were granted such a cruel, short time with that love. And I know what you must think of me."

He rose, took the torn halves of the envelope and ripped them again and again, feeling an overwhelming release, as though the ties binding him were abruptly severed and he could breathe again. The noise in his head softened to a soothing hum. He tried to find the right words but feared he would fumble and get it all wrong. He stayed silent for a few moments, looking at the scattered scraps of paper and the freedom they now represented.

"I am the man with the honour of raising Rosa," he said. "But as long as we don't know the truth, we are both her father. I want you to leave with that thought in your heart. Amina and I will love and cherish Rosa for the rest of our lives. One day, we will tell her about you, Masoud. And then … then it will be her decision."

Masoud closed his eyes and drew in his breath. "*Sadiqi*," he whispered, reaching for Dominic's hand.

Dominic cradled the exhausted body of his old rival, pulling him close, feeling the brittleness of his ribs, the clench of his sharp nails.

"Forgive me, my friend," he said. He held Masoud for a few more moments, rocking slowly, then lowered him onto the pillows.

A movement in the hall made them both turn. The receptionist stood in the doorway, holding Rosa's hand. "I'm sorry, she was anxious. May I leave her with you?"

"Rosa." Dominic beckoned his daughter over. "This man is not well, but you are a special girl. You can make anyone feel better." He coaxed her to the side of the bed.

"May I hold your hand?" Masoud asked her, wiping at tears with the sleeve of his gown.

Rosa slid her fingers into his. "I hope you get better."

"You are beautiful," he whispered.

She looked at Dominic. "Why are you crying, Papa? Are you sad?"

"No, baby, I'm very happy." He was seized by a wave of grief that made him tremble. "Come, it's time for us to leave."

He clasped his hands to his chest and bowed his head. "You will not be forgotten."

"*Ma'as salaama.*" Masoud mouthed the words.

Dominic hustled Rosa away and half walked, half ran along the corridor and down the stairs to the lobby. He asked the receptionist to tell Mrs. Mazhar they would be outside.

The falling sun had cast the date palms lining the road into long shadows. Breathing hard, Dominic slumped onto the stone wall by the fountain, the water now sparkling in the low light.

Rosa curled herself into him. "Are we going home, papa?"

"Tomorrow, my darling. A taxi is coming soon to take us to the hotel. We will say goodbye to the lady first. She won't be long."

From his inside pocket, he took out his wallet and withdrew a faded photograph of a small child with windswept curls of long, dark hair. The child was holding the hand of a young woman. Both were standing on a beach, bare feet in shallow waves, looking over their shoulders at whoever was taking the picture. He showed it to Rosa.

"Who is that, Papa? Is it me?"

"No, it's me. I was about two. And that's my mother, your grandmama. She would have loved you so much."

He saw Eleanor approaching and slid the photograph and wallet back into his jacket.

"The doctors say he will not make it through the night," she said. "It means a lot that you came." She leaned over as though to stroke Rosa's hair, then pulled back. "Such a sweetheart."

Dominic looked with new compassion at the defeated woman before him. What a strange, unhappy connection they had, he thought. All because of a chance encounter on the other side of the world.

"Your daughter? Is she—?" He realized he didn't know what to ask or why.

Eleanor turned away, staring into the distance. "We don't know. Her life here is over."

"Fate never leaves us stranded. One day she will find peace, *Insha'Allah.*"

Eleanor bit her lip. "You are too kind, Dominic. Go home to your family. Put us from your mind."

The taxi pulled up on the other side of the fountain and he helped Rosa into the back seat.

As it pulled away, he turned to see a man walking over to join Eleanor by the fountain, her husband perhaps. Both stood watching him leave. The man raised a tentative hand, as though in farewell. Dominic thought he mouthed the word *shukran* – thank you. But he could not be sure.

CHAPTER 40

The official opening or "kick-off" to the arts festival took place at one of the larger hotels near the Blue Gate, with prominent artists and creative luminaries from across the country in attendance. Aiden's impression of living in a Magical Mystery Tour fantasy sharpened. He swore once again that there must be something in his drink. It was as though the exquisite pieces of art and photography on display had bled over their edges and filled the air with great swathes of every colour imaginable, and with light and darkness, sparkle and mystery. People, all beautiful, floated by, wearing the full range of clothing from traditional, brightly patterned kaftans and djellabas to exquisitely tailored Western-style suits and cocktail dresses. They smiled, they raised their glasses and laughed, their dark hair flowing and glowing.

A painting formed in Aiden's mind, an impression of this psychedelic trip he must be on. He stared into the midst of the party, squinting his eyes to let the dominant colours and shapes surface. He was tempted to take a photograph but believed the image in his mind would be stronger and the painting more vivid if he did it from memory.

Everyone wanted to know him, it seemed, shaking his hand, clinking his glass, bowing slightly, hoping he would come back. He knew this was the work of Dominic, praising "the young artist from Canada, nephew of my good friend, the painter Steven Farrow." Aiden was surprised at how well his uncle was known, how much his work was admired … or at least that was the excellent impression these guests gave him.

There were many speeches and much excitement about the photographic and artistic entries already starting to arrive from around the world. The website and promotional material were praised for their appeal and international reach, and Zahra and Aiden were obliged to stand for appreciative applause.

Afterwards, back at the Riad Capella, Dominic and Hadir hosted another party, this one to thank staff and close friends who had worked so hard. If the festival went as planned, they hoped to attract more artists and photographers, both amateur and professional, to the country. Dominic had asked for Aiden's input on many different initiatives that would be based at their hotel: workshops, retreats, seminars, field trips—all designed to showcase the stunning landscapes of the country and its inherent artistic appeal.

Aiden sat in the colonnade, happy to watch the musicians, observe the continuing revelry, and resist all attempts to get him to dance. Hadir joined him at one point. More than a little drunk, he collapsed beside Aiden and put an arm around him.

"So, she's gone, we learned," he said. "Left the country."

"Who's gone?"

"*L'espèce de folle*. Woman who took Rosa. All kinds of trouble in Egypt."

As far as Aiden could make out, an uncle of Masoud had contacted Dominic, telling him there had been a serious family drama at Al Sayed. Something about a horse being shot. Gabriella had left the family, left Egypt for good, apparently.

"How did a horse get into all this?" Aiden asked him.

Hadir shrugged. "Who cares? *Bon débarras.* Good riddance to her."

Aiden questioned why Masoud's uncle would contact Dominic to tell him this.

"Honour," Hadir spluttered. "They know each other, this guy and Dominic. Trouble in the past. The old man wanted to put Dominic's mind at rest. Probably because he'd made that trip—you know, to Cairo, to the hospice. All very honourable." He got up unsteadily and swallowed the rest of his wine. *"Tout va bien ça finit bien.* Hey, why aren't you dancing, Aiden?"

Much later, well past midnight, when the last of the guests had left, Aiden walked across the lobby to head to the stairs and go to bed. In one of the rooms off the courtyard, he caught sight of Amina. She was lying full length on a couch, her dark blue dress falling in folds over its edge, a long yellow scarf draped around her neck. The toddler, Raif, was curled up half-asleep at her side, as though listening to the heartbeat of his baby brother waiting to be born. Aiden watched her from behind a column as she stroked the child's hair, and felt the stirring of blood she always provoked. He imagined having the courage to walk over and kiss her softly, how she would raise her arms to pull him closer. He would smell the jasmine perfume at her neck and feel the wetness of her lips on his. She shifted slightly and looked to the other side of the room, smiling. Dominic came toward her. He must have been there all the time. He did what Aiden longed to do, then took his young son in his arms so Amina could drink the glass of tea he'd brought. As he straightened up, his eyes met Aiden's, and he stopped. He didn't speak but held his gaze for a moment or two and then, with a slow, knowing smile, turned back to his family.

***

Two days later, Aiden stood on the roof terrace of the hotel, drinking a beer and finishing a small painting of the view over the railing: the honeycomb of the Medina under a cerulean sky, the distant mountains a shimmering blur in the merciless afternoon heat. Life in his Moroccan fantasy world was coming to an end. He was sad—even, if he were honest, a little depressed. He had come to love this family who embraced him as one of their own, made him feel so welcome and valued. But he was also filled with a keen sense of anticipation. The future was ringing out and, for the first time in his life, he looked forward with optimism and confidence.

One of several cats which claimed the hotel's roof terrace as their home, jumped on the railing at the edge of his view. He seized a new brush, quickly mixed two or three shades of tawny grey, and painted the cat into the scene. It was sitting comfortably, admiring the same view as he was, its tail curled into the filigree of the wrought iron rail.

"That's Bastet," said a voice behind him. He turned to see Lukas eating an ice cream. "That's what I call her. My dad loved cats. He wrote about them. One he had for nineteen years was called Copernicus."

He explained Bastet was the Ancient Egyptian goddess of cats, home and childbirth, and maybe Aiden shouldn't leave until the new baby was born. He'd miss another really big party.

Aiden laughed. "I don't think I can handle another big Moroccan party, Lukas. God knows where you guys get the energy."

As Lukas stepped closer, Aiden noticed he was wearing a chain with a silver ring hanging at the open neck of his shirt.

"That looks like a neat ring. Can I see it?" he said.

Lukas rubbed the ring against his shirt to make it shine more. "It's the Eye of Horus. My dad gave it to my mom. She loved it. And then she gave it to your uncle, but he never wore it. When he was over here that time, he gave it to me."

"Sounds like it took a while, but it was always meant to come to you."

"For sure. Cool, right? Kind of like a jigsaw." Lukas paused for a moment, as though thinking this through. "Like, you think one piece goes in an empty place. It's got the right colours, so you try to make it fit, but it won't go in. It belongs somewhere else."

He went over and stroked the cat which stretched and purred against him.

Such strange insight, Aiden thought. He would miss his ethereal young companion.

As he had grown to know them better, the El Hassan family had developed a paradoxical aura ... one of welcome, yet exclusivity, like a secret society. They were warm, even loving, ready to hug, squeeze, eager to be close. They carried their wealth naturally, no hint of ostentation, never using the success of the family business to imply superiority. But there was something untouchable about them, an invisible, uncrossable boundary. Their happiness filled him with curiosity and longing. This feeling was not jealousy or even envy, but rather the sense of a closed door, one he would never be permitted to open.

They had tried to get him to stay longer, but he felt he needed to go home. He was an outsider. He could never claim a permanent role in the fairy tale.

But he would miss them all, these strange, beautiful people.

He stood back to appraise his painting, satisfied he'd captured the goddess cat, Bastet, who clearly believed she deserved to be included.

***

On the morning of his departure, the family and staff gathered in the courtyard to say goodbye. As each of them hugged him tight and kissed him, his eyes prickled with tears and he stood, searching for a tissue, embarrassed.

"Goodbye, my cosmic twin," Amina said. "We will see each other again. I know this." He held his breath as she kissed him, willing time to stand still.

The chef, Henri, pressed a small package into his hands. "For the flight. No matter the airline, the food is appalling." He pulled Aiden close and whispered, "Find yourself a good woman of your own now. You deserve that, *mon ami.*"

"Will you paint Morocco when you get home?" Lukas asked him.

"For sure. I'm going to paint our starry night in the desert, see if I can capture that crazy feeling of being lost out there in the universe."

Lukas made him promise to send a photo of it. Aiden decided, if it was good enough, he'd send the kid the actual painting.

Dominic picked up his luggage and led him into the alleyway to head to the car. Aiden paused and turned back to wave at them all one last time.

"Hey, Aiden," Lukas called out, pushing through the others and running a few steps towards him. "No one is ever lost. They're just on their way somewhere else."

EPILOGUE

Six months after his return from Morocco, Aiden found it hard to believe he was living in his own home in Toronto, a city that once had no place for him. His uncle had been generous in lending him the down payment for this modest condominium. Working for Penelope on the management and promotion of her new gallery enabled him to pay the mortgage and live a decent life. He was meeting young, undiscovered artists, and moving in a world he had once only dreamed about. When he wasn't working or—at his cousin Catherine's insistence, socializing, he painted.

He had turned the living room of his condo into a studio. It was small but had the advantage of northern light and became a place where he felt totally centred: creative, productive, happy. The Moroccan landscapes he rendered in the past few months came from a pent-up passion he did not realize he had, a yearning for brightness, for deeply saturated, vivid hues, for kaleidoscopic blazes of colour. In the past, he would pause often, stepping back to appraise his work, looking for flaws or parts needing greater definition. But these paintings had flowed unhindered, with no photographic reference, as though he were merely the passive vehicle for their bold expression. He remembered Zahra telling him not to think, not to force the brush anywhere, so he let it do whatever it seemed to want, bringing life to the beautiful Middle Eastern world seared into his memory.

When he took stock of his life, he thought he needed nothing more.

***

On a Saturday afternoon in early Spring, he sat in the café at Toronto airport waiting for the arrival of his uncle from Vancouver. Normally

Steven would get a cab, but this time Aiden wanted to pick him up. He was coming to see Nigel and Philippe again. They had learned Philippe was now seriously ill and may not have long to live. Despite being more or less prepared for this news, it had affected Steven far worse than he expected.

The flight was delayed, so Aiden decided to get a light meal and a beer.

This morning, he had another letter from Maggie. He had spilled the truth about her to his uncle and cousin but shut down all their questions. To their credit, they respected this and did not press him. But Maggie was still learning what was going on in his life through the Amy-Catherine chit-chat, and had his new address. The letter contained the usual things he had come to expect. *I know you're back in Toronto now .... all I ask is a few minutes of your time ... I promise.*

He could not believe the words were sincere. The hurt he had endured as a child still smarted, and a part of him would always lie broken inside.

The airport restaurant was filling up. Four young children came in, chattering nonstop. They were shepherded by a distraught woman who kept telling them to stay together, not to knock into people, to wait until she could find a table. She found one across from Aiden and looked around for another chair. Aiden pointed to the one opposite him. She thanked him profusely, took the chair and told her charges to sit down, get organized and make quick decisions about what they wanted to eat.

The kids maneuvered themselves out of their backpacks and squeezed into the tight spaces. They were about seven years old, Aiden guessed. One was limping, another had a patch over one eye. Their backpacks were all the same, sporting a logo of a range of mountains and the words *Estancia Rebelde*. The kids squirmed about on their chairs, making them squeak on the floor, and shouted over each other, pointing at different things on the menu.

"Sorry about the noise." The woman leaned over to Aiden. "They're so excited. First time on a plane. I got here too early. We have to wait for the rest of the group to arrive."

He asked her where they were going.

"Argentina. A ranch. They teach kids to ride. A couple runs it. The guy is Julian something. I forget the woman's name. I think she's Canadian." She dropped her voice. "These poor little guys here… abusive families. Children's Aid were brought in. Lousy start in life. Can you imagine what a thrill this is? Hope they quieten down a bit. It's a long flight."

She told Aiden how horses can sense feelings, how they know to be gentle with a damaged child. Kids quickly feel safe when they have mastered a few basics.

"They're so proud. Makes you want to cry. Before this, they've only ever been punished … never had anything to be proud of."

A ping on his phone told him his uncle's plane had landed. He left, wishing her and the kids all the best.

***

On a sunny day, glad of a little time for himself again, he sat on his balcony and picked up Maggie's latest letter. This one had come with a few photographs. In one, Maggie and his father were standing in front of the community centre where his dad worked. It must have been winter. She was wearing a heavy coat and boots. He had his arm around her, squeezing her tight. They were both laughing. In the next one, they were sitting on a bench; his father was cradling him in his arms. Aiden's chubby baby face was creased in a smile.

He leaned on the balcony rail. The Don River wound its way south to Lake Ontario, lined with trees coming into leaf. It was the first warm day of the year. In the park below, people wore shorts and T-shirts and took photos of each other with the tall towers of the city in the background. A light wind blew through the cherry blossoms. Tiny petals broke loose and floated like pink confetti before falling to the ground.

He thought about Amina and her vicious fight for her daughter. He thought about Lukas and the tragic beginning to his life. But most of all, he thought about the children he had seen at the airport, and decided, even if something is torn apart with grief or loss or sadness, there are ways to mend it, to try to make it whole again.

Gazing at the few cottonball clouds coasting across the sky, he took a deep breath, pulled out his phone and called his mother.

-END-

ACKNOWLEDGEMENTS

This time, my first thanks must go to my husband, Jürgen, who has suffered for many years with my shushing and waving at him to go away when I'm in the middle of a thought or wrestling with a stubborn sentence. From the joyful eureka moments to the hair-pulling hissy fits, he has been unfailingly supportive of my passion to write, and I could not have managed any of it without him.

Once again, my huge appreciation goes to my fellow scribes in our First Page Writers Group, particularly to Josée Sigouin, Michelle Alfano, Tina Tzatzanis and Justine Mazin, who have hung in with me throughout the journey, offering thoughtful critique, sound advice and stimulating ideas every step of the way; and to newer members Laurie Lupton, Mathea Treslan, Brian Moore and Max Hancock who so quickly and positively influenced the way my work progressed.

Thanks to my good friends, especially Gary Hesketh and Louise Doucet, who continue to indulge my belief in both the resolve and fickleness of fate and encourage me to keep exploring its infinite storytelling possibilities.

I am greatly indebted to Shane Joseph, my editor and publisher who put me through the wringer yet again, with his usual sharp insight and no mincing of words … and yet still manages to make me like him. His belief in this story and those before it has always inspired and motivated me to be better.

Finally, I want to send a very general thank you to the wonderful people my husband and I have met on our journeys to Morocco and Egypt, two countries whose mystery and magic ignited my desire to write, became the settings for much of my writing, and created memories that will last a lifetime.

AUTHOR BIO

Liz Torlée lived and worked in England and Germany before emigrating to Canada in her twenties. She built a long career in both advertising and market research but is now devoted to her real passion: writing fiction.

Since she was a child, Liz has loved watching and learning about the stars and exploring the mythology of the night sky. She has always been intrigued by the whole notion of fate and how, through "coincidence" and other mysterious means, it makes our lives intersect in strange and far-reaching ways. The cunning tactics of fate have fueled the central ideas and themes in her work.

Along with her husband, Liz is an avid traveller, particularly enjoying any country with a desert! She is fascinated by the vast, ever-changing beauty of the desert landscape, and this has inspired many of the settings for her novels.

A Long Walk With Fate (2025), published by Blue Denim Press, is Liz's third novel. The previous two, also from Blue Denim Press, are *The Way Things Fall* (2020) and *In Love With The Night* (2022). She had two short stories published in 2024: *Flight*, in the anthology "Will There Be A Sunset?" (Chicken House Press), and "Narrowing the Field," in the *Hill Spirits VI* anthology *Change*, (Blue Denim Press.) Her story "Orion Winked" (2025), was one of four chosen to be engraved on a picnic table, as part of the Town of Cobourg's POETCHRY initiative.

Liz and her husband live in mid-town Toronto.